PLEBEIAN REVEALED

BY

DEBBIE K. LUM

Library of Congress Control Number: 2016900212

DKLit, LLC, Tampa, Florida

ISBN-13: 978-1-944463-00-7

Cover design and interior formatting by Tugboat Design

www.debbielum.com

Acknowledgments

I admit, I didn't know what I was doing when I first opened a blank document and started writing for a month. Gradually, I figured out I was writing a book. Eventually I shared my secret with Carl, Alexander, Ashton and a few friends. Most of them didn't laugh; some of them even offered to help. And now it's my turn to give them my thanks.

Sara Sepulveda, the first, only and last person to read my original manuscript.

Keri Kiefer Riegler and Amber Marcellino, my cherished beta readers.

Dr. Brandon Faza, you gave me more than a medical plausibility check; you gave me story plot lines.

Mandy Schoen, the perfect editor for a writer who had no idea what she was doing.

And my rock, my largest critic and biggest fan, Jill Reagan Healey. You went all-in with me on this journey, giving me what I needed the most: confidence. I could not have done this without a friend like you. And I know I just made you cry.

Dedicated to those
who wonder what it feels like
to receive a bouquet of flowers.

[ONE]

Lauren

Stray clouds of stage fog cling to the rafters while sticky, spilled beer claims the arena floor. The music has stopped; goodbye waves and final bows are complete. Now everything sounds fuzzy to Lauren Logan and she can't hear what the band manager is saying.

"I said *you did it!*" Davis yells, offering her a water bottle.

Her sweaty pony tail bounces with her nod. *It's over,* she says to herself. *Now breathe.* Massive knots still twist in her stomach after watching people stare at her. At least she didn't see the millions watching live on television. *Breathe.* She points to her throat, which throbs after singing eighteen songs.

"I'll get you some tea," Davis says, wearing the same blue plaid shirt and leather-laced blue boat shoes he's worn every day of his adult life. He tosses a towel for her sweat drenched body. "Not bad for a first timer!"

"And not a bad first gig you booked."

"Uh…second gig. The Academy Awards were technically first." His shoulders straighten, a bragging smile stretching his skinny cheeks.

She swipes his arm with a friendly towel snap. "No way can you claim credit for that. That was totally Johnny."

As if hearing his name, their lead guitarist flies down the backstage stairs to reach them, holding the rail as he swings down five steps at once. His eyes burn with excitement; his vintage wash black t-shirt and indigo jeans darkened with hard-earned sweat. Feet now flat on the concrete; he points two weathered, guitar-playing index fingers at Lauren. "Now that's how a first album is launched."

She squints. "And that's why I should be mad at you."

Johnny Fulton flashes a mischievous smile and pulls his hands through his wild mess of black hair. Damn if that doesn't always make her smile—just like it had back in college when they dated. Even now, after Johnny broke his promise their band Plebeian would always stay anonymous, she can't stay mad at him.

"But you did it," he whispers with soft eyes, his smile widening. "Plus you didn't suck!"

Sure. She didn't ruin it for the band or their fans. *But still…*

He rests his hand on her shoulder. "We're rolling now!"

The knots in her stomach twist tighter. She's got to talk with him. It's too much pressure, too many people staring at her. This is a far cry from the comfortable desk job she left behind. "Yeah, but…"

Too late; they're instantly surrounded by the rest of the guys in the band. Johnny completes a round of fist bumps and huddles the sweaty group together. "It's been a month since we revealed ourselves at the Oscars. No one believed we could do more than write secret songs for a movie. No one believed we could pull off a live set at the Academy Awards. No one thought we could pull off this televised concert. Plebeian may mean 'common people' but we're not common anymore. We've made it. This is the break I've waited for my whole life. These are the breaks people dream of!"

Four of the five wear cheek-to-cheek smiles.

Their huddle breaks and they quickly move toward the dressing rooms.

Later. She'll talk with Johnny later.

Up ahead, Lauren sees her tall husband of seventeen years leaning against the backstage wall. No surprise, Cory's phone is in his hand

and his blue eyes do not look up to congratulate her. His work as the Vice President of Hotel Operations at the Riverside Resort in their hometown of Tampa has always consumed his time. And since the Riverside announced a conference center expansion, the only way she'd get his attention is by lying on the blueprint plans and only then because she'd be blocking his view.

"Seven minutes to change; I need you all upstairs in nine minutes!" Davis yells. "And I know you can get up there that fast." Davis Perkins is comfortable in his commands, transitioning well from his old job as Operations Manager of the Riverside to the manager of today's hottest alternative rock band. He has invited a group of record executives, politicians, celebrities and friends to meet the band at a post-concert party.

Lauren walks next to Davis and leans closer. "Christy's group is still coming upstairs, right?" she whispers.

"She has six passes, so she should be."

Good. With the concert behind her, she might as well have some fun. And Christy, her best friend since high school, apparently brought the fun with her. Always full of surprises, Christy had gotten her good tonight by bringing old friends from high school. Some of them Lauren had known well and one of them she wished she'd known better: Andy Hayden.

Lauren had missed a few camera cues on stage when she first spotted Andy in the audience. It's been years since she's seen her high school crush. But she's never forgotten his fit, six-foot perfect body, straight sandy brown hair and brownish-green eyes that used to look at every girl but her.

"Anyone in Christy's group I know?" Davis asks, breaking the glaze forming in her eyes.

For years, Davis has listened to her blabber like a gossiping teenage girl during their workout runs together. And for years, he has kept all of her secrets. But this, her old feelings for Andy, touches something too private—"It just never hurts to take a trip down memory lane."

They pass through backstage security to reach the dressing room corridor.

Davis stops, head cocked to the side. "Yeah, but who are you tripping down your lane with?"

A thirty-seven-year-old married mother of two shouldn't be so curious to see a guy she liked so long ago. But a thirty-seven-year-old married mother of two usually isn't the lead singer of a rock band either. Crazy is her life now. Things were normal and predictable when she worked as Riverside Resort's marketing coordinator in the large shadow of her husband. Her biggest challenge used to be choosing a dinner menu to satisfy her two teenage boys and keeping the meal hot until Cory wandered home.

Things aren't so simple now. She has fame she didn't want with her ex-boyfriend, a husband that hasn't noticed and a smoldering crush on a guy she hasn't seen in years. The love categories of her life are all here tonight, and she has nine minutes until the collision.

[TWO]

Glowing blue lights pulse from inside the dark arena club; muffled indie rock music plays to the VIP crowd. Davis stands outside the door like a half-pint bouncer, turning away uninvited fans who have mischievously found the party.

Lauren rushes down the hall. Her curiosity with coming face to face with Andy Hayden has her showered, changed and arriving to the party within nine minutes.

"Damn, you're fast. And first," Davis says.

"Where's Christy?" she asks, smoothing out her black, low-cut cotton shirt that sits tight on her distressed jeans; the skinny silver hoops of her drop earrings peek through strands of her straight brown hair.

"Don't you want to see your husband first?"

"Cory is much easier to find than Christy." Lauren points to her husband, standing where she thought he'd be: close to the door and ready to leave. She heads his way and after a quick obligatory kiss, leads him into the party.

As soon as their conversations split apart, Lauren searches for Christy's long, curly, copper-brown hair. It doesn't matter that she's told Christy a million times she hates surprises. Spontaneity and living life to its fullest are Christy's trademarks. Finally, she spots her. Their smiles ignite as they wrap each other in a hug.

"Did you like the show?" Lauren asks.

"We loved it!" Christy says, bursting with enthusiastic delight. She looks over her shoulder and Lauren's eyes follow.

Brownish-green eyes, straight sandy brown hair, thin nose. *Andy!*

Lauren's arms fly open. "Hey—what a surprise! How are you?! I saw you in the audience—I sang to you!" she says, pulling away from their hug.

"What an amazing show! I loved every minute of it. You look incredible," he says, his smile simple and sincere.

Her hands slip into his in a friendly grip.

"You look great—just like in high school. And college!" she says, squeezing him. Maybe she's gushing too much but it's the truth—his fitted, blue button-down shirt lies perfectly over his pressed jeans. And his eyes. *Those eyes.* An alluring mix of hazelnut brown and olive green that light up the room. And they've ignited an old flame in her heart.

"I can't believe what you did tonight. Your music, the show, you! It's all amazing."

Lauren glances to either side of Andy to meet his wife. Certainly he married a gorgeous woman and has a perfect life with perfect kids and a perfect job. She'd like to meet the woman that captured the man she always wanted.

"You came alone tonight?" she asks. Christy nods to assist his answer.

"Long story. Divorced and not dating anyone," he says.

Her knees weaken.

Davis interrupts. "Need you over here for a picture," he says, tugging Lauren's arm. Andy just dropped a bombshell like that and now she has to go?

"Maybe we can catch up in a bit and you can tell me more," she says.

"That'd be great," he says with a smile that makes her want to hurry.

Every step away from Andy adds a question in Lauren's mind. He's here? He's single?

When the band finishes posing for photos with their record

executives, she turns to find Andy again. But a manicured hand snatches her arm.

"Lauren! Great job tonight," Amie says, offering a friendly, congratulatory hug. As usual, Amie's full figure chest reaches Lauren before the rest of her body. Those pouty lips and that body must surely give Johnny hours of endless pleasure. They have been dating since Lauren and Johnny broke up in college. It's a wonder why Johnny hasn't asked her to marry him yet.

"Thanks, Amie," Lauren says. Their embrace is cordial, their relationship sometimes cool, especially when Amie gets hung up remembering that Lauren used to sleep with her man. "It's still a little weird watching people stare at me."

Amie immediately does what freaks Lauren out the most: she starts looking Lauren over from head to toe. Her icy stare hits Lauren like the clanking ice inside her highball glass. Amie smiles, nods and turns away. Lauren grits her teeth, standing by an abandoned Johnny.

"If one more person looks at me like I'm a marketable piece of meat, I'll quit."

"You are a talented, marketable piece of meat and you can't quit. I need you," Johnny says.

Lauren turns to face her ex. "So Amie's drink—just tonic and no gin tonight?"

"Unfortunately, yes," he says, grimacing.

"Am I supposed to know she's pregnant yet?"

"No," he snaps. "I'm not ready to tell anyone else. I'm still not ready myself."

"You better get used to this, Johnny. I know it's not what you wanted, but pitter-patter here the baby feet come."

He flings a disapproving stare.

What's the big deal? Just marry your girlfriend of a million years and settle down, for once.

Lauren turns from Johnny to scan the room. There's no one here she really wants to talk to except…

Andy surprises her from behind. "A real friend would have given you a drink by now."

She spins around to find him holding two drinks and smiling like she's the only woman in the world. "Looks like an old friend just did!" She reaches for the martini he offers.

Eyes on each other, they slowly sip. Her vision blurs around the edges as she drinks in the sight of him. The sounds of the party begin to mute and even the air in the room seems to pull them together.

Get a grip and find out more!

"So, why did you ignore me in high school?" Lauren says. "And college?"

"You had a boyfriend in high school," Andy says. "And college."

"And if I hadn't had a boyfriend?"

"I would have had a lot more fun in high school. And college."

Oh how she loves a crisp, witty exchange and Andy can clearly deliver. His smoldering eyes seem to be inviting her to ask more. "Have you lived in Tampa all these years?"

"I actually moved back two years ago, from Chicago."

"Chicago? Did you move back here for a job or to get away from someone?"

"Yes," he says, an impish grin stretching his lips. Stray strands of his brown hair have fallen in his face and he moves them back with a head swing that unleashes a flock of butterflies in her stomach.

Suddenly, someone bumps her elbow, spilling her drink on Andy's arm. "Sorry, Mom," her fourteen-year-old son Aiden says.

"Come meet my old friend Andy Hayden," she says, unflustered by Aiden's mistake. She introduces Andy to Aiden and her older sixteen-year-old son, Lee.

Andy shakes off the handful of spilled martini. "Two handsome young men; you guys would be perfect for my fifteen-year-old daughter Brittney."

"Is she cute?" Aiden asks.

Andy smiles. "You're a teenager; aren't all girls cute?"

"Andy and I went to high school together but I was never pretty enough for Andy to ask me out," she says, winking.

"The true story here, guys, is while you are in high school, go for what you want," Andy says, smiling back at her. "And don't let any other guy get in the way."

Aiden and Lee shake Andy's hand and excuse themselves to finish trolling the party. Sudden fame for their mom means extra attention on them. When they are invited to parties like this they like to cruise around and collect it.

"Perfect family you have," Andy says.

Perfect? If only it was. Andy has given her more attention tonight than Cory has in a year. Her heart aches for love, both to get it and to give it. Across the room she sees Cory in a heated conversation with Christy near the bar. Even if Christy wasn't keeping Cory distracted, she doubts he would be looking for her; except to leave.

Her eyes draw back to the man in front of her. How many lucky women have run their hands through that sexy head of hair? His hazelnut-olive eyes have surely seen faces more beautiful than hers. And the scent of his cologne; a spicy leather fragrance she's not sure what it is but it's making her lean closer to breathe in more of it. *Damn, what a great surprise.*

Some friends wave their goodbyes. All parties peak and this one is ripening.

"Tonight's concert really was amazing, Lauren. I'm glad we got to see each other again."

"We should have lunch sometime; catch up some more," she says, surprising herself.

"You have time for a new, old friend in your life?"

"My schedule is crazy, but lunch sounds fun."

"Let's do it. I'll get your number from Christy."

Time seems to stop with their eye-locking freeze. Inches apart, they hold empty glasses, standing in a room filled with friends and family; strangers and enemies. Curiosity and excitement fills her mind but for some reason, an odd feeling of fear sours her gut.

Andy leans closer. "I wish I would have had more fun in high school."

Lauren breathes in his words. "Me too."

Her smile comes easy. Turning and walking away is what's difficult.

And from the other side of the room, Johnny watches.

* * *

He comes home and reaches deep into his jeans pocket for the concert ticket stub.

He lays the ticket on the dresser and methodically strokes it. Finally the creases surrender, allowing the paper to lie flat.

He can't believe that he finally saw her.

After all this time, he got close to her.

She is more beautiful than he remembers.

Tonight, she was right there; in front of him.

She sang to him.

If only he could have gotten closer.

But tonight was close enough.

For now.

THREE

Blue hydrangeas bloom under shade trees in Central Park while choirs of chirping birds compete with taxi horns on this beautiful summer day in New York City. Too bad the members of Plebeian have only seen a dark photography studio all morning.

While props are being reset for their publicity photo shoot, their broody, tall bassist Oliver Brinks scans a tabloid newspaper. A wet, chewed cigar lies on the table beside him as he reads his daily horoscope. Out loud.

Lauren looks up from her phone. Her toes curl with the sound of Oliver's voice. Actually, everything he does has that effect on her.

Davis tries to talk over him. "Two months since the album debut concert and look at this."

Johnny reads from the tablet Davis holds. "Our platinum album is still number one. Nice."

"And according to this," Oliver says, his bony hand pointing to a story in his tabloid, "Johnny and Lauren are still in love. Ah…the old lovers that people can't get enough of."

Johnny grabs the newspaper and smacks Oliver with it.

Keyboardist Michael Casper launches his snarky smile; a perfect set of pearly white teeth offset by the dark complexion of his African-American skin. Michael used to play the organ while Lauren sang the solos in church. She suggested him for Plebeian's keyboardist when she and Johnny formed the band. Big framed and packed with a brain full of incredible music, Michael now composes most of their hit songs. "You'd think since you and Amie announced you're having a baby they'd stop those stories now."

Lauren glances up from her phone again. You'd think since she's married those stories would have never started.

"You'd think," Johnny says, unfolding the tabloid. Before he reads it he looks across the room at Lauren.

Oh no…don't you dare.

He gently kisses his fingertips and blows her a kiss.

"That's cute," Michael says.

No, it's not. His air kisses have been annoying for years. And when will these Johnny stories stop? She's got enough on her plate keeping track of her workaholic husband. She's trying to stay relevant to her kids, but she just reminded Aiden and Lee to do homework they've already done. Plus, it's been difficult to ignore her constant Andy daydreams since she saw him at the concert two months ago. There's no mental space left to fight romantic rumors of her and her old college boyfriend.

Still, she can't resist.

She sticks out her tongue, slowly licks the palm of her hand and gently blows a lick back to Johnny.

"You guys are sick," mumbles their drummer Doug Maggio.

All eyes snap towards Doug. He spoke! It's rare to get any words out of him, so add those four to the list. Single, short and humble, Doug taught percussion at Lee and Aiden's high school before Lauren convinced him to join Plebeian. Even as a teacher he never spoke much.

Lauren wants to change the subject. And wash her hand.

"After this we head uptown to the recording studio, right?" she asks Davis.

"Yeah, we start recording this afternoon and should wrap by noon on Saturday," Davis says. "We better wrap by then because I've got me some Yankees tickets for Saturday night."

She looks down at her phone and an incoming text.

"You are not going to believe this: I've got to meet with a new financial client next Thursday. I have to cancel our lunch again. Ugh!"

It's more bad news from Andy. Since Plebeian's concert, the two have not been able to find a day for their lunch. Lauren texts back:

"This has been crazy trying to find a day that works!"

"I know. Now I'm heading to New York City for a financial advisor's conference through the weekend. My schedule has been as crazy as a rock star like you."

Andy's coming here? She smiles and texts him back:

"Guess where I am? Any openings for lunch while you are here?"

"Are you seriously in NYC? I've got sessions all day, but nothing for dinner Saturday night."

"Then I think our lunch just turned into dinner. Put me down for Saturday night."

"Dinner with Lauren Logan in New York City on Saturday night? I never imagined words like that on my calendar."

"I never imagined the words 'dinner with Andy Hayden' in any city on any day on my calendar either!"

She clutches her phone to her chest. *Perfect!* She'll have to add a night to her hotel and text her pilots to schedule her plane to leave a day later, but finally seeing Andy will be worth it.

Her chiming phone and smiling face catch Johnny's attention. He moves to sit on the couch next to her. "Busy bee over here."

"Nosy bee over there," she says, slipping her phone into her purse.

"Someone has your attention." He nods toward her bag.

"Someone did, but you have my attention now."

He smiles. "You've been brave today."

"Thanks. A photo shoot like this is fine. Standing on stage and seeing people stare at me is what I can't handle."

Oliver plops down between them. His wild brown hair desperately needs to be combed. Cut and washed too. Of all the bass guitar players Johnny could have chosen for the band, he picked *this* old drinking buddy. Oliver peels back the top of a vending machine pudding cup and starts licking the lid. "It's awesome our lead singer doesn't like to be on stage."

Lauren tries not to stare at the freakishly long length of Oliver's tongue. "I love to be on stage. I love the energy of a concert. I love to sing. Just take away all the creepy people staring at me and I'm fine."

"Good idea; creeps can pay for a concert and then leave before we play," Oliver says, stuffing a heaping spoonful of pudding in his mouth. "Hey," he mumbles with his mouth full, "at least creepy people will be looking at you in different languages when we go on a world tour."

World tour?

"Look, I never wanted us to be revealed. Not what I signed up for, okay? The movie studio knew people would go nuts trying to find out something that was a secret. It was a great marketing idea. I was happy as an unknown. But now look at us! Top of the charts and we have to back it up with concerts. Now I'm the one going nuts! I'm center stage being sized up by my weight, age, hair, clothes and I don't like to watch people staring, judging and drooling at me!"

The room of men has fallen silent.

"Sunglasses," says a voice from the back of the room.

All heads turn to look at Doug. He raises an eyebrow and looks at Michael.

"Great idea!" Michael says. "Just wear sunglasses on stage and you won't see the creepy people. Maybe they'll work so well, you'll never see Oliver again."

Oliver throws his spoon at Michael and finishes the assault by playfully tossing the empty pudding cup at him.

Ugh. She ignores them by playing with her phone. They don't get it. She trusted Johnny when he said their band would stay anonymous. It seemed impossible to keep a secret like this in today's 24/7 gossip-fueled world, but they did it. Their plan was working. Then when the Oscar nomination for Best Original Song surprised them, Johnny wanted to reveal Plebeian in the live performance. It was the right call, but sometimes it takes awhile for her to come to terms with a decision. The same thing happened when she and Johnny broke up in college. They both agreed it was the right call, but Lauren didn't come to terms with the decision until she stopped by Johnny's house one night, uninvited. When he didn't answer the door, she walked around to his bedroom window and boldly peeked through a crack in the blinds. She saw four feet in Johnny's bed. That's when she knew her place with Johnny was now the ex-girlfriend.

"We'll be ready in five minutes," the photographer says, preparing for the next phase of the shoot.

Lauren glances up from her phone. *Dang it.* She had just found a great online site for designer sunglasses. Then an incoming text draws her eyes back down.

"I just confirmed that Saturday night is blocked off on every calendar I own. There's nothing to keep me from having dinner with you. I'm so looking forward to this!"

Her chest drums at the sight of Andy's text. Forget the drama of Plebeian or the prying eyes of fame. She's hungry to fill up her emotional tank, drawn dry from an inattentive husband, maturing kids that don't seem to need her anymore and the demands from the band. Why not enjoy a nice evening with an old friend?

"Texts from Cory making you smile?" Davis asks, walking past her.

Her face drops. Cory! Dinner for two on a Saturday night looks more like a date than a weekday lunch. And she's in New York City! With every step outside she risks being photographed by paparazzi.

Then she sees a solution. He's sitting across the room, leaning back in a chair, reading a tourist guidebook. She walks over, sliding into a chair next to Michael.

"Hey, you and Sunny are staying until Sunday to do some sight-seeing, right?" she quietly asks.

"Yeah, we're staying all weekend. Sunny's never been here before."

"I'm meeting an old friend for dinner on Saturday night. Can you two join us?"

"Sure, but why?" he asks, putting the guidebook on the table.

Lauren doesn't really want the extra company but she doesn't need a scandal either. Rumors could hurt her family. And that might happen if there's a photo taken of her and Andy alone.

"If I go to dinner alone with a guy, you know, Cory might think that's weird."

Michael smiles. "So where are we going?"

And across the room, with his chin resting in his folded hands, Johnny watches.

* * *

He can't stop thinking about her eyes, her hair, those lips.

It's been so long since he's seen her, too long.

But now he knows she's closer, she's down there somewhere.

His face peels away from the oval window as the plane begins its descent.

In minutes he'll be on the ground and one short cab ride away from New York City.

It won't be long until he finds her.

He always does.

[FOUR]

Andy

Andy glares at the conference room clock. The second hand sweeps painfully slow, the minutes nudging closer to the end of this derivatives trading breakout session. Judging from the tapping feet and clicking ink pens throughout the room, no one thought this speaker would drone on this long.

He sits still, but anxious, scribbling on a piece of paper and regretting his choice to sit towards the front of the room. What a waste of time. He could have been enjoying this Saturday afternoon out in Manhattan, visiting two Gothic revival buildings he has yet to study. Interesting architecture fascinates him. Instead, one of those buildings is just a doodle on his paper.

At least he doesn't have to rush to the airport like the others tonight. He flies home tomorrow because tonight he's having dinner with Lauren.

Dinner with Lauren. His face warms. *Lauren Logan.* He still can't believe he will be with her tonight. After seeing her at the concert, the past two months have felt like quicksand. As soon as he thinks about the soft, merlot color of her lips, her shiny, long brown hair and those tight leather pants she wore on stage, he's sucked in. And some days he can't get out.

She remembered him that night. That was unbelievable too.

Especially since they led parallel lives in high school and college. He tried to talk to her back then, but her penny-colored eyes would always snap away; focused on her valedictorian, smart-ass boyfriend. At least she never married that guy, or her college boyfriend Johnny. *It could have been you.* If only…

He glances up at the presenter. At the rate this guy talks, Andy may only have five minutes to get ready for dinner. Across the room, he notices the batting eyelashes from a vibrant, thirty-something redhead wearing a white blouse bursting at the buttons, her blue suit jacket pushed up at the sleeves. *Delicious.* Her smile invites him to smile back. He does. *But that's all, honey.* Tonight, he's taken. *Dinner with Lauren Logan, international rock star and a friend. Yeah.*

He's learned his lesson anyway: beauty isn't what it's cracked up to be. Right after college, his ex-wife Janie caught his eye that way: wearing short, tight skirts to the travel agency where she worked, right across the street from his office. Their first date was hours after he asked; they slept together that night and got married a few weeks later. Too soon. Janie quickly became the beautiful stunner from hell, dominating, abusive, calling the shots on everything from how they'd have sex to what clothes he could wear. He couldn't tie his shoes without asking and began to doubt that he could tie a shoe at all. Ending it was the best decision he ever made. Even though how he ended it may not have been the best.

His phone vibrates with a text.

"Hey! Michael and Sunny got stuck at a museum and will be late to dinner. Don't want to lose the reservation and it's awkward when I arrive someplace alone. Can you come to my hotel and ride with me?"

He gulps down his excitement. *Lauren!* And…hell yes.

"Sure! I'll meet you at your hotel. 7:30."

Andy lowers his phone just as the speaker concludes. Good timing because now he's gotta fly.

He's out the door before the redhead can sink her fingernails into him, walking with adrenaline-powered steps through the hotel conference center. *Shower. Change. You got this: move.* Elevators in sight, something catches his eye at the hotel gift shop. He comes to a halt.

Fresh flowers.

Should he buy a bouquet? Those flowers look as happy as Lauren. She'd probably love it! *No, it's too over the top.* But he can't arrive empty-handed. After all, she's an old friend. *Do it!* He steps towards the shop to make the purchase and then stops cold.

Can't. Shouldn't.

He lowers his head.

She's married.

Lauren

The lounge chairs on the penthouse terrace are begging Lauren to sit in them. And she could, forever, watching the busy water traffic on the Hudson River. Of all the hotels in New York City, The Burberry—a boutique, neoclassical, restored hotel—is her favorite.

But right now, she doesn't have time. This morning's recording session ran well into the afternoon. Johnny, Oliver and Doug were late for their flight home, Michael got delayed with his museum tours, Davis was late for his Yankees game and she was rushed to shop for a new outfit for tonight's dinner with Andy.

She sweeps into the penthouse bedroom and begins cutting tags off her new clothes. No way would Cory ever notice an outfit like this, but something tells her Andy will. She puts on the gold, wrapped-lace shirt, a little tight and see-through if you look at it hard enough, pairing it over a tight, short black skirt. Her three inch high, gold strapped sandals should be tall enough to get her eye-to-eye with Andy. Who's she kidding? He's a little over six feet tall and she's all of five foot three on a good day.

She catches her reflection in the mirror. Her hair looks good; full for once. And finally, she's perfected smoky eye makeup on both eyes. Usually, she can get one eye close to perfect, but then the other eye has that "been partying in a club until 4 a.m." smeared look. Her professional makeup artist helped teach her those skills, one perk of being famous. But still, in her reflection she feels like an average woman, born in a small town in central Florida, raised in a middle class family with a younger brother. Her father was a scrappy entrepreneur, offering contracting services to small businesses in town. He once helped a struggling friend double the revenue of his barber shop just by moving the front door to face a busier road. It seemed that everyone in town was seeking his services and his popularity paid off when he later became president of the local bank. Her mother was the shy spouse, rarely seen in the social circles. Quiet and dutiful, she lived simply and uninterested in her husband's business. When he died years ago, he left a few surprises. Their family was already worth millions from a land inheritance he had received when he was a boy. Then he left a surprising trust fund in citrus investments that Lauren received when she turned twenty-one. Her values are reflective of her father's loyalty and her mother's strong sense of obligation, those obligations she carries heavy herself.

Obligations. Lauren checks her phone again. She texted Cory earlier to ask how his day was and to tell him who she was meeting for dinner. Still no reply. She tucks her phone into her Fendi purse. Forget obligations. Andy is on his way to ride with her and will be here any minute.

Her pacing has worn a path on the carpeted floor. Someone knocks at the door and her heart starts to pound.

Opening the door, the sight of Andy makes her tummy leap. His black sport coat and pants look as incredible as his welcoming smile. No tie binds his pale-blue dress shirt collar; the extra undone button exposes a hint of his smooth upper chest. She's smiling; he's smiling—this is going to be one hell of a night.

She opens her arms as he steps toward her. "My escort!" she says, pulling back from their hug. The smell of his delicious cologne now weaves through the lace on her blouse; her perfume now surely rubbed on his shirt.

"Such a beautiful woman to accompany," he says confidently, yet the shy peeking of his eyes tells her that he's nervous too.

They steal glances of each other as they walk to Lauren's waiting town car. Their steps together are fluid and perfectly timed. Her eyes sweep their surroundings as they approach the car. *Good!* Still no paparazzi or fans have found her hotel, even after several days here.

They arrive on time to Ink, a popular restaurant Lauren's been dying to visit but Cory never wanted to try. Their booth has heavy steel gray curtains draped on three sides. In the background, the smooth sounds of remixed electronic music plays. Simple white candles help Andy and Lauren see each other as they sit together on one side, waiting for Michael and Sunny.

"Never been a fan of same side booth sitters," Andy whispers, grinning.

"You hate that too! How do people eat and talk to each other when they sit like this?"

"I guess how we are doing right now." He turns more towards her.

The waiter approaches their table.

"Martini okay?" Andy asks her. She nods.

"Vodka, up, perfect with a twist for us both," Andy says.

She doesn't hear him. She's too busy watching his lips as he talks.

Within fifteen minutes Michael arrives, with his beaming smile and feisty girlfriend Sunny. Their table fills with lively conversation and laughter, making them in no rush to order their appetizers and entrees. Under the table, Lauren's leg keeps accidently brushing against Andy's but she's starting not to care since her second martini was served.

"This tastes amazing. Try it," Andy says, offering her a bite of filet from his fork.

"So good," she says, swallowing the filet and the sensory overload from this evening. How he looks, how he laughs, how he turns his body towards her when she talks. He's making the ache for attention she's felt for years disappear tonight.

"Hey," Sunny says, finishing up her cheesecake dessert, "let's walk a few blocks to the river to see the Statue of Liberty!"

"You guys can go and be discovered by photographers; I'll pass," Lauren says. "Really, this long day has caught up to me." She stands and hugs her goodbyes to Michael and Sunny, and then turns to Andy.

"Would you like for me to ride with you to be sure you get back okay?" Andy asks.

She was hoping he would. "That'd be great."

It doesn't matter that she's tired; the ride back to The Burberry with Andy energizes her. The city lights are magical, the music in the car seductive. They sit close but not touching, leaning together to show each other family photos from their phones.

Her town car stops at a red light one block from her hotel. She's one minute away from saying goodbye; sixty seconds from ending the most enjoyable night she's had in months. *Invite him up? What's the harm?* He was already in her suite when he picked her up, so it's no big deal to ask him back up. *Right?*

The driver pulls up to the curb. She quickly glances around for photographers. What's the point of asking friends to come to dinner for cover and then get caught walking into your hotel alone with a guy? *Damn optics.* But luck is with her: the coast is clear.

"Would you like to come up for a drink and more conversation?"

His eyes smile from the corners. "I was going to offer to walk you up to be sure you are safe. So sure, that would be great."

Andy extends his hand to help her out of the car and stays a step ahead of her to open the door and call the elevator. Once upstairs, they step into the penthouse.

"Wait till you see this view at night," Lauren says. "First though, martini?"

"Would love one." He begins to take off his jacket. "May I?"

"Of course. Get comfortable."

She fumbles around the wet bar. *Crap…is it vermouth in a martini? Olives, right? Gin…no…vodka? Why didn't she listen when he ordered their drinks?* Then her bumbling mind goes completely blank seeing him roll up the sleeves of his blue dress shirt. She splashes her hand with the drink she was stirring. *Next batch, use a shaker. And don't look at him when making it.*

She finishes making the drinks and then opens the terrace doors. A stiff summer breeze blows across the rooftop as they step to the glass ledge. Andy leans closer, pointing out the architectural differences between her neoclassical hotel and nearby buildings. Soft music from inside mixes with sounds of the aggravated city below and his eyes seem to be getting lost in the distant city view.

"You almost look sad," Lauren says, gesturing for him to sit down.

He eases onto a lounge chair next to hers, looking down at his drink. "It's like all of my bad choices come rolling back to me, here, on a beautiful balcony with a breathtaking view in the company of an amazing woman."

She absorbs his compliment like a dry sponge. But his first comment has her attention. "What choices?"

"I wasted so much of my life, always attracted to the superficial. I took what came easy. And look where I am now? Good career but a failed marriage and a broken relationship with Brittney. I never learned to start with love. I never loved deep. If it was difficult I left it behind and if it wasn't pretty, I never looked at it twice in the first place."

Do you nod or shake your head at that? Is he really that shallow? He takes a sip of his drink and she watches him with uncertainty.

"Then I see you on TV. The cute girl in high school that always had a boyfriend. I never got close to you because you were taken. I never bothered to fight for what I really wanted."

He...noticed her then? Wanted her then?

"Your book isn't finished, Andy. Life's lessons are supposed to be learned, right? People are worth more than skin shows. You will feel true love once you crack the surface with the right person."

She raises her glass to offer a toast. "To life in love."

"To loving life," he says, smiling as their glasses gently touch. His smile fades as his eyes retreat to his lap.

"It's okay, you can tell me more." *She wants to hear more.*

"After Janie and I got married, she ran my life. Over the years, she said I was worthless and I started to believe her. Just like my parents had done years ago. I believed them, and then I believed her."

He raises his drink for a sip.

"When Brittney was born, we turned into a calendar of family transactions. I was always told I wasn't a good father. Even though I tried, it was never enough. It all came down to one night. One night..." He pauses. "Twelve years of marriage and I'm washing the dishes one night. Janie starts screaming that I screwed up the cast iron skillet because I washed it with dish soap. A skillet she's worried about! I just stood with my hands in the soapy water while she screamed. It was like a switch was flipped. I was done. Washing that cast iron skillet was the last straw.

"I wanted to get out of Chicago so fast. It caught Janie by surprise. I filed for divorce that week and gave her full custody of Brittney. I thought my daughter would be better off without me. The only thing I asked for...all I wanted, was that cast iron skillet."

"And from what I've already seen, you've turned out strong like that skillet."

He smiles a little, his eyes warm and appreciative.

"Do Janie and Brittney still live in Chicago?"

"No, they moved to Tampa a few years ago to be closer to Janie's mother."

"Then if Brittney is close by, you have a chance to fix the mess with your daughter."

He nods. "I see her. I try. I also went back in time and found some of my old high school friends. Do you remember Chase, Bobby and Cheryl?"

"Wow, yes! Chase was the football player who partied all the time and Bobby and Cheryl were the cute baseball player and cheerleader couple. They were with you and Christy's group at our concert, right?"

"Yeah, we all sat together. They've really helped me regroup. They remind me of a better time in my life when I had my act together. They tell me life is too short and if I left something behind, I better go back and get it."

"Did you leave something behind?"

"Regrets for not fighting for what I really wanted." His saddened eyes turn to her. "Sorry for unloading all that; guess this long day has caught up to me too."

"I'm glad you are comfortable with me. I'm happy to have someone to talk to." She notices his empty glass. "And I'm glad you like my martini. Let's make another round."

They move inside, shake up fresh martinis at the wet bar and kick off their shoes. They settle into the living room sofa, he on one end with his legs stretched out, she on the other, as if they have done this a thousand times before.

"I do like getting to know you better," she says. "It's a shame we didn't talk more in high school or college."

"You got married after you graduated college, right?"

"Yeah, Cory and I got married not long after Johnny and I broke up."

"You had kids right away, like I did."

"And that was another thing that happened too soon. Don't get me wrong, I love my boys and Cory has been a good father to Lee and Aiden, but..."

"But?"

"Cory was distant even before I became famous. It's not personal, it's just the way he's always been."

"You have a distant marriage; I had a controlling one."

"So opposite, right?"

"Now, from what I saw at the concert and post-party, he doesn't seem to like your new job."

"Cory didn't want me to work at all but I liked working at the Riverside. Then Johnny's friend in Hollywood asked him to write the soundtrack for the movie he was producing. Johnny played in the house band at the Riverside, so I'd see him from time to time at hotel events. It seemed easy to say yes when he asked me to sing the soundtrack. Why not, right? Johnny wanted a clean start with a new band and Cory didn't care about any of this because we were only doing six songs. Everything was fine when we were unknown. Then when Plebeian was revealed, everything changed."

"Now you are a world famous singer who just wants to be noticed by her own husband."

Yeah. She finds comfort in his words and in the nervous swirling of her glass.

"Yesterday, leaving the recording studio, I was in the town car heading back here for the night. My driver stopped at a light next to a sidewalk flower cart. I noticed this young guy in his twenties leaving with a bouquet of flowers. I thought whoever is getting those flowers is the luckiest person in the world." She pauses to sip.

"I have everything I want now, right? Fame, fortune—I could buy that whole damn flower cart if I wanted. But I'm so jealous of whoever got those flowers. I don't remember what it's like for the man I love to bring me a simple bouquet of flowers."

Andy nods. "Flowers are your cast iron skillet."

Her skin tingles.

He's nailed it.

He gets her.

"And I wish I could pull a dozen roses out of thin air and give them to you right now."

His offer is as generous as his smile. "I wish I was as brave as you," she says.

"Brave enough to give you flowers?"

She chuckles. "No, brave enough to make a change like you did. To abruptly end what isn't working and move on."

"You are one of the bravest people I know! You walked out on stage at the Academy Awards in front of a million strangers and sang. Not many people could do that."

"But I've been told—I've been raised—that once you make a certain commitment, you can't make a change."

"Ah: you grew up in a no-divorce household."

She nods. "My mom would have left my dad in a heartbeat but she stuck with him even though she was miserable. So now the choice I made when I was barely out of college, I have to keep forever."

"It depends."

"Depends on what?"

"It depends on how badly you want flowers." His grin stretches; hers does too.

"We've got to get off this subject because I'm drinking too much." She holds up her empty glass.

"Agreed to change the subject but not to stop drinking!"

Even though she's perfectly fine with his warm legs next to hers, the next batch of martinis calls. They untangle their legs and move to the wet bar.

A familiar retro song comes on, *I Just Want To Be Your Everything* by Andy Gibb, and any song by any brother Gibb makes her sing silly out loud. The song and Lauren's ridiculous singing lightens the mood.

The shaking sound of ice for their martinis seems quiet compared to their blurting voices; they point and laugh when Andy breaks into a falsetto voice trying to sing louder than her.

He sets the shaker aside and grabs her arms in a lighthearted embrace and she matches his hold, the two dancing barefoot, fueled by the drinks they've already had.

He suddenly stops. His eyes read happy but his lips look hungry. He leans down and kisses her. Her eyes fly open as stabs of excitement sear through her body. His lips are so warm, so delicious and *so on her right now*!

She pulls away, breathless. *Damn...that was...so good.* Her body softens at the sight of his eyes, his hair, everything Andy Hayden. And she wants more. Her lips dive back to his and he doesn't resist. Pleasure surges through her, dangling her on the edge of wanting more. Suddenly, reality smacks into her. *You can't kiss him! You're married!* She steps back; eyes ground in a shy focus on the floor.

Catching his breath, he gently squeezes her arms. "I shouldn't have done that. I'm so sorry."

She stares at the floor which seems to spin as fast as her racing mind. *He's sorry? She's not!*

She looks up into his anxious eyes. "That's too bad. I'm not sorry and right now I'm thinking that was the best kiss I've ever had in my life."

His eyes widen.

"But...even though that's the truth, I shouldn't have done it," she says, "and it can't happen again."

He takes a deep breath. "Okay, I'd like to tell you the truth." Another deep breath. "That was the best kiss I've ever had in my horny little life and while I know I shouldn't kiss a married woman, I can now die a happy man because it was worth everything."

Happy chills run down her body. *Love his honesty.* "But...it can't happen again."

He frowns. "It won't." He pulls her in for a friendly hug, his crisp dress shirt crunching against her cheek. She can barely stand up in his arms. She's melting with the thought of how tragic this is. He'll never hold her so close again. She can never kiss him again. But everything about being in his arms feels...perfect.

A long moment later she pulls away. "So, horny little life, huh?"

His clumsy choice of words makes them both laugh. "Hey, if you were married for twelve years to someone who told you when, where and how long, you'd be horny too."

They step apart.

"I should go now," he says.

"You don't have to go because we…well…you just made this drink!" She points to the wet bar and their full martini glasses.

"I just kissed the lead singer of my favorite band. The *married* lead singer. I probably shouldn't stay and finish that drink," he says, smiling. "Besides, it's late and I have to get up early to catch my flight." He reaches for his shoes and jacket.

"Hey, why don't you fly back on my plane with me?"

His head turns. "A private plane ride with you sounds more fun than commercial."

Lauren glares at the door; the last thing she wants to do is open it. She turns around just in time to watch Andy's muscular shoulders squeeze inside his jacket. The sight makes her tummy do that leaping thing again. "I enjoyed everything about tonight."

He swings his hair off his face, clearing her view of his wide smile. "You have no idea how much this evening meant to me." He steps into the hallway.

"Eight a.m., curbside of your hotel. Be there or you'll have to fly commercial."

"Oh I'm flying with you." He glances back with eyes that don't want to leave and a smile that clearly wants to stay.

His eyes: there's something about them. Cool but hot, edgy but safe. His stare doesn't bother her like the stares from others when she sings on stage. But it does make her wonder what he was staring at. Maybe her lace blouse was see-through, after all.

For the next hour Lauren paces the penthouse suite.

She sits where Andy sat on the sofa and outside chair. She washes his glass. She stands in the center of the room where they shared their kiss; a kiss she will never forget.

He was here, with her, together for a night. She learned so much and she shared too much.

Morning is drawing closer. She lies in bed with the terrace door cracked so she can hear the sounds of the quieting city. Andy must be back at his hotel by now. Wonder what he's thinking about tonight. But what if he had stayed here? How would he be holding her if he was lying with her now?

She rubs her face in her pillow to erase her cheating thoughts.

This might be getting complicated.

Maybe she's making this complicated.

[FIVE]

"Good morning, Lauren," her pilot Craig yells as she steps out of the town car. She nods, but the high-pitched sounds of the jet engines make it difficult to hear.

"Welcome aboard, Andy," co-pilot Henry yells as Andy steps on the tarmac.

They hurry onto the Gulfstream jet so they can hear each other again.

"I texted Craig and Henry this morning so they would know who you were," Lauren says.

Andy's eyes explore the inside of the plane as he takes a seat next to her. "Epic way to travel," he says, fiddling with the foot rest.

"Leasing this plane was one of Cory's good business decisions," she says, leaning over to help him. Andy's cologne still lingers on her blouse from their welcome hug this morning. And as she moves closer to him, that scrumptious spicy leather scent gets stronger.

"You can fly with me anytime, you know," Lauren says. "I mean, you can track my plane with the TracFlight app and pretend you are flying with me. You can track any plane by their tail number."

"You tease," he says. "Though tracking your flights sounds like fun too."

Craig and Henry have the plane up within minutes, leaving Andy and Lauren alone in the cabin. They recline the seats; lying across from each other.

He says nothing of his past and she says nothing of her present. They talk about ordinary things in a conversation that takes up the entire two and a half hour flight.

They begin the descent to Northrop, an executive airport in north Tampa close to Lauren's home. Her driver Bill will have an extra car ready to take Andy to Tampa International Airport, where he parked for his original flight.

As soon as the wheels hit the runway, two cars drive to meet them. She presses her face to the window for a closer look. It's her black Chevy Tahoe and Cory's black Mercedes S600 sedan.

"Oh…no," she slowly says. "Cory's car is pulling up with the Tahoe and he never lets anyone drive his car. He's never picked me up at the airport before."

Andy grins. "It's not like we're having an affair. You and I just had dinner, maybe drank a little too much, shared the best kiss of our life and then you gave me a ride home. Simple!"

Andy's damn smile is anything but simple.

The plane slows to a stop. Of course, he's right. They shared one spontaneous kiss and everything between them is now in check. She just needs to hide her *I dig Andy* vibe. Her vibe spikes when Andy gently rests his hand on her knee.

"The ride home was fantastic and last night was even better," he whispers, giving her two quick pats. "I'm really looking forward to meeting Cory!"

Her gut tightens.

A mix of sounds fill the air as the airplane door opens, the cars pull up and people get out. Lauren greets Cory with a quick kiss. "So… this is Andy Hayden, my rescued friend," she says, turning to Andy, her cheerful tone hiding her nerves.

"Yes, rescued from the tortures of commercial flight." Andy greets Cory with a handshake.

"Glad you had fun." Cory hasn't even released Andy's hand before he turns back to Lauren. "Ready?"

"Yeah, let me get Andy set with Bill," she says, leading Andy towards the Tahoe.

Bill has already loaded Andy's suitcase into the car. Craig and Henry have the plane ready to be towed to the hangar. How sad is this? Her time with Andy is over.

"Glad we could meet for dinner," she says.

"We can still meet for lunch this week too. My Thursday meeting was cancelled so now I'm open."

"Seriously? Perfect. Put me on your calendar."

Andy wraps her in a friendly hug. Her eyes close as she tries to memorize it.

"See you later this week." She turns away, unable to control the runaway smile spreading across her face. As she steps closer to the Mercedes her smile fades. Cory sits in the driver's seat, not bothering to open her door. She grudgingly climbs in the passenger seat.

"Thanks for picking me up."

Cory nods and says nothing, driving through the airport's automatic gates, while Lauren watches the rearview mirror and the car she'd rather be in. Cory turns right towards their home while Bill turns left with Andy towards Tampa International.

Her gaze sinks into a depressed stare out the window.

"So why were you in New York again?" Cory asks.

Her eyes squeeze closed. It's a wonder he still remembers her name.

* * *

It's Monday morning and after an aggressive, stress-releasing run with Davis, Lauren takes her coffee out by the pool. It's time for work. At least she doesn't have far to commute.

Plebeian's studio is a generous space attached to her north Tampa home. Money from record sales, Lauren's trust fund and generous bonuses Cory has earned were enough for them to build their twelve thousand square foot, two-story house. Their neighborhood only has twelve homes, all about the same size as Lauren's, and a security guard mans the neighborhood gate 24/7. She and Cory were just finishing the house when Academy Award nominations were announced. She wanted to move to the safer home immediately, catching their good friends in their old neighborhood by surprise when they suddenly moved before even listing their old house for sale.

Everyone in the band has the code to open the back gate of their home, giving them access to the poolside studio at any time. All the guys are here this morning, but none of them have unlocked the studio. They are too attracted to what Tish is offering.

Tish smiles with delight, her eyes peeking from behind her stylish, choppy blonde bangs. Tish manages Lauren's house and handles everything from accepting deliveries and scheduling service calls to whipping up meals for the family. It's not a full-time job, but it is a busy one. She loves fussing over Lauren's boys: the two teenagers and these four from the band.

"My favorite banana bread!" Michael says, sitting down at the outdoor table to eat.

"You made the egg thingy with the sausage," Oliver says, rudely thrusting his fork in the casserole.

Tish politely slides a plate towards Oliver. "I know you've all been traveling, so I wanted to make Monday special."

The solid breakfast was a good start to the unusually early morning. Their record company just told them they have to choose the lead off song for their second album.

They gather in the studio after breakfast. "Okay, last vote," Johnny says. "Hands up for *Tonight's Good Night.*"

All hands go up.

"Finally! We all agree. Then *Tonight's Good Night* it is," Johnny says.

"We seriously just voted like preschoolers?" Oliver asks.

"Next, Tish will bring us juice boxes before nap time," Michael says, grinning.

Lauren thought it was a stupid way to vote too but she likes the choice. *Tonight's Good Night* is about new beginnings. When she helped Johnny tweak the lyrics she realized the song is more about his reluctance of impending fatherhood.

Johnny hasn't even made the call to the record company and his eyes are already lost in thought staring out the window. After a couple of hours working in the studio, Lauren notices his mood hasn't gotten better. Maybe it's her turn to be the nosy ex. When everyone else heads out the door to leave, Lauren touches Johnny's arm.

"You've had a couple of zoned-out funks this morning," she says.

"Just a lot on my mind."

She knows what's on his mind. And since she's a mom, maybe she can help.

"Why don't you stay for lunch? It's been a while since we talked."

Not long after Johnny and Lauren have settled in at the poolside table, Tish brings them sandwiches and iced tea. It's a hot Florida day, but that's not why Johnny's pulling on his t-shirt.

"Do you think I'm wearing clothes that a daddy should wear?" he asks, tugging at his vintage wash black t-shirt.

"You're wearing clothes that look good on Johnny Fulton, and so if Johnny Fulton happens to be a daddy, then yeah, you are wearing good clothes."

"I'm just not feeling it, that's all. I think I'm too old to have kids."

"You're only thirty-seven, like me!"

Johnny looks down, circling a sliced lemon around the lip of his glass. "I've waited so long for a band like this. Everyone we picked is perfect. I've got dozens of songs already written. We're about to release a second album, right on the heels of our first. And now with Michael and all his talent, we could easily turn out new songs for years to come. How's a squirmy baby gonna fit into this?"

"You'll figure it out, just like I'm trying to figure something out." *Oh crap.* She looks down, not wanting to look him in the eye. *Why did she just blurt that?*

"What are you figuring out?"

Of course he heard her. Maybe she should blurt *I need to get rid of my husband*, but she's still not sure if that is what she should do. She looks up. "All is good. Actually, really good."

"Well, one thing we have to figure out is your confidence for live performances," he says.

She straightens.

"We need a tour to get to the next level and your stage fright is holding us back. You never had this problem back in college when we'd play on campus or at the clubs and stuff."

"I loved people looking at me then. It's different now."

"You're the same person, same great voice. What's changed?"

"Look, I don't think I've got some freaky clinical phobia. I just…"

Johnny's eyes tighten. "Just what?"

"I don't feel good about myself, okay? I'm always doing things for Cory or the kids. At the end of the day, there's nothing left of me. It's run me dry."

If she could hide between the bread slices of her sandwich, she would.

"I have a great stylist. Lara can do my hair, clothes and makeup and people think I've got my act together. But I don't! When people stare at me, it rips me up inside. It takes more than make-up for me to feel good. For years now I've had no emotional investment in myself."

"Then let's start investing," Johnny says, his wavy black hair picking up the slight afternoon breeze.

How can she admit what she's thinking? Andy is a great investment for her. When she's with Andy she feels confident, special and heard. There's got to be some way to get closer to Andy but still stay married, especially for the kids' sake. Plus, if she stays married, it continues to prove a secret point she's been making for years to Johnny.

"I think I know the best investment," she says. "I need the right people around me."

"You mean people in the band or people that help you, like Lara?"

"Neither. I think I need someone closer."

His jaw clenches. "Like the guy you gushed over during our concert after-party?"

"I didn't gush. He's a friend. An old friend from high school."

Johnny's smirk tells her: he doesn't buy it.

"I have no problem investing in people to help you but you need to be careful, Lauren. Don't play with fire."

Line crossed. Andy isn't fire! And what's this "I have no problem investing" crap, like he's the boss of her?

She leans closer. "If fire fixes my problems, I can handle the heat."

His eyes flare.

Ugh! She doesn't want this argument now! Johnny has always kept one critical eye on Cory and somehow he's doing the same with Andy, even though they've never met! She wants to get back to their original topic and ease this tension down.

"Look, Johnny, we are both going through new things now. I don't think either of us was looking for it but sometimes you play the hand you're dealt." She reaches for his hands, so dry and hardened from years of guitar playing. Johnny's exterior may be tough but she knows his heart means well. "Your lead singer here will figure out her problem," she says, smiling. "I may not be the best example, but I know you pretty well. You should think about marrying Amie. You might feel the whole family thing coming together when you're married."

"Well, look who's here," a voice bellows behind them. Cory has come home early—at lunch time? Lauren drops Johnny's hands. Shoot, this must look like a cozy, romantic lunch date!

"So, Johnny, are you enjoying…lunch?" Cory says, his voice dripping with his usual snide undertones. There's never been a day when Cory's liked him.

"Sure am. Lauren's coaching me on having a baby. Not making a baby, Cory, but having a baby."

"Come home early to check up on me or something?"

"Just wanted to spend an afternoon at home."

The thought unsettles her. He has been so distant for so long, why spend time at home now?

Johnny takes the hint and stands. "Lunch was great, Lauren. Thanks for the chat." He flings a stiff, departing smile to Cory as he steps away. Then, looking back at Lauren, he smirks.

Don't do it, Johnny. Don't...

He blows her a kiss.

She shakes her head.

Cory turns towards the house. Lauren dutifully follows him inside, where Tish has left the kitchen in perfect order and already left for the day.

He immediately heads to his den. The few times he wanders out, he barely talks and when he does it's about nothing of particular interest. The two of them alone in their own house feels awkward.

Eventually, Cory plops down on the family room sofa to watch a news program and Lauren stops reading her magazine to sit next to him. Neither she nor the program captures his interest and he quickly dozes off. This is her chance—her only chance—to touch him the way she used to. Slowly, she reaches for his hair, softly trailing her fingers through his coarse strands. She was once madly in love with him; now he's a man she barely knows. What made him drop work on a Monday to come home? He obviously wasn't seeking an afternoon romp in the sheets with her.

Is it because Johnny was here? That can't be it. Johnny has been to the house a hundred times now.

Is he wondering about Andy? She's never brought a guy back on the plane before.

She moves her hand off Cory's hair.

Stop! Once again, she's worried about Cory: what he's thinking and why. She's spent too many years carving out space to accommodate his needs and his career while she's barely received a compliment in return.

Plebeian will force her to face her fears. Johnny's right: they can't go on tour if she doesn't have the confidence to be on stage. She didn't want fame but now she doesn't want to hold back the others. But there's no way Cory would travel with her. Just thinking about leaving her kids behind and being alone on a world tour makes her chest ache.

Cory's gentle snoring brings her thoughts back from a world tour to this sleeping man on the couch. Look at what happened today: an afternoon alone with her husband. Would an afternoon like this, at home alone with Andy, be different? Would she be doing something other than watching him sleep?

She knows what she would be doing.

And she's close to getting rid of the last obstacle keeping her from it.

* * *

He does not want a sausage sample and the old lady offering it is as irritating as the dorky music playing in this grocery store.

He just wants to be left alone.

He has work to do.

He walks down the candy aisle, reaching the magazine display.

His eyes anxiously scan the covers, his skin moist and clammy from nerves, his heart beating faster in anticipation of what he will find.

Bingo: two new issues.

His fingers shake when he picks them up, holding the magazines closer.

She's on the cover of one of them and there's a photo spread inside with that story. The other issue has photos and a long article.

Good. Something enjoyable to keep him busy tonight.

[SIX]

Lauren tugs down her white sleeveless sweater dress, buckles the straps on her silver platform sandals and grabs her Balenciaga envelope clutch. It's the perfect late summer outfit for lunch.

She's a coordinated match to her car, a white BMW M6 Gran and today, she will drive herself. Usually she has Bill drive in case fans or paparazzi are following her. But today, she doesn't want anyone else involved.

Today, she's having lunch with Andy.

Andy has already arrived at the South Tampa seafood restaurant; his engaging smile is the first thing she sees. Their booth is towards the back of the restaurant, nicely tucked behind a wall of tall potted plants.

"Lucky for me that business lunch of yours was cancelled," Lauren says, putting her napkin on her lap as she takes her seat.

"I still can't believe we conquered our calendars for dinner and now lunch," he says, smiling. "I feel like the lucky one."

The look in his eyes warms her from head to toe. They may have agreed to put their spontaneous kiss behind them, but his eyes seem to want to change the deal. Is he as interested in her as she is becoming in him?

They talk about his work projects and she encourages him to tell his boss about his office restructuring idea. She gives him the inside scoop about a new song she's working on and he suggests a clever line for the lyrics. They debate which artificial sweetener is healthier and why people would risk botulism by eating raw oysters. No moment is without words that interest them both.

Andy's cheeks blush with his smile. "You are a good influence on me."

"Me? How so?"

He straightens. "I'm going on a date this weekend."

Her shoulders melt. "A date? A…A big date??"

"I don't know about big, but I finally asked her out," he says. "She's been dropping hints for a while and until I talked with you about my past I really never thought about dating her. She's cute, a bit younger than me and works downstairs in Human Resources. What the heck, right?"

What the heck, *wrong*! Andy is *her* crush and she liked him just the way he was: single and interested in her.

"Wow, this is a big move for you," she says, swallowing a gulp of nerves. "Tell me more about her."

He does, but she doesn't listen. She can't. No words make sense right now; her head spins in a blur. Did he just say they are going out Saturday night? This Saturday night? Why so fast?

Fake smile. "You know what Andy, I'm happy for you. Are you nervous?"

And again, his words sound like muffled blah, blah, blah's as her mind races. He's telling her this because they are just friends. Right? She *told* Andy they can never kiss again. She's married. He's single. Andy *should* be dating others. Then why can't she see straight right now?

"Lauren?"

"What? Oh sorry. Just got distracted."

Their lunch is winding down yet Lauren's mind is ramping up, obsessing about Andy's interest in this other girl.

He walks with her to the valet and in seconds her M6 pulls up.

"You didn't valet?" she asks.

"I'm in the lot right there," he points across the street.

"Jump in. I'll take you to your car."

He slides in the passenger seat. Their drive only takes a few minutes but Lauren wishes it was longer.

"Right there…the blue BMW," Andy says, pointing to his car.

"A 7-series. Nice car for a single thirty-seven-year-old guy," she says, pulling up beside his BMW.

He smiles. "A nice car might help me not stay single."

She cringes. Why can't his blue BMW be some plain, practical four-door sedan no other woman would notice? She pats his knee. "If you need a pep talk for Saturday night, I'm here for you."

"Good, I might need it. Maybe I'll call you Sunday with the recap?"

Her teeth clench. "Sure! I can't wait to hear the juicy details."

"Lunch was fantastic; let's schedule another one soon." He kisses her cheek and steps out of her car flashing a warm, departing smile.

Lauren drives away, her cheek stinging from the soft touch of his lips and her mind indignant. Within a few minutes she is on the interstate heading home, driving fast, but not as fast as her mind is racing. Andy kissed her in New York City—didn't he still have feelings for her? Wait, maybe he really doesn't have a date and just wanted to see her reaction?

She glances in the rearview mirror and the reflection of her angry eyes. *What a hypocrite.* How can she be outraged Andy is interested in someone else while she drives to the home she shares with her husband?

Lauren's bad mood worsens as the day wears on and reaches epidemic proportions by Friday. All of her feelings are bottled up with no one to talk to. Normally, Christy would be the first person she'd call for advice, but Christy's on a cruise and can't be reached. Michael and Davis have met Andy, but they don't know how mixed up her feelings are for him. She's already confided way too much to Johnny. Besides, Johnny can't even figure out if he wants to be a dad to the baby he's fathered with his girlfriend. Worse, she has no plans for the weekend. All she has is a husband who has suddenly remembered his home address but still hasn't realized his wife lives there too.

Saturday is a picture-perfect Florida summer day and after a brief afternoon thunderstorm, it turns into an unfortunately beautiful evening. Now nothing can stop Andy's date. And nothing can get her mind off of it.

No one at home wants to do anything with her tonight either. Aiden is practicing his drums in their studio and Lee is getting ready to hang out with some friends from their old neighborhood. Cory is still at work.

Maybe fresh air and a long run will help clear her mind. She laces up her favorite pair of running shoes, slips on a hat and new pair of sunglasses to help hide her identity and then heads out the door.

Her feet pound the sidewalk as she runs, the sun slicing through the canopy of tree branches overhead. With every step she feels like she's running towards Andy. And it feels good. Options seem unlimited with him. She feels happy and heard; he fits her life now. He's exciting; a known but unknown. With him she feels confident, beautiful and alive. But it's too late. Tonight, he's offering his options to someone else.

When the sun begins to set she stops running and glances at her watch. Her heartbeat is fast and heavy and she's not sure if it's from the exercise, her massive nerves or both. Andy's probably with his date now, having a wonderful meal at a trendy restaurant, where the music is edgy and the food is sparse. It should be her. Why can't it be her?

On Sunday morning, Lauren wakes up under a wad of bunched up sheets. She's dying to know how Andy's date went. He *had* offered to call her with the juicy details, and she'd really like some of those juicy details now. She waits all morning but her phone never rings. Then after lunch, she texts him:

"How was your date?"

About a half hour goes by before he replies:

"It's still going on."

Her grip goes slack and she drops the phone. Still going on? It's almost one p.m.! He spent the night with her?

The game is off, just when Lauren realized Andy is the guy for her. She was close to walking away from a seventeen-year marriage to be with the man who gave her the best kiss of her life. But now…her head drops in disappointment.

She couldn't have Andy Hayden in high school or college and she can't have him now. He really may have been the love of her life. No man has ever made her feel this way before.

Distant thunder from a passing rainstorm adds to the gloom of this Tuesday evening. Lauren hasn't heard from Andy since his brief text on Sunday. The dinner dishes are all washed and she closes the stainless steel warming oven, the trusty appliance she uses everyday to keep Cory's dinner warm, since she never knows exactly when he'll be home. Aiden and Lee have left to hang out with friends. All alone in this big, lonely house, she seeks a smaller space and wanders out to the studio.

Johnny's favorite Hummingbird acoustic guitar hangs in the corner and seems to be inviting her to pick it up. She rests the smooth wood on her bare legs as she softly strums. The wood feels as cold as her spirit. She put no effort into choosing the denim cut-off shorts and white t-shirt she's been wearing all day. Did she even take a shower? The twangs from the guitar sound odd; she doesn't know how to play. She strums the strings anyway, letting her mind get lost in the sad, pitiful sound her fingers make.

Her problem is larger than her lack of guitar-playing skills. She's unhappy and unloved. She started to imagine a life without her husband and the growing crush she had for Andy gave her hope for an exciting new chapter. But now Andy isn't an option.

But why stay married and unhappy? She'd rather be without a man and be happy. She just started an exciting new career. This should be one of the happiest times of her life!

Lauren stops her pathetic playing to rub her eyes. Being a single woman in a rock band? The stares she barely tolerates now would become more intense. Instead of being a marketable piece of meat, she would be a single, rich, meaty slab.

No options are good without Andy.

Suddenly her phone chimes with an incoming text.

"If you are available I need to see you. Tonight. Can we meet somewhere at 7?"

It's Andy! But this can't be for her. It's six thirty. He wouldn't ask to see her that quickly. It took them two months just to find a day that worked for dinner!

"Did you mean to send this to me, Andy?"

He immediately replies:

"Yes, Lauren. I want to see you as soon as I can. Can we meet at Burton's Coffee in the parking lot?"

Her face warms, her heartbeat rises.

"Sure. I will leave now"

* * *

After the fastest shower of her life, Lauren pulls into the parking lot at Burton's Coffee, next to Andy's blue BMW. He's sitting in the driver's seat, clenching the wheel, and nods for her to join him. She opens his passenger door and climbs in, scrunching the back of her still damp hair. His eyes look flat and strained with stress but his clothes are casual—dark jeans and button-down shirt with the sleeves rolled up—so he didn't come from work.

"I just need to drive," he says. He pulls out of the space and his quick acceleration pushes Lauren back in her seat.

What the heck? "Everything okay?"

"I just wanted to see you. I want to talk with you. Somewhere private."

They drive a few miles south to a waterside park facing the bay. He puts the car in park, his eyes darting like a guilty little boy unable to admit his mischief.

"Are you…mad?" she asks, curious but nervous. She tilts her head to see him better.

He turns to face her. His hazelnut-olive eyes and thin nose are inches away, his lips looking more mouth-watering than when she first tasted them in New York City. He slowly nods.

"Wow…what happened?" She braces for some horrible story.

"Want the short answer? I turned on my TV one night and saw you." She pulls back. *Her?*

"It's you; you. I just…I just stumble along with my life, making mistakes left and right and then there you are: my high school memory on TV at the Academy Awards one night. You're the voice in the band that plays the music that I love. You are larger than life—full of life and I can only dream of you remembering me. And then you do, you do remember me, we have this connection, you help me, you listen to me," he says with words so heavy with emotion they seem to hang in the air.

"It's not your money and it's not your fame. It's how you encourage me. You believe in me. No one has ever believed in me.

"I want your laugh and that look from your eyes. I want your interest in me. I know there is a line I'm not supposed to cross but you have to know I want to. You have to know all I imagine is my life with you."

Elated flutters fill her belly. She sits back, stunned. All she has dreamt of for the last five days is Andy saying something like that. And now, he actually is.

"What do I have to do? What can I say? How do I get closer to you?" he asks.

Now her heart pulses as fast as her stomach flutters.

"I…I…" she stutters. "I thought you found a new girlfriend. Your date the other day; I thought you found someone more interesting than me."

He inches towards her, reaching for her fidgeting hands. His warm touch calms her flutters. She stares in disbelief at their touching hands.

"There's no one better than you. Lauren, there's no one *but* you."

This…is happening?

"We have to figure this out," she says. "But it can't be now. I'm…I just can't do this now."

"I didn't try hard enough for you when I was younger. I accepted that you had a boyfriend and didn't try. No more. I'm not going to sit back and not try. I know there's a line but I have to keep trying."

"But my line, Andy, doesn't get redrawn overnight."

He reaches for her hair and the spinning world seems to stop as he softly strokes down. Her scalp warms where his fingers trail; she can't see anything but him.

"Then I will wait for the line to be redrawn."

She can't speak. He will wait until she's ready? *Is she really ready?*

She looks around the car for something to focus on to calm her nerves and break the tension of Andy's stare. Then something catches her attention. Off in the distance across the bay, she notices the lights of a cargo ship leaving port. The sight of the ship draws the perfect comparison to what her brain and her heart are going through. Her brain is like the cargo ship—dutiful, purposeful and loyal—it reminds her that she's already in a committed relationship with Cory. But her heart is different. She imagines another ship sailing beside that cargo ship: a cruise ship. Her heart is more like a cruise ship—exciting with a party on every deck—and right now she really wants to take a cruise with Andy. Temptation is urging her to jump over this car console, throw herself on his lap and start redrawing some lines right now. But her brain is calling for common sense to keep her on her side of the car. For now, the cargo ship wins.

She turns back to face him.

"What…what happened the other night with your date?" she asks, so curious why he spent the night with someone but now wants to be with her.

His slight laugh tells her this is going to be a good story.

"Dinner was fine, but compared to you, she was boring. She tried to drink martinis with me but after two she switched to red wine. That was a bad call. I drove her home after dinner and she threw up when we got to her apartment. I got her on the couch but she passed out. I felt sorry for her and tried to clean up as much as I could.

"It was late and I wanted to go home so I took her key and locked up behind myself. The next morning I called her to see if she was okay and she never answered. I was worried, so I went back. I knocked but she didn't answer, so I used the key and found she had fallen off the couch. I woke her up and told her this was not my idea of a good date and wished her luck with the cleanup. It was embarrassing; I didn't want to text all that."

Wish he would have because this is hilarious. "All that time I thought she was in your arms and little did I know your arms were cleaning up her vomit." She struggles to hold back a laugh but it's no use. They both burst out laughing.

But the clock on Andy's dashboard reminds them of reality. "I know we have so much unresolved, but I've got to get home now," Lauren says softly.

They start the drive back to Burton's, the moon filling the night sky, the silence in Andy's car making them more aware of each other.

Finally she can feel the layers peeling away from the one remaining obstacle to a new life with Andy. The question of her strong tradition to obligation has been called. She's not a failure if her marriage ends. Her mother warned her that divorce should never be an option. Lauren married Cory anyway, rushing into marriage to prove she was over Johnny. She tried to make her stale marriage work, burdened by the obligation of her vows. But now the larger obligation is to her happiness. Chances are Cory won't even miss her. And her boys have grown up to be fine young men; they will understand this. There's no need to prove she's over Johnny anymore either. It's time to work on her happiness.

She reaches for Andy's hand, threading her fingers between his, pressing her palm tight against his. He glances down at their hands while he drives, holding the steering wheel in his left hand while Lauren squeezes his right.

"I don't know what the future holds, but I do want to find a way to get you in it," she says, pressing his warm hand tight.

He breathes in deep and smiles. They drive in silence, their fingers woven together in a simple yet powerful touch.

Good thing she left the house so fast tonight; she didn't have time to put on her wedding ring. It would have made holding hands with another man more awkward.

A hand hold and a promise to figure something out are as bold as Lauren wants to go right now. She has more than Cory to worry about. She has two kids and a public image. At some point here she's going to have to get a lawyer involved. And Johnny.

* * *

Traffic seems heavy for this hour of the night.

Still, he's able to pass that stupid silver pickup truck that just cut him off. Now he's back behind her white BMW again.

Her brake lights shine brightly as she brings her car to a gentle stop.

From the traffic light's glow he can see her face in her rearview mirror.

He can see her eyes.

She's so beautiful.

He tightly grips the steering wheel, his palms wet with nervous sweat.

This really isn't a good idea; she shouldn't be driving home alone in the dark like this.

It could be dangerous.

Someone like him could be following her.

[SEVEN]

Lauren wakes to the sounds of running water and a toothbrush being thrown in the sink.

"Ridiculous," she hears Cory say.

She rolls out of bed and steps into the bathroom. "You okay?"

"Whatever," he says, looking down and reading something from his phone.

"What time are you coming home tonight?" she asks. She always asks. This time though, she asks because she wants to have a serious talk.

"It's just too hard to tell," he grumbles, leaving the room.

No morning kiss. No departing one either. Cory never even looked her in the eyes. He's certainly making one decision easier for her.

Lauren steals a page from Cory's playbook and pours herself into her work while she sorts through her next steps. Plebeian is heading to Phoenix to do three full days of recording for their second album. This Phoenix studio specializes in ensemble recordings where musicians record all parts together. This less fabricated sound is exactly what Johnny wants for these songs. Everyone needs to be completely prepared because if one person messes up, they all start from the beginning again. This is a lot different than when Lauren records vocals alone in a booth.

These recording sessions will be intense but they are also planning some relaxation time at the desert resort where they will be staying. Everyone is bringing someone on this trip. Amie is coming with

Johnny, Michael is bringing Sunny and Doug is bringing his brother Jason. Oliver is bringing a friend since his wife Mary can't come, but then again, Mary never seems to come to anything. There will be a full complement of security, drivers and background musicians. Davis will be there, as will their production manager Trent Driscoll and their publicist Lynette Brooks and her assistant Lesley Baldwin.

At the same time as their Phoenix trip, Cory has planned a business trip to Germany with three coworkers. He is researching a resort that offers first-class, kid-friendly amenities, so he and his colleagues are each bringing their kids. Lauren can't help but visualize him traveling hundreds of miles east while she travels hundreds of miles west. It's the perfect example of their marriage: heading in totally different directions.

She's already made plans to fly to Phoenix a day early to relax in preparation for their recording session. Her suite is supposed to have a large private terrace with a Jacuzzi, and soaking in a hot tub in the desert air sounds like heaven. Actually, sharing this trip with Andy is what sounds like heaven. Everyone else is bringing someone, so why shouldn't she bring a friend?

She calls him. "I know this is short notice, but can you run away with me in three days?"

"If you gave me only three minutes I'd make it happen," he says.

She gives him the details.

"I finally get to meet the rest of the band," Andy says, sounding excited. "I've never been in a recording studio either. This will be so fun to watch you!"

Every minute listening to him makes her excited too. The uneasiness in her gut is gone. And by the time they hang up she feels braver.

Brave enough to ask Davis to book Andy's room close to hers, and to tell Davis not to ask any questions.

* * *

Because of time zone changes it is still early morning when Andy and Lauren arrive in Phoenix.

A personal butler shows Andy his room first. Then the butler and Lauren continue down the hallway to her suite, just six doors down from Andy's room. A generous VIP welcome basket with fruit and wine is placed on the dining room table and through the dark mahogany framed glass doors she sees the private terrace and sunken hot tub.

When the butler leaves, she texts Andy:

"Jacuzzi on the terrace! Get your swim trunks and come down!"

"Be there asap."

She rushes to the bedroom, quickly unzipping her suitcase. Her clothes are off in seconds, replaced with a black bikini and sheer sarong cover-up, though the sheer black fabric really doesn't cover much up. She steps outside to the terrace, a beautiful, open yet private space with two half walls, and the other two sides opening to the suite's bedroom and living room. The Jacuzzi jets hum while she grabs some towels, two plush bathrobes and then passes the time twirling the strings on her bikini while she waits for Andy.

Finally, there's a knock at the door.

Lauren opens the door and both of them drop their mouths in surprise.

Andy's already visited the lobby bar, bringing up a shiny silver tray with two martini shakers and two glasses. Guess he didn't want to wait for the butler to bring drinks! He looks Jacuzzi-ready in blue-and-white striped board shorts with a white polo shirt.

"Are you trying to get me drunk this early?" she asks.

His mouth hangs open. "Wow, you've changed to a great new outfit!"

Their eyes teasingly look each other over. She welcomes him into the suite, leading him to the terrace where the bubbly hot tub awaits. He sets the drink tray on a side table as his eyes greedily admire her attire.

"That really is a great swimsuit."

She steps closer to him, so close his warm breath tickles her cheek. "Too bad you won't see it when I'm underwater." She tosses him a daring smile and unties her sarong, letting the sheer fabric fall on his feet. She snatches the glasses and one shaker and turns, knowing his eyes are following her, and steps down into the swirling pool. "Water's great! You should be in here with me!" She pours her martini.

In seconds, his shirt comes off. Now she sees proof of the time he makes for his fitness; his tight abs and bulging biceps are covered in smooth, tan skin. She squeezes her martini glass at the sight.

Andy steps into the water, gliding to the submerged seat across from her.

Her smile can't be contained. She pours his martini and hands him his glass.

He sips, smiling. "Mmmm, this drink is nice and cold. This water's hot!"

"Temperature sure went up when you got in," she says, sipping.

"This water is still not as hot as that bikini." His eyes lower as he takes another sip.

She finishes off her martini. Now she has an empty shaker, an empty glass and a warm buzz from drinking so fast. *Keep the martinis and cheesy lines coming!*

"Can you pour me another?" she asks, knowing the second shaker is on the side table on far side of the hot tub. He'll have to step out to get it. And one of those wet and now see-through white stripes on his swim trunks is right where she wouldn't mind another glance.

He moves for the steps and she tilts her head to watch.

"Hold on." He turns around and dips back under the water. "What are you looking at?"

"Nothing," she says, lowering her eyes guiltily and raising her glass to hide behind a sip. Her eyes flash down to the glass. It's empty. *Busted.*

"Uh huh…" he says, smiling. "I guess a man's white swim trunks are to a woman what a little black bikini is to a man."

"Is there anything wrong with that?"

"Not from where I'm sitting." He raises his martini glass in approval.

"My glass is still empty!"

The water parts as Andy moves closer, his eyes searching the bubbles for a glimpse of her bouncing chest. Every inch closer makes her breathe faster.

His wet fingers stroke hers as he slowly takes her glass out of her hand. He places both glasses on the side of the hot tub and now, empty-handed, turns to look back at her. He bites his lip and his eyes darken. Her insides melt.

"Look, I know there is this line between us, and I respect that," he says, his eyes blazing. "But I want you to know…I really want to cross it right now."

She gulps.

Bubbles swirl around them, her mind spinning as agitated as the water. She's gone too far; she's led him on. She flaunted bare skin covered in mere inches of fabric while he's half naked. He's right there, ready for the taking. She can't.

Damn her promises! Damn the years of mistakes! Damn him for looking so freaking hot!

She exhales one of the most frustrating breaths of her life. "Can you cross it…when I'm ready?" she whispers.

His grin softens her frustration. "I won't cross anything if you aren't ready."

Steam from the water and the heat of her surging emotions are making her dizzy. Why should there be a line for him to cross anyway? Why can't she be happy? Free? What the hell is she waiting for?

"I'm going to get rid of this line," she whispers. "As soon as I get home, I will see a lawyer. I don't want anything to stand between us."

His eyes widen and his smile broadens. "Us?"

She nods. "I want us."

"I'm going to make you happy," he whispers.

Relief blankets her. "Andy, you already do."

[EIGHT]

"Greek omelet, no onions," the waiter says, placing a steaming plate in front of Lauren.

"And for you, sir, the breakfast combo with turkey sausage," he says, putting a plate in front of Andy.

"So perfect, thank you," Lauren says, reaching for a bottle of hot sauce to make a perfect omelet even better. The hotel café has a view of the morning sunrise from the back windows and a view of the lobby from the front. But she can't take her eyes off the man in front of her. And the image from those wet, white stripes when he finally stepped out of the hot tub yesterday has yet to leave her waking thoughts either.

Andy rotates his plate so the sausage is closer to him. "I'm starving after last night!"

"For real," she says, scooping up a heaping forkful of spinach, egg and mushrooms with a dash of hot sauce.

"Look," he says, cutting his scrambled eggs into a quarter of the serving. "That was how big my entire meal was at that fancy restaurant last night."

She holds up another forkful of omelet, laughing. "Does this remind you of how much food was on my plate too?"

"Why is it that the fancier the restaurant, the smaller the meal?"

"I'll never know," she says, smiling. "I'm just glad I was able to share the stingy, expensive meal with you."

Andy sips his coffee. Even his eyes look like they are smiling. "A hot tub swim, lunch by the pool, a fancy dinner and now breakfast with you? This weekend is amazing."

Clarity in her life, Andy's company and the promise of a future with him. This weekend has been amazing for her too. Except the frustrating part of sleeping alone last night, especially knowing he was alone in his room right down the hall. At least they're together now. But she knows they won't be alone for long.

Her phone chimes with a burst of incoming texts.

"Your boys again?" Andy asks, looking on.

"They should be having dinner in Berlin by now," she says, looking down. A sarcastic grin covers her face. "Yeah, it's the boys all right. My band boys. Charter flight just landed." She holds up her phone.

"Wake up…we're here!" texts Michael.

"Your suite better not be bigger than mine," texts Johnny.

"Are you sleeping alone because if you are I'll be right there," texts Oliver.

"You have no idea how long this plane ride has been," texts Lynette.

Lauren laughs. "When the publicist says the plane ride has been long; then it's been long." She looks again at Oliver's text. *Oh my God; perish that thought.*

By the time Andy and Lauren have wrapped up their meal, their private time is over.

Michael spots them first, bounding across the hotel lobby, a cross-body satchel carrying his music bouncing off his hip with each step. "Order anything for us?"

Sunny catches up, adjusting her slipping purse strap. "Honey, you don't need a second breakfast."

Davis appears from behind them, his signature blue boat shoes and plaid shirt matching the vibe of this resort much better than when he wears them during a concert. He scans Lauren's empty plate. "You didn't order anything with onions did you? Vocals need to be perfect today and I don't need you…you know…burping."

"Unless burping is written on my music as something for me to do, I have no plans to entertain you with any today," she says, smiling. "Davis, this is Andy Hayden, my…friend."

Davis shakes Andy's hand. "Everything good with your room?"

"Perfect; everything has been perfect."

Doug, his brother, Oliver and his friend arrive. Lauren completes her introductions of Andy. Andy seems a little awkward meeting Oliver, but only because Oliver is awkward to know.

Davis distributes room keys. "Do what you need to do in your rooms and get back down here in fifteen for the shuttle to the studio."

Like candy to hungry kids, the guys grab their keys and head off to their rooms.

Then someone's hand rests on Lauren's shoulder. It's Johnny.

"Hey, Johnny, Amie," Lauren says, standing. "This is, um, my good friend, Andy."

"From high school, right?" Johnny says, extending a hand and a long, reviewing look.

Andy stands. "It's true; that long ago." He smiles his hello to Amie.

Lauren stands between two strong forces in her life. And she's got her fingers crossed that Andy will get along better with Johnny than Cory did.

Johnny turns to Lauren. "We need to go over some stuff before we leave. Now, maybe?"

"Hey, I'll go up to my room and be back here in a few minutes, good?" Andy says and Lauren nods.

"I'll go check out our room," Amie says, giving Lauren a tepid glance. Amie's tight t-shirt hugs the curves of her growing belly. As she begins to walk away, Lauren tries not to stare at Amie's surging, hormone-amplified chest. *Geez, even Amie's pregnant body is perfect, times ten.*

Lauren turns to Johnny. "What's up?"

He squints. "Just curious; I didn't realize you came out here a day early, you know, with your friend."

She stands taller. Good lord, if she was a pie, she feels like Johnny would claim every slice.

"It wasn't a secret and coming out a day early was…amazing for me."

"Amazing, huh? What's going on?"

What the…? "I'm ready to lay some tracks today. What's going on with you?"

"Just making sure you're okay."

Relax, Captain Control!

"Never been better," she says, cheeks pulsing. "And I've got the sudden urge to get busy recording all day."

They look at each other that way that they do. Sometimes Lauren thinks she could send a complete sentence through her eyes to Johnny and he would understand it.

"Okay, as long as you are okay." He nods and they turn to rejoin the others now gathering in the lobby.

And where does Johnny look when they turn around? Straight to take a laser sharp good look at the man now walking back towards Lauren.

This feels like the beginning of one very strange day.

A steaming cup of tea feels warm in Lauren's hands; her eyes close after taking a long, soothing sip. After singing for hours in the studio today she was supposed to rest her voice and stay quiet. Instead she just spent an hour on the phone with her attorney Pamela. After watching Andy's inviting eyes stare at her from the observation room all day, she was motivated to make the "how do I begin a divorce" call.

She sits on the sofa in her suite, bending forward to buckle the straps on her evening sandals. Two more days here and then she'll be home. She'll talk with Cory and then explain everything to the boys. Nothing about this will be easy, but it will be over. And her new life will begin.

Soft knocks sound on her door and her face flushes as bright as her coral knit dress. Andy is coming to walk her down to tonight's poolside reception with executives from the recording studio and Plebeian's record company, Platinum Plate Records. Then the group will have dinner in a private room in one of the resort's restaurants.

She opens the door and gasps.

Andy stands with a smile, holding a bouquet of peach roses.

"I'd like for you to know what it feels like to get flowers from a man."

She opens the door wider. He wears a white button-down shirt and dressy jeans, she thinks. She can't really see because her eyes are filling with tears.

She bites hard on her lip to hold off a full-blown cry, looking down at the flowers. "Wow—you remembered."

Andy steps closer. "Line or no line, I will never let you wonder what this feels like."

He slides his hand under her chin to push her head up. His eyes fill her with the love she has craved. He pulls back, adjusts his hair with one of his irresistible hair swings, and then places the bouquet in her quivering hands.

With Plebeian business to attend to, they walk together to the poolside reception. Some resort guests are standing nearby and taking pictures as they arrive. It's no big deal if she arrives with Andy; others have arrived in groups of different people.

The desert evening is warm and clear; the wood-burning fire from the restaurant's grill fills the air with a mouth-watering cedar scent. The setting sun has painted the sky in shades of honey and the private party is filled with music and conversation.

Andy waits for her cue and then picks up conversations with everyone they meet. Lauren gives him a "game on" stare as she approaches their record company representatives. Everyone in the band knows Platinum Plate wishes they had more than just a license deal with

Plebeian. Lauren didn't need the record company's capital, which gives Plebeian more copyright and ownership of their own material. Their deal made Johnny, Lauren, Oliver, Michael and Doug rich. Then again, Plebeian's success has put Platinum Plate Records on the map.

Lauren gets stuck in conversation with one of the record executives and loses track of Andy. She scans the crowd and sees him at the other side of the pool, alone with Johnny, whose flailing arms seem to be doing the talking. *Damn!* She quickly excuses herself and rushes to the bar to order their favorite drinks: a beer for Johnny and a martini for Andy.

"Interrupting anything?" she asks, stepping up to them. She hands them their drinks, still not sure what they were talking about but certain it was about her.

"Look, there's a lot of change coming for me," she says, rotating her eyes to each of them, "but one thing I know is my life has room for both of you."

Johnny's eyebrows wrinkle. "Hey, Andy, would you mind if I talk with Lauren for just a second?"

Andy leans towards her. "You okay if I leave?"

"It might be good if he and I talk," she whispers. Actually, she's not interested in a friendly chat; she wants to shut down this possessive, ex-boyfriend thing right now.

Andy excuses himself and walks towards Michael and Sunny.

Johnny leans closer. "So, you are choosing to play with fire."

Her arms cross. "I told you before, I can handle the heat."

"Are you sure this is a good idea?"

"Me being happy? Yeah, it's a good idea."

"Is this supposed to be secret or are you kicking Cory to the curb?"

"Cory's been on the curb."

"This will be big news when it comes out."

"And right now, there's nothing *to* come out."

From the corner of her eye, Lauren notices Lynette and Davis heading toward her, their expressions serious. They come face-to-face with her and Johnny and pull them into a close circle.

"There's a situation," Lynette says, eyes wide, catching her breath. Lynette must be the calmest publicist in the world; never ruffled. So if she says there is a situation, it's a safe bet something isn't good. She looks Lauren in the eye. "Some pictures have come out."

Lauren sucks in a breath and her head rolls back. Pictures of her and Andy already? Alone? At dinner? Breakfast? Oh God, not in the hot tub?!

Davis pulls up the photos on his phone.

"From Germany…" Lynette says.

Lauren's head lurches forward.

"Cory has been enjoying another woman's company," Lynette says.

Lauren hears Lynette's words in slow motion. Cory? Another woman? Davis holds up his phone with the photos. There are several of Cory and a young brunette that Lauren recognizes. He works with her! They are kissing in one photo, he is kissing the side of her face in another and they are dancing in some club in another. Cory dances?

"They were taken tonight in Berlin and just posted on this gossip website," Lynette says.

Johnny swats down Davis's phone.

"People might be watching us right now; fans over there, other people in this party," Johnny says. "Someone could be taking pictures of Lauren seeing these for the first time."

"We've got to get you out of here now," Lynette says.

"Let's get her back to her room," Johnny says.

They quickly leave the reception without saying goodbye to anyone, walking from the pool area back up to Lauren's suite.

Once inside, Lynette uses her tablet to show Lauren the pictures in larger view. Lauren's mouth falls open in shock. Cory was making out with this girl in a public place, looking like a fool.

"Okay, she needs to stay in here until this is figured out," Johnny says, launching into crisis management. "Davis, you need to tell our record execs at dinner that we've got a situation but she's okay."

"We're going to need a statement from you because without one people will speculate on what you are thinking and feeling and it can get out of control," Lynette says.

Lauren looks up from the tablet. They are troubleshooting her spouse's public cheating scandal at the same time she was on the verge of becoming a cheating spouse herself.

"Oh no, Andy!" she says. "Someone needs to get Andy up here!"

Davis hurries out of the room to pull Andy from the reception downstairs.

She turns to Johnny and Lynette, shaking the tablet as if Cory was inside it. "I don't care if it's the middle of the night in Germany. I'm calling him." She stomps to the bedroom.

A sluggish Cory answers the phone.

"You got caught, Cory! The photos are everywhere."

"What? It's no big deal," he says sleepily. "It's not like I'm running around with my old college lover all the time."

"Johnny? Really, Cory? What does Johnny have to do with your tongue down the side of another woman's face tonight?" she yells, pushing her tired vocal chords over their limit. "Get Aiden and Lee out of there now! You do whatever in the hell you want Cory but get Aiden and Lee home now!"

She disconnects the call, throwing her phone on the bed. As it tumbles it lights up with incoming texts from worried friends who are starting to see the photos. In minutes this has gone worldwide.

She doesn't know who might be in the living room of her suite but there's a good chance they overheard her yelling. When she emerges from the bedroom she sees Andy first. *To hell with optics now.* She runs into his arms.

"Can you believe this?" she asks.

"To me it's a dream come true," Andy unapologetically says, squeezing her.

She quickly turns to see who else is in the room. Only Johnny is there, sitting on the dining table, his legs swinging as he tosses up an apple from the hospitality gift basket.

"Well sure it's a dream for you, Andy, because evidently I get the blame," Johnny says. Then he looks at Lauren. "And, if you were going to bust up your marriage anyway for a new guy, it's not so bad that your husband went public with another girl first."

Johnny is right. She has just been handed the perfect public relations disaster.

[NINE]

Dim lights warm Lauren's hotel suite; it's well after midnight and she just heard her suite door close.

She softly steps out from the bedroom. "Who was that?" she asks Andy.

He turns, holding a room service tray of salty snacks, chocolate and wine. "Reinforcements."

She lays a hand over her heart. *This* man is a keeper.

He sets the tray on the table. "Did it help to rest a bit?"

She nods, walking toward him with her hands deep in the pockets of a plush hotel bathrobe. "Thank you for staying, and for helping to get Johnny out the door."

Andy holds her shoulders. His eyes glimmer with understanding, patience and if she's reading them right, love. "Johnny would have stayed all night. He just wants to help you."

"I know. He means well."

"It was good for us to talk. I think he relaxed a bit, with me."

"I didn't want to listen to him getting all strategic with the band, already figuring out how my crisis can be turned into a positive. I know he said it's fine, but he's probably pissed I can't finish these recording sessions."

Andy looks down. "When do we leave?"

She pushes up his chin to look into his eyes. "First thing in the morning. I want to get home before the boys."

"I'm sorry you had to go through such a surprise. But I have to be honest; I'm glad it happened."

"A few paparazzi pictures and boom, our line disappeared," she whispers.

"I understand if you need time to process this. Even though it's what you wanted, it probably still hurts."

She shakes her head. "It hurts and I'm sad, especially for my boys. But my marriage has been over for awhile. I don't need more time. And since we're only here a few more hours, the only thing I want to process…is you."

His gaze deepens.

She glances over his shoulder. "And maybe some of that chocolate and wine…"

His smile is already heading for the tray.

"…and actually, that chocolate and wine in the hot tub would be nice!" She tugs the belt of her robe, opening it. She's wearing her black bikini.

"My lucky day and my favorite suit!" he says.

Her grin turns mischievous and she races towards the hot tub. In seconds, she's got the water swirling, her robe on the terrace floor, and her skin covered with warm water and soothing bubbles. Andy follows with the tray, placing it down beside the pool.

He stands at the edge of the hot tub, still wearing his dressy jeans and white button-down shirt from the reception. "My swim trunks are back in my room."

She sure doesn't want to wait for him to get them. "Aw…too bad." She swats water his way.

His teeth clench. He kicks off his shoes, uncorks the wine and starts unbuttoning his shirt.

Time for a show!

Soft moonlight shines on his bare chest and on his hands as they slowly unbutton his jeans.

*Mother of God…*she's about to get a full view of what was under those white swim trunks. His fingers…undoing…buttons…zipper… down…thumbs pushing jeans down…boxers dropping. She thinks she hears a choir of angels singing. She can't breathe; blink; move.

Wearing nothing but a smile and a healthy arousal, he steps into the hot tub.

"Wine?" he offers, pouring a glass of merlot.

A shot of whiskey might work better right now. She reaches for the glass, smiling, sipping, and then sipping again.

Water laps at his bare chest as the Jacuzzi churns and her goose bumps grow.

"Chocolate?" he offers, holding out an unwrapped bar.

She can't take any. One hand holds her wine and the other one is wet. But her mouth is available. Smiling, she parts her lips. He grins and clutches the end of the bar with his teeth. Coming closer is a sweet chocolate scent, his glowing eyes and a burning urge to put *anything* he offers into her mouth. Nose-to-nose with him, she sinks her teeth into the most erotic bite of chocolate in her life.

He slowly licks chocolate from his lips, his smile so wide he's barely able to sip his wine.

Rich chocolate melts in her mouth like a libido-surging sugar rush. She's buzzing from her finished glass of wine. He sets down his empty glass. The bubbly water glistens as he moves closer again. Only this time he has no chocolate.

He takes her glass out of her hand and sets it aside.

"Look, I know there was a line between us, and I respected that," he whispers, "but the line is gone and I want you…now."

He grabs her shoulders, pulling her into a chocolate and wine flavored kiss. She throws her arms around him, opening her legs to straddle his waist.

Reckless passion takes over, water splashes as their hands begin to explore. They twist in the steamy water when she pushes him against the side of the hot tub, tugging at his wet hair. He groans and pushes her back against the ledge, his tongue against hers. She's overheating with his kissing, becoming undone and delirious with want.

Andy pulls away, putting his wet, warm fingers on her lips to stop their kissing. *What? Why?* He flips his head to sweep his wet hair from his eyes and turns for the hot tub steps, climbing out and putting on a plush hotel robe draped over a nearby chair. He turns to face her, his body a sexy, dripping mess wrapped in a cuddly, thirsty and wide open robe. It's easy to see the size of the pleasure that awaits her.

He grabs the second robe and reaches for her.

Ah…time to give him something to memorize. She tugs the strings of her bikini top and the fabric falls into the water as fast as his mouth drops open. Then with every hip-twisting step out, she slowly reveals her topless body. Grinning, he covers her back with the robe, helping to thread her arms through the oversized sleeves.

The soft cotton robe has dried the water off her skin but she still feels wet wearing her bikini bottom. It's time to get rid of it. Eyes on him, she bends forward, slowly pulling the bikini down until it falls to the floor. "No lines now."

His eyes drink in the sight of her naked body. "No lines."

They stand face to face, toe to toe, open robe to open robe. Then lips to lips they exchange soft, engaging kisses.

She's got him—she's finally got him and she's not waiting any longer. She pulls back from their kiss.

"I'm yours. Please—take me."

His inhale makes his shoulders rise. He grabs her hand, squeezes hard and leads her from the terrace. He can't see her smile as he guides her through the suite living room and into the bedroom, never once looking back.

Stopping at the end of the bed, he faces her, staring with adoring wonder. The taste of what will happen next fills her mouth. Andy turns and dismantles the bedding and she can't help but softly giggle as he wildly tosses the pillows to the floor and rips back the crisp white sheets. He turns to face her. *There it is.* His invitation to join him in bed and she is so ready to be his lover.

"I didn't bring swim trunks, or…anything else…"

She hushes him with a finger to his lips. "I've got it covered." She's prepared; she sure isn't going to end up with a surprise in nine months like Johnny has.

His warm hands claim her, starting on her bare chest then slowly sliding up until he gently pushes the robe off her shoulders. Her moves are more primal, yanking the shoulders of his robe until it falls to the ground. Their bare bodies meet each other for the first time, falling on the bed.

All they feel is warmth; all they kiss is skin. All they make is pure love as they release their inaugural pleasure.

[TEN]

The ringing doorbell at Lauren's home sounds like a blaring telephone amplified with the boom of a gong.

"Damn, girl. This new intercom is loud!" Lynette says, getting up from a barstool at the kitchen counter.

"Yeah, I'm still getting used to this new security system," Lauren says, heading towards the front door.

It's Wes, the manager of her favorite deli.

"Mrs. Logan!" he says, handing her a white paper bag. "Glad to see you smiling. I read about…I mean…sorry about what happened last weekend."

Lauren takes the bag. Everyone in the world seems to know about the Cory photos. "Thanks, Wes. Some things work out for the best in the end."

Lynette peers over Lauren's shoulder. "Did you remember my extra sour cream?"

Wes smiles. "I figured you were here too when I saw the order. Yep, extra sour cream for your baked potato plus a bag of your favorite jalapeño cheese puffs. Do you, like, dip the chips in the sour cream or something?"

Lynette snatches the bag from Lauren and turns away. "I don't have to reveal my secrets."

Lauren gives him a generous tip. "You are the best, Wes. Thanks!"

Lynette and Lauren head back to the barstools.

"Mmmm…this turkey melt always helps me feel better," Lauren says, unwrapping her sandwich. "What a week, huh?"

Lynette smirks. "Sure was one of the busiest of my life. I have to admit, Cory made it easy though. Amicable agreement with you, papers signed, new house leased and his stuff already gone. He could have dragged this through the tabloids and he didn't."

"He doesn't want publicity and he never wanted my fame," Lauren says. "Sad fact is he didn't want me. But I still don't buy his excuse that he 'misjudged' how much he drank that night. I heard he hooked up with her months ago. If that was true, he should just own it. Drunk or not, she was there."

"Speaking of 'she', that reminds me of 'he'. Have you seen Andy since your flight home?"

"No and it's killing me. I have to keep this quiet a little longer. Aiden and Lee's world has already been overturned and I don't want to bring a new guy home this soon."

"Good," Lynette says, putting down the cheese puff she was drowning in sour cream. She pulls her laptop over.

"Good? How so?"

"Look at this." Lynette opens a document. "Plebeian record sales are through the roof. Pity is bringing in money."

Lauren leans over to see. "Oh my God…album sales too?"

"Johnny has paparazzi following him everywhere now. Doug got followed to the gym by some website blogger. Michael and Sunny were at dinner last night and a photographer popped up in the window. I've got a two-inch stack of fan mail to go through before I give it to you."

"This is unbelievable. Plebeian has become more popular because my husband had one wild night in Berlin?"

"Scandal sells," Lynette says. "That's why I said it's good to wait before introducing Andy. This is not the time to roll him out."

"But we plan to see each other tomorrow."

"Here?"

"No. He booked a suite at the Sand Club on Clearwater Beach."

"Lauren? A public place?"

"We'll be low-key. I can't go to his house because his daughter Brittney doesn't know any of this. And he can't come here yet. Even though the boys will be at Cory's helping him unpack, they are still really mad at him. What if they ditch Cory and come back here? I can't risk them catching me with Andy."

"Are you two arriving together?"

"Give me some credit," Lauren says. "He'll get there first to check in and then I'll drive myself. I don't want to ask Bill to drive me."

"You are the hottest tabloid story this week," Lynette says, dunking another cheese puff into the sour cream. "You better drive invisible, arrive invisible and stay invisible."

Lauren nods. She will. This should be easy. She only has to worry about getting there and leaving without being noticed. Because once she's in Andy's arms, she's not planning on getting out of bed.

* * *

Berry-blue water, flat waves and towering palm trees. This drive from Tampa over the causeway to Clearwater Beach is filled with beautiful sights. But today, Lauren can't enjoy it. Her eyes keep flashing to her rear view mirror.

She sucks at being invisible.

She weaves in and out of traffic at a normal speed, trying to throw off two cars that are trailing her. Paparazzi, probably. She keeps a steady speed so they won't realize she knows they are there.

Andy has already checked into the Sand Club. And she just called him and said she might need help. While he works on a parking plan, she's going to try a bit of aggressive driving to lose her stalkers first.

Up ahead is a roundabout, a confusing piece of roadwork merging arriving beach traffic with thru traffic with departing beach traffic. Add a huge, misty water fountain in the middle and it's a wonder that any car can make it around safely.

She needs to turn right to get to Andy, so she approaches the roundabout in the left lane. She quickly merges into the right lane and one of the cars follows. At the last second, she veers left, just a few feet in front of the second car. The car behind her was too late to react and had to make the right turn. *One down!*

Her foot crushes the gas pedal and the second car can't match her sudden speed. She spins around the circle twice and shoots out heading in the direction of the Sand Club.

The first car she ditched has turned around and is racing back towards the roundabout. Lauren passes them. Even if they saw her, it will take them a few minutes to complete the circle to catch her. She's free and heading straight towards Andy.

"Dial Andy!" she calls out to her car's Bluetooth system.

Seconds later, he answers the call. "You okay?"

"I lost them!" she says, her pulse racing. "But I think one of them saw me come this way. I may only have two or three minutes."

"Pull in to the valet; the manager Gregory will take your car," Andy calmly says. She's already driving up the hotel's palm tree lined brick driveway by the time they hang up.

She barely puts the car in park before flinging open her door. A valet driver jumps in and her car disappears in seconds. Behind her she sees a fleet of valet drivers in various cars pulling up. Gregory has dispatched at least five other valet drivers in cars to clog up the entrance of the hotel with an instant traffic jam in case her pursuers were close.

She smoothes out her skirt and takes a deep breath to compose herself. She quickly walks into the hotel, not exactly sure where she is supposed to go, until she spots Andy leaning carefree against a marble wall by the elevators. He's calm and cool but damn he looks sexy and hot in his tight jeans and a white shirt with rolled-up sleeves. Within seconds they're alone, safe inside the rising elevator cab.

"Oh, you're good." She melts into his hug.

"I know," he says, greeting her with his sweet, sweet lips.

They walk down the eighth floor hallway and Andy opens the door to their suite.

It's as if they stole all of Lauren's imaginary beach house dreams and designed them into this suite. There are two balconies overlooking the gulf and she immediately opens the glass doors to let the fresh air in. Linen drapes blow into a room with two plush sofas, a dining table beside a stylish kitchen and a fully stocked bar. On the other side is a giant, king-sized bed, angled to take in every inch of the water view. She hasn't even put her purse down before their suite doorbell rings.

Gregory has personally brought up her suitcase and Andy invites him inside.

"I appreciate what you did," Lauren says, shaking his hand. "I probably needed a driver today, but I am just trying to get away for a quiet weekend."

"There is no worry, Ms. Logan. In fact, I'll adjust room assignments and put fewer guests on this floor. I'll assign a personal butler to you too," Gregory says.

"We appreciate your discretion," Andy says.

"Discretion is everything to us, Mr. Hayden," Gregory says, walking towards the door.

"One more favor," Andy asks. "I would like to know if any paparazzi come around the hotel. I'd like to know what might be out there in case we go for a walk."

"Absolutely. I will keep an eye out for them," Gregory says.

The sound of the suite door closing behind Gregory means Andy and Lauren are finally alone.

His lips stretch to a wide smile. He claims Lauren's hands, pushing her backwards toward the bed. She tugs him down with her; their bodies sinking into each other as they start the enjoyable task of reintroducing themselves.

[ELEVEN]

Lauren doesn't remember what time she fell asleep but she knows what time it is now. It's midnight and she just woke to Andy's lips on her ear.

"I've got a crazy idea," he whispers. "Let's go for a walk on the beach."

She cracks open a sleepy eye. After having sex three times he wants more exercise? Her eye closes. "Mmmm…I'd rather stay in bed and sleep with you."

His lips press her ear harder. "Let's go on a beach date."

Both her eyes open. "You are completely irresistible."

He's already out of bed, peeking over their balcony to see if the beach is clear.

"Gregory said there were no paparazzi hanging out here, right?" she asks, sitting up.

He pulls on his jeans. "He said two suspicious cars came by earlier. One had two photographers, but they left. The other was a guy who came inside and asked employees if you were here. Gregory kept an eye on him and watched him leave."

She shimmies out of her blue halter slip and into a pair of jeans, a white tank top with a sheer white blouse and sandals. "Then let's go!"

The stiff breeze feels so good on Lauren's skin, almost as good as the warm grip of Andy's hand. They walk for a while, still within eyesight of the hotel until finally finding a spot by some sea grasses to sit down. Andy spreads out a sheet he grabbed off of the bed and wraps his arms around her while she comfortably sits in between his legs.

They listen to the sound of the waves and let themselves get lost in the rhythmic beat of the gulf. The salty air feels refreshing on her face; the stars burning bright on this clear night. He turns her around to face him and picks up her hands.

"Listen, this time I spent away from you this week drove me crazy," he says, trying to swing his blowing hair from his eyes, "and I was hoping it was driving you crazy too."

Drove me nuts. She nods.

"I know it might be a while until the world knows we are together so I had an idea. I wanted to have a piece of you with me, and you to have a piece of me with you, so I got these."

He pulls out two beautiful, simple, wide-band silver rings from his pocket.

Whoa! "Andy, are you serious?"

He nods, stroking her left hand and her empty wedding ring finger. "I know this finger is taken until the papers are final," he picks up her right hand, "so I was thinking this was a good spot for me."

Use of the English language leaves her as he slides the ring on her finger.

"So until such time that we can be together publicly, I'd like to be a part of you here," he says as he pushes the silver band over her knuckle.

She throws herself at him in a wild kiss of approval. "This is the best idea anyone, ever, has ever, ever had," she stammers. She snatches his matching ring from the palm of his hand.

"Ok, then, I would like to make a presentation." She snuggles closer in a playful squirm. She grabs his right hand, slipping the ring over his right ring finger. "Until such time that we are publicly together, I'd like to be a part of you here."

Her eyes are an inch away from his, in a look promising as much potential as these rings. He gently cups her chin. "Until such time, and after we are revealed, until forever." His soft kiss seals the ring exchange.

"Lauren…" he says, eyes twinkling through the strands of his long, straight hair. "I love you."

Words she never thought she'd hear; words she never dreamed she'd earn. She squeezes his hands. "I'm glad you finally came around because I've always been in love with you." One by one she slowly kisses each of his fingers.

They keep admiring their hands as they walk back to the hotel. Simple silver rings that now unite them strongly.

No one has noticed their midnight escape, and they slip back up to their suite to continue their secret weekend.

*　*　*

Monday brings the typical beginning-of-the-week dread; especially today, after having to say goodbye to Andy.

Lauren stands alone in her kitchen with her eyes closed. She sees him when she closes her eyes. She clutches her arms, deep in a fantasy, remembering how he touched her. Oh, how he touched her…

The side door opens and Davis's voice interrupts. "Why are you hugging yourself?" He's come down from the office space above the garage that he shares with Tish. A step behind him, Johnny follows with Lynette.

Team Reality has arrived.

"I hate to talk business, but I need to know when we can schedule your vocal make-up session," Davis asks.

"We also need to know if you're up for public appearances with the band," Lynette adds.

"And I think we all want to know what's the latest with Andy," Johnny finishes.

"A few things on your minds, huh?" Lauren says. "I am fine!

Schedule the session whenever you need to. Andy and I plan to tell the kids this week. If you think this is a good time, we are ready to take it public."

"This weekend is good," Lynette says. "Enough time will have passed since the Cory scandal and there's an awards show in Hollywood we all will attend in three weeks. You might as well go public now, before the show."

Lynette and Davis begin to chat about details of the Hollywood trip while Johnny reaches for Lauren's elbow, pulling her aside. They walk to the living room and he leans in close.

"This has all happened so fast—you and Andy and you leaving Cory. Are you sure you are okay with everything?" he asks.

"Are you worried about me, Johnny?" She smiles, poking him in the chest.

"You know I am."

"I'm good—real good. Andy has opened a whole new life inside me that I thought was gone. It's been so long since I was this happy."

Johnny's cheeks pulse. "Andy is okay with me as long as he is good to you."

She almost laughs. Johnny just decreed it permissible for her and Andy to proceed with their love? His intent is sweet though.

"He is good to me, Johnny. And we are good for each other. He will help me a lot with my issues."

"Good. Davis has already started working on our first tour. By early next year, we'll be on the road."

"I'll be ready."

She watches Johnny walk away with the confident swagger he uses when he knows he's right. And he is right—again. This has happened so fast; she has barely gotten started with Andy. He doesn't even know where she lives! She hasn't met his daughter Brittney. She has to take a relationship the equivalent of a seed and grow it to a strong tree within six months if she wants Andy to be with her on tour.

She looks at her silver ring. Until such time? There's not much time.

She needs to blend three kids in a new family, add in a new lover, all baked in the hot spotlight of fame while she's served to hungry fans on Plebeian's tour. That's the new recipe for her life. None of this is going to work without a key ingredient, one that she left out before: herself.

[TWELVE]

Saffron-roasted chicken fills Lauren's home with a holiday scent. The wet bar is stocked with Icelandic vodka, Spanish olives and a bottle of Andy's favorite French dry vermouth. Aiden and Lee are staying late at school for band practice and Tish is finishing up in the kitchen. Lauren leans over the kitchen table, lighting two white tapered candles, her blush colored silk shirt tucked into a pair of skinny jeans. *Ready.*

Tonight, Andy is coming over for dinner.

Lauren's neighborhood within Arbor Palms is gated and staffed full-time with a guard, one of the reasons she and Cory chose this street. With only twelve homes here, the guards know everyone very well. She calls up to the "hut", the nickname they call the guard house, and lets the guard on duty know Andy Hayden is expected and to add him to her permanent visitors list. At exactly seven p.m., the guard calls to let her know Andy has come through the gate.

Lauren leans against the frame of the ten-foot tall glass front doors as Andy's blue BMW glides under the portico of her Mediterranean-style home.

"Welcome home," she says, smiling.

His grin leads him out of the car. "I'd live in a shack with you," he says, kissing her and offering a bouquet of pink and white roses with white lilies. He glances at the house. "Though this place has potential."

She bites her lip watching him as he looks around her foyer. Andy looks like he fits here, like he built this house with her. He looks at home.

She takes him on a tour of the sitting room, to the right of the foyer, and to her study, which is to the left. Andy points out some design features she's never noticed.

"You know so much about buildings and design, why aren't you an architect?" she asks.

"Required too much math." He winks.

"But you invest people's money—that's not math?"

"Different math. Besides, admiring design is just a fun hobby for me."

Hand-in-hand they walk to the living and dining rooms, to the right of the front doors. The living room is the width of the house and large windows curve at the end of the room, showing the leafy green queen palm trees outside. Patio doors in the back of the room open to a walled courtyard, the concrete privacy walls lined with crawling bougainvillea vines blooming with bright pink and purple flowers.

"It was probably good to show you my house before you bring Brittney in a few days."

"No kidding. I'm not sure what will impress her more: you or this house."

She snatches his hand and leads him down a back hallway. Windows line the hall and follow the outside walled courtyard, leading to the kitchen. Tish is finishing up dinner and turns to meet Andy.

"Lauren, you are a cheater!" Andy says, seeing the meal Tish has prepared.

"I only cheat with the best," she says, giving Tish proper credit.

The kitchen has two islands, one for food prep and the second one surrounded with padded barstools. At the end of the room sits a large, oval breakfast table that faces a wall of windows. From here, Andy can see the outdoor kitchen and pool.

"I think you can take it from here." Tish grabs her keys, tosses Lauren a wink and leaves for the day.

"Smells wonderful. Thanks again," Lauren calls after her. She and Andy start lifting lids from pots to explore the feast Tish left. They kick off their shoes and sit at the breakfast table enjoying roasted chicken and yellow rice.

After dinner, she shows him the pool lanai, which is really the heart of her Florida home. From here he can see the Plebeian studio, adjacent to the second garage and facing the lanai.

"So this gate here, everyone just comes in here to get to the studio?" Andy points to the steel gate.

"Yep, whenever they want. The hut just tells me when someone is on the way. Usually though, only Michael and Johnny are regulars."

They tour the home gym next to the studio and then the poolside guest house. "So…is this where I would stay if I ever spent the night?" His eyes lower, as adorable as a puppy begging to come inside.

"Oh, I have a special place in the main house if you ever spend the night."

She tugs his arm, leading him to the double chaise lounge chair by the pool. "This is my favorite spot," she says. He grabs her by the waist, pulling her down to the padded citron-colored fabric.

"Perfect for me too," he says. They lie in the chaise for awhile, holding hands, talking about the house and the memories they plan to make here.

She pulls his arm to get him off the chair. "Let's go upstairs," she says, eyes lowering.

He grins. They continue his tour upstairs, seeing the boys' bedrooms and three other guest rooms and a game room over the second garage.

Finally, she walks backwards towards the double doors of the master suite. "I've saved the best for last."

She opens the doors and Andy's eyes look at her bed the same way he hungrily looks at her. He scans the sitting area with sofas, and the double shower and soaking tub of the bathroom. With any luck she'll lose count of how many times they will make love up here.

"I finished redecorating this last week. You know—new beginnings."

"Looks like the only thing missing is a pillow with my initials on it to mark my territory," he says, smiling and pointing towards the bed and the mountain of decorative pillows in various patterns of black, white and gray.

"Oh? Mark *your* territory, huh?" she pokes him in the chest. "Well, one room off limits to you is my closet." She winks, stepping in to the walk-in closet with floor-to-ceiling rods and shelves filled with clothes, shoes and purses, with three crystal chandeliers and two sets of mirrors. He steps up to the waist-high island of drawers with a clear glass top displaying her collection of bras and matching panties. "Black, red, sequins, prints—are you sure these are off limits to me?"

"Those? You can put your hands on those anytime."

"So, what color is not in this drawer right now?" His eyes are already undressing her chest.

She beams. *Come find out.*

He pulls her to him, fingering and tugging the bottom of her silk shirt while his face softly presses into her hair. "I love solving a good mystery," he whispers. In a swift move he pulls her shirt up and over her head and steps back to see her blush pink lace bra.

"You…and that…are so beautiful."

The house tour ends and the body tour begins.

"Um…wait…" she says, disappearing around a shelf of dresses. She quickly ditches her jeans and panties, and grabs a pink pair of Gucci pumps. *He'll love these.* She returns to face him, wearing nothing but the blush lace bra and high-heeled pumps. "I wanted to show you my shoe collection."

He's not looking at her shoes. He grabs her bare waist with hungry hands as his lips find hers. In a split-second he's unclasped her bra, while she slides her fingers inside his waistband to unbutton his jeans. With a raised foot she pushes his jeans and boxers to the floor.

He presses her against a shelf of purses. God, she wants him right *here and now.* Still standing, she grabs the shelf with one hand and a fistful of his hair with the other.

He relentlessly kisses up her neck…higher and higher until he finds a turn-on spot under her ear that she never knew she had. *Oh… there!* She crumbles. *Bulls-eye, baby.*

"Andy…" she moans, as he begins to make love to her.

"There are…so many things…I want to do to you," he breathes in her ear, his heart pounding heavy with the thrusting of his body.

"This…" she whispers, squeezing the shelf, "…is a…good start."

Their groans of completion lead to their collapse on the floor. They lie on the carpet, tangled up with each other, catching their breath.

Andy rolls to his side, smiling. "Look where the secret lovers just did it."

"A closet!" she laughs.

He rolls on top of her, his fingers softly moving her hair from her face. His chest still beats heavy with his racing heart and the look in his eyes makes her want to stand up and do it all again. "I was wondering," he whispers, grinning, "do you ever wear those shoes to bed?"

Her chin rises with her grin. "For you, any pair you want."

They would have taken a shot with another pair, but it is close to the time Aiden and Lee will come home. Standing in the foyer, Lauren and Andy are pressed tight in their goodbye.

"I wish I could say hello to the boys tonight," he says, his forehead pressed to hers.

"Then that's not fair to Brittney—she's never met me like you've met the boys."

"Once the kids meet, then our new life can begin."

She whispers in his ear, "When the kids are settled, I want you to stay here with me. Here in this house, everyday. Your car in the garage, your clothes in the closet and your body in my bed. Move in with me."

"I love you so much," he whispers. "I'll gladly claim my spot in your bed, as long as you are sure we aren't moving too fast."

She shakes her head. "It's not fast enough."

He grins. "Save me a spot in that closet too."

You bet. "Just one small step to go," she says. "Two teenage boys meeting one teenage girl."

"What could go wrong?"

She stiffens. It depends on how much Brittney is like her mother.

* * *

As their Thursday family dinner draws near, Lauren had it so much easier than Andy. She only had to tell Aiden and Lee that the guy they met at the post-concert party was someone she likes and he's bringing his daughter over for dinner. Andy needs to tell his daughter that his new girlfriend is a famous rock star and multi-millionaire.

Lauren stands by the glass front doors, watching Andy and Brittney pull up under the portico. Brittney steps out of the car, a beautiful girl wearing a tentative smile. She looks a lot like Andy with long, straight brown hair and a thin nose. Her black-and-white knit leggings don't really match her long, green tank top which doesn't really match her coral notched crop top, but it all looks surprisingly good together. Her eyes look unsettled and wide.

"I waited until after we pulled through the hut to tell her who you were!" Andy says while giving Lauren a warm welcome kiss and a dozen long-stemmed yellow roses.

Poor girl! He could have given her a couple blocks' advance notice, not ninety seconds! Her body feels like mush when Lauren hugs her.

About an hour into the visit, Brittney's smile has grown, giving Lauren a hint that she's comfortable here. Lauren catches Brittney watching her and Andy as they grill chicken and jokingly debate the best way to brew iced tea. Even during dinner, Brittney is smiling.

After dinner, Lauren goes back out to the grill to clean up and Brittney follows.

"I know this was a big night for you; full of surprises," Lauren says.

"I didn't know why my dad wouldn't tell me about who he was dating so I just thought he was seeing another sketchy woman. When he turned in here and told me it was you I just died."

Lauren swallows her words. How many sketchy women has he dated? That must be an exaggeration from a teenager.

"I'm crazy about your dad, Brittney, and I have been for a long, long time."

"My mom is gonna freak."

"Well, I'm not worried about your mom," Lauren says. "I'm worried about your dad and keeping him happy. And that means you being happy too."

In the family room, Lauren catches Andy in a similar moment with Aiden and Lee. He comes over to help when he sees Lauren and Brittney coming inside. Then the boys offer Brittney a tour of the house, leaving Lauren and Andy alone in the kitchen.

"This is normal. And nice." She flirtatiously bumps her hip against him while rinsing dishes in the sink.

He grabs her from behind, wrapping his arms around her. "I'm becoming overwhelmed by how much you have changed my life. I've never had love like this. Even as a kid I've never felt this much love. You don't yell at me. You don't criticize me. You let me be me." He squeezes her waist. "Plus, you don't make me do the dishes."

"I'm not one to yell," she says, squeezing his arms. "But after you move in, buddy, you better take your turn with the dishes."

As he embraces her she closes her eyes and takes this all in. Soapy bubbles fill the sink and her waist is wrapped with the arms of the man she loves.

After their goodbyes, Lauren huddles with Aiden and Lee to get their take on the evening.

"Andy is okay, Mom. It's weird having him here and not Dad anymore, but he's okay," Aiden says.

"I have to admit Andy's alright, but really, Mom, having Brittney around is not going to work very well," Lee says. "I've got a brother. I don't need a sister too."

"Having a girl around will change things," she says. "Even though Brittney lives with her mom she does sometimes stay with Andy. And I'd like for Andy to stay here more often. We will see more of both of them, but it doesn't make Andy your new dad and Brittney your new sister. It only means my heart is opening with love for them both. And maybe in time, yours will too."

It does not take long for the boys to become distracted by something else, and soon it's time to say goodnight. Lauren heads upstairs and steps into her bedroom where her eyes fly open. On the center of the bed is a small, gray square pillow embroidered with a large white "H". With it is a note:

> *My territory is now marked; your redecoration is complete.*
> *I cannot wait to share this bed with you.*
> *I love you,*
> *Andy*

How did he…Who cares? He did! She falls face-first on the bed and buries her cheeks in the H pillow, breathing in that sweet, Andy Hayden smell.

By this weekend they will be out on a date and the world will meet Lauren Logan's new man.

* * *

The bartender pours him another drink.

He turns on his barstool to look again at the beautiful Sand Club lobby.

He sips slowly, the biting, warm alcohol easing down his throat.

This looks a lot like the resort in Phoenix and now that he has seen them both he has a better idea of her tastes, her likes.

He needs to know what makes her happy.
He has to make her happy.
He leaves the bar to walk outside, lighting up a cigarette.
A stiff Gulf breeze blows his cigarette cold.
Fucking wind.
He grimaces as the beach sand blows in his face.
He hates the beach. But if she likes it, he will now.

[THIRTEEN]

Andy and Lauren have kept their romance private, until tonight. Their round of telling close family and friends is complete. Lauren's family knows, including her mother, brother and even Cory. Christy says she's ready to plan the wedding. Andy's sister in Houston knows. The guys in the band know. Andy has told his boss. They're ready to step out in public and will meet Michael and Sunny for dinner at a South Tampa steakhouse.

Lynette has rewarded one of their usual paparazzi photographers, Franz, with a juicy tip: Lauren will be going to dinner tonight with her new boyfriend, Andy Hayden. Franz will make a lot of money selling their first photos. Lynette's no fool; she knows one day they may need a return favor.

Michael and Sunny have already called to say they've arrived at City Grille and are waiting in the bar with their cocktails. When Bill is not driving Lauren, she always calls ahead to the valet to let them know she is coming. The manager prefers to park her car himself and tonight, he is waiting as Andy drives Lauren's white M6 up to the valet station, a busy area adjacent to the steakhouse and a large upscale mall. Andy puts the car in park and Franz approaches the car window.

"Here's to the end of your normal life." Lauren pats Andy's leg.

He bravely steps out of the car.

"Andy! Andy! Over here, Andy!" Franz calls out, snapping his camera. Bystanders take notice. You can almost read their *"who is*

Andy?" expressions. Then Andy opens Lauren's door and she steps out to the buzzing sound of Franz's camera.

"Lauren! Good to see you—over here. Andy—over here," Franz encourages while they walk hand in hand towards the restaurant. They finally look his way and he takes his money shot.

As they near the restaurant door, Franz lowers his camera. "Thank you, Lauren."

"Go make some money, Franz." She winks.

Inside, the restaurant is crowded but they quickly find Michael and Sunny. They feel the stares and hear the whispered conversations as they make their way to the table. At last, they are seated, enjoying drinks, knowing their new romance is being publicized.

They raise their drinks for a toast.

"To New York City," Andy says.

Lauren smiles and meets his glass. It was New York City where they had that wonderful dinner with Michael and Sunny. It was the evening of confessions and their first kiss. It was the moment she knew she never wanted to be without him.

Lynette sends only one text to Lauren during dinner:

"Huge story; just huge."

After their two-hour dinner, the manager comes to their table to let them know quite a crowd of photographers and on-lookers have gathered outside.

"Are you ready for the feast?" Lauren says and Andy gives a confident nod. They hold hands and walk out through the revolving doors of the restaurant and into lights flashing as fast as lightning. They hug Michael and Sunny goodbye and then Andy helps Lauren into the car. He can barely walk around to the driver's side while paparazzi press closer and yell his name.

An hour later, Andy and Lauren are back at Lauren's house relaxing with Lee, Aiden and Brittney. The kids are checking out their social pages, watching news of their parents' love life spread.

"You should see how many posts I'm getting," Brittney brags, elbows on the kitchen island. "I'm telling everybody I'm sitting in your house right now!"

But there's a little problem with *where* she's sitting.

Brittney swivels back and forth on Lee's barstool. Lee tries to move her with threatening stares. He glances to Lauren with a look that says: "Make her move." *What is she supposed to do? Put name cards on their placemats and favorite cups now?* Ultimately he takes the high road, silently retreating from the room. She doesn't know the first thing about blending families. And she has to start blending now because Brittney and Andy will stay overnight with them. The security guard at the hut will keep paparazzi away. Heaven knows how many photographers have camped out at Andy's house.

Their family time gets interrupted when Lynette calls.

"A photographer has a picture when you grabbed the car door leaving. You have matching rings," Lynette says. "Do you want to tell people what that is about?"

Lauren repeats Lynette's question to Andy. Andy takes Lauren's phone.

"We do have matching rings and they have a special meaning that we'd like to keep private," he says.

Nothing fans the rumor flames more than a secret you can see. By morning, stories of Andy are everywhere but the biggest rumor spreading is about their rings.

Andy reads the stories on his tablet as he lies next to Lauren in bed. "They think we're engaged! They want to know everything, don't they?"

She snuggles to his side. "I'll never get used to living in the public eye. It makes me numb."

He puts his tablet down, wrapping his warm arms around her.

"They will never know what happens here, in this bed, between us. I want you to always feel safe here."

"I do. I feel safe, loved. Everything I want is right here."

His smile widens and he rolls to his side. "Everything?"

Damn his morning hair and that wide, sexy smile. "Everything I want. Right here." She moves his hand between her legs and presses her thighs together. "So what exactly happens in this bed?"

With a grin covering his face, he breathes deep, rolls on top of her and demonstrates.

* * *

Light from his tablet casts a bright glow over the dark room.

Too much damn light.

His finger trails across the tablet, lowering the brightness setting.

He doesn't want to disturb anyone else.

He's already too disturbed himself.

He swipes the tablet screen, each swipe bringing up a new photograph of her.

So many photos.

So many new, beautiful but unsettling photos.

His heart races. He loses his grip on the tablet and it slips from his wet, clammy hands.

He's not sure he can handle this now.

[FOURTEEN]

Tonight's full moon shines a clear, bright light on the interstate. Few cars share the road with Andy and Lauren as they speed down the highway. Andy grips the steering wheel tight with one hand, his other holds Lauren's hand.

"Is anyone following us?" she asks.

Andy glances back in the rear-view mirror, again. She's asked him the same question three times already.

"Amazingly, still no."

For the first time in two months, no one is following their car. Since Andy and Lauren stepped out with their romance, they've been mobbed by photographers. Andy was so challenged arriving and leaving work, they had to have Bill drive him every day. Even during the holidays, they were greeted with fans and photographers wherever they went. Plebeian fans love Lauren and Andy together, even though it still hasn't stopped the nagging rumors about her and Johnny.

But tonight, Lauren hopes for a bit of peace, for Johnny's sake. Amie's water just broke and Johnny is on the cusp of becoming a father. Andy and Lauren are now minutes from the hospital where baby Anna will be born tonight.

When they arrive, the hospital waiting room is already filled with Amie's family. They hug their hello to Amie's youngest sister Ashley, but Amie's parents give them a searing stare. Lauren and Andy slip into seats near the door.

"I should just offer a knife to Amie's parents so they can stab me dead," Lauren whispers to Andy.

"I noticed. I wonder what their problem is."

Lauren overhears Amie's older sister Allison whispering about her.

"Did you hear that?" Lauren whispers to Andy. "Allison just said I go wherever Johnny goes."

"I don't get that; it's not true."

"I know I'm not Amie's best friend but I'm here for her and Johnny."

"I'm glad we didn't bring balloons; all this negativity could suck the helium out."

A nurse comes to get Amie's mother. Everyone looks at each other.

When Amie's mother returns, a few friends gather around her and whisper.

Something isn't right and this family isn't about to clue them in. Andy and Lauren leave, walking down a series of hallways to find Johnny and Amie themselves. They pass by the nurse's desk in the labor and delivery area, pretending to know where they are going, until they spot one of Amie's family members leaving a room.

Lauren boldly presses her face to the small, rectangle window of the door. In the room's faint light she can see Amie sitting up in bed, holding baby Anna. Anna is here! But Johnny paces wildly next to her. And she recognizes his pacing. He's mad. But mad at what?

A nurse walks through the doors, exposing Lauren and Andy standing in the doorway. Johnny notices them and his mouth opens with surprise. Lauren has never seen his face this mad, or sad, maybe he *is* happy? For once, she can't read him. Johnny hurries over to them and steps outside the door.

"Hey, congratulations," Lauren says, reaching to give him a hug. He grabs her and collapses in her arms, burying his face in her shoulder. Andy puts his hands on Johnny's back and Lauren's still not sure if this is a happy hug or what.

Johnny pulls back from their hug. "Anna's here," he says, his face weighted with sadness. "And she's going to die. She's not going to live."

He shakes Lauren's shoulders with every group of words he blurts out.

Her face stretches in horror. Andy leans closer.

"She has anencephaly; no brain. No functioning brain. She may be here for an hour, maybe less."

There are no words Lauren can make herself say. Shock numbs her. Anencephaly? Isn't that something they know in advance? *Oh no.* She makes the bizarre connection at the same time Johnny starts to explain.

"She knew. Amie knew. But she didn't tell me," Johnny says between the beginning of soft sobs and gritted teeth. "She thought I'd want this. She thought I'd want Anna to die. She knew I wasn't ready to be a father so she just didn't tell me. Never told me."

Lauren's crushed from the weight of his words. This—this—is way too much to handle so quickly. He came to the hospital expecting a baby, a baby he won't be taking home and worse, his girlfriend knew it all along. She had time to prepare. She had time to bond with Anna while she carried her. She had time to say goodbye before Anna was even born! She never gave Johnny a chance.

Andy leans in. "Johnny, you don't have a lot of time. Get in there and be with your girls." He points to the room.

Lauren grabs Johnny's hands and pushes her face close.

"Anna. Anna is your priority. Got it? Anna—nothing else but Anna now."

He nods and walks back in the room, his shoulders sunken with sadness.

Lauren's arms flail. "Who would ever be able to keep a secret like that? If she thought he wanted this, why didn't she tell him right away that Anna was going to die? Why wait until the day she is born—what was she thinking?"

Andy walks Lauren across the hall to an alcove and he pulls her close. "Let's stand here and wait," he says, the safety of his arms calms her.

Within minutes a nurse asks them to leave.

No! Lauren doesn't want to go back to the waiting room and leave Johnny! "There are photographers in the waiting room," she lies. "Can I please stay here?"

The nurse narrows her eyes, considering the options. She opens an empty delivery room across from Johnny and Amie's. Until the room is needed they can stay here, she says.

Lauren and Andy leave the lights off to better hide themselves. She finds a wheelchair stored in the corner and positions it so she can sit and watch across the hall.

Andy uses Lauren's phone to make some calls. He starts with Lynette and works his way through the band, personally calling everyone rather than having Lynette or Davis do it. Andy even calls Cory. It's a task keeping him busy while Lauren sits in the wheelchair, rolling forward and back with nervous energy. Forward and back. Forward and back.

"We'll never have kids together," she whispers. Andy sets the phone down.

"That ship has probably sailed for us, huh?" he says, leaning over the edge of the wheelchair and holding her shoulders. Even though they could physically have a child, the idea of starting again with a baby when they both have teenagers seems unlikely.

"I would have never hidden something like this from you," she says.

Andy squats so they are eye to eye. "Amie is not as strong as you, Lauren. We really don't know what she's been through."

His defense of Amie could be right. They don't know what might have snapped in her mind when she learned the baby she was carrying was going to die. She may not even be processing it all right now. *Oh God, this is so horrible for both of them.* Maybe Amie's family turned that confusion into anger towards Johnny for some stupid reason. Anger towards Johnny must mean anger towards her, Lauren assumes.

Their attention turns back to the hall and a flurry of new activity.

Amie's parents, her sisters and two nurses come and go from the room. Finally Johnny comes out and looks around the hall. She and Andy lean into the hall so he can see them and he joins them in their secret hiding room.

He rubs his face. "She's gone."

Lauren opens her arms and Johnny falls into them. She struggles to hold his weight as he leans hard on her body and starts a shallow cry.

Tears sting her eyes and roll down her cheeks. Through her blurry eyes she looks for Andy, now standing in the corner with his hands on his face and eyes full of tears.

She holds Johnny for as long as she can, until his weight becomes too much for her. Then she pushes him up and he staggers to a straight stance. She cups his wobbly head.

"You...you will always be Anna's daddy," she says, squeezing his head.

Johnny stiffens straight and wipes his eyes, slowly nodding. "I would have been a good daddy."

He buries his head back on her shoulder.

Two photographers lurk in the parking garage, taking pictures of Lauren and Andy leaving the hospital in the early morning hour. "Boy or girl?" they shout. Lauren and Andy walk without comment, tightly holding hands, trying to hide the devastation of what just happened. They quickly get into the car.

"By far, this is the saddest thing I have ever experienced," she says on the drive home. He acknowledges the same by saying nothing, his eyes focused on his driving.

Interstate lights pass by in a blur as a sliver of the rising sun fingers its way to the horizon. Her mind starts to fill with thoughts about Johnny and Amie; their sadness tonight and the healing that needs to come. So many thoughts, so many words.

"Michael," she softly says. "Later this morning, I want to see Michael."

And by nine p.m. that evening, the song *One Night with Anna* is born.

FIFTEEN

Soothing sounds from an acoustic guitar fill the studio. Johnny sits on the sofa, strumming his favorite Gibson Hummingbird. Even now, two months after Anna's death, he still seems lost in thought. And today, he hasn't made any suggestions for new lyrics.

"I got some great lines," Oliver says, shoulders straight. "Eeny, meeny, miny, moe. Catch a tiger by the toe. If he hollers let him go. They don't make rhymes like this no mo'."

"And that is why you do not write our songs," Michael says. Doug laughs from behind his snare drum and for once, Oliver gets quiet.

They are rewriting lyrics for a song before they head to Dallas next month. Plebeian has another live televised concert to debut their second album. This time, they are following it up a week later with their first U.S. concert tour.

Plebeian has hit marketing gold. Audiences in their thirties relate to Plebeian's lyrics and the real life struggles of Johnny and Lauren. Their music has made those fans relevant, a demographic that had been stuck between pop music for high-school kids and old-school rock from their parents' era. And fans in their thirties are itching to open their wallets for a sound that belongs to them, purchasing entire albums, not just singles, driving up record sales. Plebeian's success with their first televised special has also uncovered a new niche for televised album debuts.

For the tour and televised special, Trent Driscoll is back as their production manager and Thom Stewart, Johnny's friend in Hollywood who gave them their movie soundtrack break, is the promoter for the tour.

But Davis's smartest move was hiring Frank Allen to head up Plebeian's security. Frank worked for twenty years with the FBI and retired as an agent on fugitive recovery teams. He's short, about Doug's height, and even at fifty years old his cut muscles bulge from under his shirts. Frank manages the big picture for Plebeian security, and now he personally handles Lauren. Already he's made some good, smart changes. Lauren's house now has someone stationed in the office above the garage twenty-four hours a day to protect her and the kids and monitor the million-dollar studio. Security personnel have been assigned as needed for the guys in the band.

Everyone has noticed more fans hanging around odd places and sometimes their intrusions are a problem. They push uncomfortably close for autographs or to hand off their homemade demo CDs. Michael had a strange encounter in the produce section of the grocery store with a creepy woman who later asked him to take her home. Oliver nicknamed her "Banana Girl" and Michael will probably write a song about her someday. Having Frank now to watch for weirdness like this will be helpful.

Their studio work now finished for the day, Johnny lingers after Oliver, Doug and Michael leave. Lauren links her arm with Johnny's, walking by the pool. Andy comes out of the house to join them. Andy works from home now as a consultant, not a financial advisor, because his celebrity status became a distraction. All of the firm's clients had been requesting him as their financial advisor.

Seeing Andy means: *it's on.* She drops Johnny's arm and races Andy to their favorite chaise lounge, where they collapse together.

Johnny moves a little slower, eventually reaching them and stretching out in a nearby chair. He wears his pain on his face, still recovering from the loss of Anna plus dealing with Amie's breakdown. After learning of Anna's condition mid-way through her pregnancy, Amie tried to control an out of control situation by keeping it from Johnny. The weeks that followed Anna's death proved too difficult for Amie to handle, and she checked herself into a clinic two weeks ago.

"Amie's coming home in four days," Johnny says. "And I'm going to disappear for a couple of days when she does."

"Good. I'm glad she's doing better," Lauren says.

"While I'm gone, are you going to be getting ready—completely ready—for the Dallas concert and this tour? My girlfriend just lost it; I don't need you going nuts."

No. Not ready. Never ready. "I got this," she says with a fake smile. "I'm not the one you should be worrying about; worry about yourself. You and Amie need to start working on each other again."

"Don't start with me about marrying her," Johnny says. "Not when you are still single living with your boyfriend."

"Hey, at least I gave Lauren a ring!" Andy lifts Lauren's right hand to show off her silver band.

"Wrong hand, pal," Johnny says.

* * *

"We love Plebeian!" chants a group of attractive, young women to the TV cameras inside the Dallas arena. "Johnny's my favorite!" a curly haired brunette screams. "No, Doug! Doug!" yells another while a woman behind her waves a "Marry Me Michael!" sign.

Backstage, the guys and Lauren wait in the dressing room, watching the live pre-concert coverage. "Look, we have smart fans," Michael says. "None of them like you, Oliver."

His eyes lower from his drink. "My fans are too cool to scream."

Davis sticks his head in the door. "Opening act is about to start, so be ready in twenty."

Lauren's entourage of teenage fans—Lee, Aiden and Brittney and their friends—already have their seats. A few other family and friends came for the show, including some friends from Lauren's old neighborhood and Andy's only close relative, his older sister, Cindy. All of them, and Andy, will be seated off stage left so Lauren can see them. That is, if she's brave enough to look.

Walking out of the dressing room, the knots in her stomach twist hard enough to give her a headache. Still, she lowers her head in their pre-concert huddle, arms on shoulders, for their pep talk tradition.

"This is a little different than our last concert, huh?" Johnny says. "Some things have happened in our lives and we have new material to bring to the stage. Let's show them how a second album is done."

Their huddle breaks and Doug looks to Michael, raising his eyebrow.

Michael nods. "Yeah, just us two go up first."

Doug nods and he and Michael take their stage positions.

Johnny looks baffled. "How does he always read Doug's mind?" He shrugs and heads up the stairs to the stage.

Lauren catches the scent of alcohol as Oliver stands beside her. Maybe she should have relaxed with a drink too. She looks down at her tight black pants and over-the-knee boots, adjusting the wide band of her leather belt. She doesn't need a drink. She's Andy's lover, and that feels good. She slips on her Dolce & Gabanna sunglasses in the dimly lit backstage.

"Seriously? You're wearing those?" Oliver asks.

"Seriously? You are going on stage smelling like a liquor cabinet?"

"Thank God I had a drink. It's helping me not laugh at you right now. I thought you only wore sunglasses in rehearsals as a joke."

"Trent?" Lauren calls out to their production manager, standing right next to her. "Trent, I thought I just heard Oliver, but I can't see him. Doug and Michael were right! These glasses work so well I'll never have to see Oliver again."

Oliver punches her arm and runs on stage. Trent smiles. "I could use a pair of those." He nods for Lauren to go.

Energy drives her confidence on stage; she catches the camera exactly when she's supposed to. Stares bounce off of her like ping-pong balls. *You're. On. Fire.* And the hot guy staring at her from stage left is the only person she cares about. She's sung towards Andy three times now, squatting in front of him for one song while her kids cringed and he bit his lip staring at her over-the-knee boots.

Halfway through the concert and right on cue, Johnny puts his guitar in the stand and steps off stage with Doug. Lauren introduces the next song, standing next to Michael and Oliver.

"Life is about change, right? Some things you plan and others you don't. Some things work out well and others don't. This next song is about losing what you didn't think you wanted. It's called *One Night with Anna.*"

Michael begins on piano. Silence blankets the arena of forty-five thousand fans, all waiting to hear this rumored song dedicated to Johnny's baby. Emotion cracks through her shaky voice. Through her shaded lenses she sees people crying. Oliver's violin, his second favorite instrument behind his bass guitar, weaves the perfect sound of sadness.

Now finished, Lauren turns to hug Michael. Who else but Michael could take her ramblings the day after Anna died and put such beautiful music to it? Johnny begins walking back on stage and the applause grows. He slowly nods, his wave slight as he straps on his guitar for the next song. But the applause only grows louder.

Finally, Johnny grabs his microphone. "You know…one night is better than none." The audience erupts.

"I hope Amie is watching," Lauren whispers to Michael. She takes off her sunglasses, setting them on Michael's piano.

He cocks his head, "You sure?"

She nods, "Yeah. I got this."

Closer begins. Johnny's fingers light up his guitar as Doug unleashes on the drums and Oliver arches his back, digging into his bass. Emotion fuels them as they rip into some fun. *Love this song!* Lauren skips to the far edge of the stage, squatting closer to the crowd as she sings. Some scruffy guys she noticed before have their hands in the air, reaching for her. All except one. His hands are down his unzipped jeans, his arms thrusting as his evil eyes devour her. *Shit!*

She stands too quickly and her head spins. She loses her place in the song. *Words! What are the words?* Johnny snaps his glance towards her; they play on while she freezes. She turns from the jackass and sees Andy on the other end of the stage. His eyes are wide with concern and he nods, encouraging her. *Andy.* The words return to her brain and she begins singing again, moving back to the safety of center stage.

She plasters on a fake smile. *Pretend nothing happened.* She sings on, glancing back at Michael's piano, where her sunglasses lie. *Maybe no one noticed.*

When the last encore is finished, she rushes off stage and sees Frank, hands on his hips, eyes glaring. "We got that guy who was jerking off. He was arrested by the time the song ended."

She lowers her head. "I froze. I completely lost it. Did anyone, like, really notice me?"

Frank's eyes sadden. "Evidently 'Plebeianfreeze' is already trending."

Doug pats her back and Michael squeezes her arm.

Oliver walks past. "Keep your sunglasses on next time."

Johnny gathers them for their traditional huddle. She can't read his eyes because he hasn't even looked at her!

"It was a good show. Thank you for what you did for me—that's all I want to say," Johnny says, their circle locked tight with their arms.

"Speechless for once; I think I like that," Oliver says, already chewing the end of a cigar.

They break apart and move quickly to the cars—two limos and three Suburbans waiting for the group. They have a runner tonight, a caravan with police escort. Andy has already grabbed Lauren's arm, heading for the Suburban that Bill is driving. The kids and their friends rush into one of the limos. Lynette grabs the seat behind Bill and Frank lets one of the new security guys he's hired, Ryan, take the front passenger seat. They're rushed but Andy takes the time to hold open her door. *Best part of the night.* She slides into the middle of the back seat. They roll the second Andy shuts his door.

"All the kids got in the limo, right?" Lauren asks Ryan.

"All three—I watched them," Ryan says.

She turns to Andy. "How bad was…"

"Doesn't matter," he says. "It's done. They got that jerk. It's time to relax."

How in the hell can she? Johnny must be so pissed she froze like that. He's told her before to never stop singing, no matter what distractions happen in the audience. How can she ever go on stage again and look…at people? She rests her head on the back of Bill's seat as the caravan speeds forward. She still sees that creep in her mind; the image feels like ice knives stabbing her nerves. Andy gently rubs her back and her tired eyes close.

"It really was a good show, baby," he whispers. "At least tomorrow we can…"

BAM!

Deafening sound; scratchy glass; pressure—tight pressure on Lauren's head and right side. Lynette screams. Bill shouts.

They've been hit.

Lauren's chin feels embedded in her forehead, her head wedged against the driver's seat. Andy presses tight to her right side. *God, there's so much yelling!*

She can't move her head but she can move her eyes. Lynette tries to open her car door and Frank paws at the window, trying to find a way in. Her eyes dart to the right. *It's so bright!* Andy's head is almost in her lap, his body oddly bent and his hair splayed all over. *Oh God… Andy!*

Damn this bright light! She rolls her eyes towards it.

It's another car.

There's another car practically sitting on Andy and she's inches from the headlights.

Dizziness is creeping in but she fights to stay focused. She's got to know if Andy is okay. She drops her hand under Andy's nose, desperate to feel his breath on her fingers. He's breathing! She touches his cheek. *Please, baby, feel me!* A pounding in her head starts to take over.

Ryan's legs are trapped but Bill and Lynette have escaped. Frank moves in where Lynette was sitting.

"Lauren?" he yells, touching her face. "Can you look at me?"

Her eyes roll towards him, still unable to move her head or talk.

"She's looking at me! She's looking at me!" Frank yells.

And Frank is the last thing she sees.

* * *

"Lauren?" A strange man's voice calls out. He leans in to help her eyes find him. He looks like a doctor. "How do you feel?" he asks, smiling.

"Tired," she growls. She does feel warm and comfortable, very comfortable. She's clean; not sweaty from the concert. She hears people moving and voices coming closer.

"Mom?"

Lee stands next to her bed. There's a blur of voices. She squints and sees Aiden, Michael, Johnny—she can't see the rest.

"What happened…" she whispers.

"Your car was hit and you've had a head injury," says the doctor. She focuses to see him better. He's a tall, African American man, impressive in the way he stands and holds a clipboard of papers. "I'm Doctor Russell Tobias. I treated you last night."

She's having trouble processing his words.

"The boys?" she asks.

"Fine, right here," Johnny says. That's right. She just saw them.

"Andy?"

"He's here too, we're all here in the hospital," Johnny says. Questions are filling her head like warm water inside her brain. But sleep wants to take her over.

"Good," she says, closing her eyes again.

Six hours later, sunshine fills the room and she's greeted again by the same doctor.

"Good morning. Let me check your eyes," Dr. Tobias says, shining a rude white light on her pupils. "You have a contusion; a brain bruise. As long as the swelling keeps coming down, you won't need surgery."

"I hit my head?"

"Yes. Your vehicle was hit on the back right side. There were actually pieces of the other car where your head would have been, had you not been leaning forward."

"Where is Andy?"

Dr. Tobias shifts his weight. Already she doesn't like the answer.

"No. Here's how this works. You tell me exactly what happened and don't sugar-coat the details." She rallies a fair amount of conviction for a woman wearing a flimsy hospital gown, lying immobile in a hospital bed, in a city that she's already forgotten the name of.

His expression twists, part smile, part serious. "Andy's injuries are more severe and he remains in the Intensive Care Unit. He has lacerations of the liver and the spleen and just came out of surgery. He has a few rib fractures too."

"Can I go see him now?"

"You need to lie still, with your head straight. Don't bend your neck or there could be complications you don't want."

"Fine, I'll rest today. Then tonight you can take me down to see Andy."

"We'll see if you are able to rest," he says, smiling as her room fills with Aiden, Lee and others.

Reporters, photographers and fans now swarm outside of the hospital. Some fans came straight from the concert and still haven't left. The trend #Plebeianfreeze has been replaced with #PrayforLaurenAndAndy. Lynette, who walked away with bruises and minor cuts, has set up an office in a conference room to deal with the media.

Andy's sister Cindy has been comforting Brittney and the boys. Johnny, Michael and Davis have been going from Lauren's room to the waiting room of the Trauma ICU, seeing doctor after doctor. Earlier in the morning, Oliver, Doug and the rest of the Plebeian crew flew home as there was nothing they could do here.

Lauren's aggravation grows throughout the day. The diuretics they've given her to reduce her body fluids require bathroom trips every half hour. She has an irritating compression bandage on her head and a headache from it, plus the right side of her body feels like it was ripped off. None of that matters to her; she wants to go see Andy.

Davis visits with Lauren in the afternoon to give her more updates.

"Andy's going to be in the ICU for a couple of days and need rehab, but he'll be okay," he says. "Ryan's right leg is broken, but his wife is here now and he'll be fine."

"This is going to be an irritating recovery," she says, trying to sit still and look straight ahead as Tobias requested; her bed is elevated to reduce pressure on her brain.

"At least you have a recovery," Davis says. "The driver that hit you died on the scene. He was drunk. Left behind a wife and kids, who are terrified we are going to sue. I'm not sad for the driver but the wife and kids, they don't deserve what he gave them. The media is all over her."

"Someone died that close to where we were?"

Davis nods.

"But that someone almost killed me and Andy. I really want to be with Andy."

Davis breathes in deep.

As the day passes, one thing is clear: Lauren Logan will be one of the worst patients ever in the history of known hospitals until she sees Andy. She refuses to eat and buzzes the nurse every ten minutes, asking if she can see him. Dr. Tobias has taken high interest in his feisty celebrity patient, visiting often in the day, his presence the only thing able to calm her down.

Finally, at eleven p.m., Tobias comes to her room with a wheel-chair. "Someone woke up and he would like to see you."

She's so nervous and happy she cries while Tobias pushes her down the hall. Her head starts to hurt but she doesn't care—Andy is finally awake.

The lights are low in this late hour, the normally busy hospital halls are silent. Tobias quietly wheels her around the corner of the Trauma Intensive Care Unit; his presence makes her an exception to the unit's strict visitation hours.

Tobias points to Andy's curtained room and her eyes find him. His swollen body is surrounded by complicated machines and her gut tightens as if she can feel his pain too. Tobias wheels her to the left side of Andy's bed and finally, he notices her. He slowly blinks a few times, wincing at seeing the bandages on her head. He straightens his arm, inviting her into his bed. She tries to stand on her quivering legs and Tobias gently reaches to balance her.

She awkwardly slides into the mere inches of bed space available, careful not to touch Andy's heavily bandaged chest. She rests her head gently on his shoulder, her tears already dampening his hospital gown. He bends his bruised arm around her.

They lie like this, without saying a word, and close their eyes.

[SIXTEEN]

"You ready for lunch?" Tish calls out in her usual chipper fashion. Her spiky short blonde hair catches the sun as she walks out of the house, heading towards the black steel gate by the auto courtyard.

Lauren stretches her arms. She gently nudges Andy awake from their nap in the double chaise lounge by the pool.

Wes from the deli has brought lunch.

Tish unlocks the back gate and Wes walks over to the poolside table.

"You're looking better, much better!" he says, setting up drinks, napkins and spoons for their turkey melt sandwiches and potato soup.

"Wish I felt it," Andy moans.

"Time, right? Time heals it all," Wes says. "As always, anything I can do just call."

Tish locks the gate behind him, returning to inspect the spread of food. Andy and Lauren move like sick, slow people towards the table.

"Sleep, eat, sleep: our new normal," Lauren says. The familiar headache she's been suffering from these last three weeks has started to return again today. Hopefully eating lunch will make it go away.

"At least you have a concert tour motivating you to get better," Andy says. He wears the same grimace he's had since coming home. Good sleep has been hard for him to get. And getting him in a good mood is even harder.

"But your bruises are getting better," Lauren says, trying to cheer him up.

"I hate them; hate this surgery scar even more."

She rubs his shoulder as they take their seats.

Their lives have come to a halt, as has Plebeian's inaugural concert tour. Concerts in six cities have been cancelled and in another week they have to decide whether to cancel another six. Lauren told Davis she can put up with pain, but the deafening sound of their concert music might make her head explode.

While Andy and Lauren recover, it seems everyone else is moving on. Michael and Sunny visited one night, bringing them a barbeque dinner and a big surprise: they're engaged. They want to get married in spring, which should be well after the tour's rescheduled concerts.

Johnny and Amie have been regular visitors too. Amie has thrown herself into a new passion: cooking. She loves to bring her creations over and Andy and Lauren love to eat them. Johnny and Amie are not following Michael and Sunny's lead with an engagement though. And Lauren is surprised. After watching the horrible accident she was in and experiencing the loss of Anna, she thinks Johnny would realize how short life can be.

* * *

The spring of the accident turned into the summer of recovery and now the fall of return.

Dr. Tobias gives the green light for Lauren to tour. He has flown out several times at Lauren and Andy's request. They both love Tobias's bedside manner and he has been very helpful in getting them established with local doctors for their long-term care.

On the evening before she leaves, Lauren and Andy sit hand in hand, reclining in their poolside chaise.

Andy will miss the first ten-city leg of the tour. "I don't get it; I still feel so weak."

"I don't want to do this tour without you. I always imagined if there was a tour, you'd be with me."

"Lauren, just remember, every guy looking at you is just another guy that can't have you."

Thinking of those stares makes her shudder. But thinking about Andy being home without her makes her sick. "You sure you will be okay here?"

"I'll be fine."

"I'll fly home as much as I can," she says, resting her head on his shoulder.

Memorize this moment: the warm feel of Andy's hand holding hers, his breath softly tickling her cheek, snuggling together on their favorite chair. These moments don't seem to happen much anymore. And when she's gone, these memories will be all she has.

* * *

Muffled music from the opening act filters into Lauren's dressing room. In fifteen minutes, Plebeian will headline this Baltimore show.

Her blank face stares back at her from the dressing room mirror. False eyelashes, thick eyeliner and tan stage makeup as thick as clay. Looks good; feels fake. She may look ready but she would only feel ready if Andy was here.

She called him a few minutes ago, but he didn't answer. She just wanted to hear his voice again. Maybe he had nothing to say since they talked three times earlier today.

Three soft knocks on the door interrupt her brooding. Frank sticks his head in.

"Just checking on you," he says, smiling.

Loyal Frank. His eyes wrap her like a protective blanket, keeping watch over her and her surroundings. She enjoys Frank's company too. "Please come in."

He pulls up a stool beside her.

She smiles. "I'm good, I guess. I might not wear the sunglasses tonight," she says, twirling her favorite pair that she sometimes wears, especially if *Closer* is in their set. Since seeing the pervert at the Dallas show, can't sing that song without sunglasses.

"We're sold out again tonight," Frank says.

"Davis must be happy."

"Listen, I wanted to let you know of a small change I made at the house."

"Is something wrong?"

"No, probably not. But earlier today, Tish went out to get the mail and she noticed several crushed cigarette butts in the gutter."

"Like, someone is standing in front of the house smoking?"

"Could be. It may have come from the yard crew since that's where they park their trucks. But the yard crew had already come a few days earlier."

How weird. "What did the camera show?"

"There was a blind-spot right there. The front and side cameras didn't capture that corner. So Ryan adjusted them."

"Did Ryan talk with Andy?"

"No, he didn't. I wanted to talk with you first. Unless you tell me differently, you still call the shots at your house. I come to you for all the decisions."

"Well, that's probably good. Andy is in such a strange place right now. He doesn't need to be bothered with things like this."

"I think he's safe. The boys and Brittney are safe."

She glances away. *Safe. Just as long as everyone is safe.*

"Still…let me know if you find out anything."

Her door cracks open and Michael's smiling face sticks in. "We're on fire!" he says. Frank quickly stands. "No, Frank, no, not real fire. Our tickets sales are on fire."

Johnny, Doug and Oliver follow Michael in.

"Davis saw a news report that some tickets for this show sold for over a thousand bucks!" Michael says.

"Since we cancelled the shows after your accident, the resale market has been hot," Johnny says.

"It's probably me," Lauren mumbles. "I'm the accident on the side of the road everyone wants to slow down and stare at. Now people pay top dollar to stare at me."

Oliver smirks. "I think people want to see you because they're glad they're not you."

Doug frowns.

Oliver's rude, but right. All eyes are on the lucky woman who keeps having bad luck.

* * *

It's Sunday morning and Lauren's enormous smile seems to be piloting her plane home for this four-day break. Maybe Andy's watching her flight on his plane tracking app. Hopefully he feels better; rested and happy again. He still hasn't come to any shows yet, but she may be able to talk him into flying back with her for the next one or two. *Fingers crossed.*

Lauren arrives home in time for a family Sunday brunch. Tish has rolled out an impressive spread: smoked salmon quiche, colorful fruit salad and a roasted turkey sandwich platter. The kids rush downstairs to eat while Lauren rubs Andy's neck as she takes a seat next to him.

After updates from Lee on his grades, Aiden on the Florida Snowboarders club he joined and Brittney's announcement that her best friend Kayla is dating a jerk, Lauren turns to Andy.

"I don't have anything new to tell you." He looks under the bread slices and grimaces at his sandwich.

"What about the new consulting projects?" Lauren asks.

"It's easy stuff; really not challenging," he says of the work his old boss has given him to keep him busy.

"Did you like the new personal trainer?"

"Yeah, he was okay. He's been here twice. But he didn't really show me anything new."

Wow. His hole of wallow is deeper than she thought. Maybe she should ask if he's tried to relax by taking up smoking in the front yard but she better leave that alone.

"Are you still taking all your medicine?"

"Nothing is helping. I am so tired of not feeling well but I don't have the energy for anything new."

She reaches under the table to pat his leg. Somehow, she has to snap him out of this funk.

Andy

By early December Plebeian's first tour is complete. And Andy only made it to one show. Now the aggressive, possessive Lauren that was born in the Dallas hospital has come home.

"Andy?" He hears Lauren's muffled voice calling from outside. "Andy!"

What now? He breathes deep, opening his eyes from his nap on the family room sofa. If he doesn't get up and see what she wants, she'll find him anyway. He swings his legs off the couch, plants his bare feet on the wood floor and rubs his unshaven face.

"Hey, Andy? Come here!"

He shuffles outside. The sky is clear and blue, the air cool. Someone in this world must think this is a nice day. He squints just as the bright sunlight gives him an instant headache.

"Look!" Lauren says with the energy of a thousand people. "I found the extra Christmas lights!" She stands next to a storage bin, unthreading a string of knotted lights she wants the yard crew to put up.

Crap. He was hoping she wouldn't find those. There are way too many lights in the front yard now. No need to turn their home into some cheesy holiday attraction. It reminds him of the epic fights he used to have with his parents when they forced him to put up decorations every year. The outside of their tiny home was drenched in holiday spirit while the inside was really holy hell.

"We've been through this before," he mumbles. "It will make the house look stupid."

Her shoulders deflate. "I don't agree. I think we can add twice as many lights to the front yard and not look stupid."

Just tell her yes. It will make her stop. Or, stand your ground and fight. Just do something to end this and get back to sleep.

"It's stupid and pointless and will make the house look ridiculous."

She drops the strand. "Gee, Andy, did you not take your medicine today?"

Not again! "Damn, Lauren, stop asking about my medicine."

"I noticed all the pill bottles have been moved from the kitchen. How am I supposed to know if you need refills?"

"I'm a big boy. I can figure that out."

"Speaking of big boy, how come you cancelled the personal trainer again?"

"What? How do you know? Can't I do *anything* around here without you knowing?"

"That's not the point! I'm trying to help you."

"It's frickin' Fort Logan here. Stop obsessing and *that* would help."

"I'm not obsessing! I'm trying to help!"

He kicks the plastic tub, abruptly turns and stomps back to the house.

Please don't follow; please don't ask questions!

He wants to rest.

He wants space.

He just wants to feel better.

[SEVENTEEN]

Lauren

The northern winds blow stiff on this cloudy January day. Palm trees sway, their fronds bending as they surrender to a rare cold front. Even the peaceful pool water has turned into a tiny sea of irritated whitecaps. Lauren watches the weather from inside the studio, where she, Johnny and Michael have been working on a new song.

"I guess we'll call it a day," Johnny says, hanging up his Hummingbird on the rack.

Good. She wants to get back inside the house and check on Andy again.

"Thank you, guys," Johnny says. "I finally got that melody outta my head and recorded."

"Just in time for you to split town," Michael says. Amie and Johnny are leaving in two days for a winter getaway to their North Carolina cabin.

Lauren's gaze remains focused outside.

"Hey, you okay?" Johnny asks.

"Crappy day, that's all."

Michael straddles a chair beside her. "Is Andy doing alright?"

She snaps her head towards him. "Why?"

"I tried to talk to him the other day and, like, he still doesn't seem right," Michael says. "I asked him if y'all want to go out to dinner tomorrow night and…"

"And what?"

"He said he didn't want to go anywhere."

Johnny takes a deep breath.

"It's just been a long recovery," she says. "I'm helping him through it. We'll be okay." She reaches to pat Michael's leg, adding a fake smile. Andy might be okay once he agrees to see a therapist. She plans to ask him again, for the fifth time, later today.

They step out of the studio; Lauren wraps her sweater around her chest when she feels the chilly air.

"Have fun at the cabin," she says, giving Johnny a goodbye hug.

She turns to Michael. "Let's plan on that dinner tomorrow night. Lee and Aiden will be in New Orleans with Cory this weekend and Brittney will be with Janie, so it will be good for Andy to get out of the house," she says, hugging Michael. "I'll call you tomorrow for the details."

Johnny and Michael turn for the auto courtyard and that's when she spots Frank. He's standing by the back door to the family room, arms crossed, eyes stern.

"Whoa, what's wrong?"

Frank opens the back door and leads her into the family room. "Did Andy mention he was going anywhere today?"

"No, why?"

"He left about an hour ago. I was in my office watching the cameras and saw him carrying an overnight bag."

"What?"

"He hasn't returned my calls and his phone tracking app is off. I thought you might know where he was going."

"No…no, I don't," she says, looking around the family room. "His app is off?"

Frank nods. "Very strange."

"And…an overnight bag?"

He nods.

She pulls out her phone and calls Andy. It goes to voicemail. "What the heck?" She looks around the family room and kitchen for any sign of where he might have gone. Finding nothing, she heads upstairs, Frank behind her. In the bedroom, tucked under the H pillow, she sees a folded note.

"Oh good," she says, reaching for it. "I knew he wouldn't leave without a note!" She smiles, unfolding the paper.

Everything feels like it's closing in around me. I've been on this trip before. I've got to find some space and I can't find it here. I need a new start. It's time for us both to move on. You'll be better off if I'm not around.

Andy

Her eyes blur and her hands begin to shake. She tries to read it again but the paper is shaking too hard. Frank steadies her hand and leans over her shoulder to read.

"Move…on?" She turns to Frank. She can't breathe. "Can't be."

She reads the note again.

"We need to find him," Frank says. "He needs more help than you and I can offer."

"This…this just can't be for real. I'm sure…I'm certain…he just wanted to go for a drive or something. He'll be back tonight." She folds the note and places it on the bedside table.

"I'll ask Ryan to try to find him."

"Not right now," she says, breathing deep.

"At minimum I want to call Lynette."

"Why do you think my publicist needs to know that Andy went for a drive?"

"That's not what this note is saying," Frank says. "We need to let her know you are dealing with a serious matter."

"Let's just give him some space," she says, walking toward the bedroom door. "I just think he needs some space."

By sunset, the howling wind whips at the family room windows, the darkness of night making the sound even creepier.

Lauren sits on the sofa, hugging her knees to her chest, staring at her toes. It's after ten p.m. and she still hasn't heard from Andy.

But at least she knows where he is.

About two hours ago a credit card charge appeared on their shared account for a hotel in Ft. Lauderdale. And seeing it removed the weight of the world from her shoulders. He's safe, at a nice hotel. *See? He just needs space.* He can relax, spend some time on the beach. Heck, let him look at some bikinis and then when he comes home to her, she can model his favorite black bikini and they can have some fun. Like they used to.

She turns off a lamp and slowly steps upstairs. Forget what the note said. This will only be one night. After all, he only packed an overnight bag.

Lauren wakes up at seven a.m. and throws her arm across the empty bed. *Ugh.* No morning kiss from Andy. A few deep, wake-up breaths later, she realizes Andy should come home today.

The security intercom by her bedroom door buzzes with Ryan's voice.

"Lauren, Lynette has come through the hut and will be here shortly."

She crawls out of bed and presses the button that confirms she heard his message. This is their standard procedure, one Tish usually handles when she is here.

Guess Frank told Lynette about Andy's note. But a 7:10 a.m. visit? Then Lauren smiles when she realizes why. She must be bringing her a breakfast surprise. Lauren's favorite doughnut shop is near Lynette's house. Lauren instantly craves the chocolate cream filled doughnut she likes.

She throws on some clothes and meets Lynette at the side door.

"Hey," Lynette says, juggling her phone and laptop bag. "Can we go to the study?"

They walk to the study where Lynette spreads her devices across the desk. But there's no doughnut box.

"You haven't turned on the TV or anything yet, right?" she asks.

Lauren groans. "Don't tell me you've got a situation."

Ryan's voice comes through the intercom on the panel in her study. "Lauren, Davis has come through the hut and will be here shortly."

Lauren presses the confirm button. Now she's almost amused. What band drama has brought them here so early? But she's more bummed that she's not getting that chocolate cream doughnut.

Lynette's eyes dart all over the room, finally zooming at Lauren.

"We have…um…a Berlin situation."

Berlin? The last time Lauren heard Berlin was when Cory got caught sucking face with a coworker in Berlin the night she and Andy first got together.

"Oh, crap! Cory is in New Orleans with the boys. What did he do now?"

Davis hurries into the room out of breath.

Lynette looks at him, then Lauren.

"No, Lauren, not Cory," she says. "It's Andy."

A bar, a blonde. Andy's face is all over hers and her face and other body parts are all over his. At least twenty different photos hit gossip websites overnight. An old friend of Andy's from high school, Chase, appears in some of them, a stupid smile on his face and another woman on his lap. The photos make Cory's Berlin romp look like a fourth grade playground date.

"Obviously…I don't like this," Lauren says, using her calm "mom" voice. She clicks on each image. "But I'm not surprised. Andy needed to blow off some steam." She tilts her head to figure out whose hands are where in one of the photos. "Really though, did he have to do this in public? And why do my men like to kiss other women in public?"

Davis shares a concerned look with Lynette. "Andy needs to lay low today or he's going to get slaughtered by the press," Davis says.

"Look, Andy made a bad call. I'm sure when he wakes up and sees how big of a mess he's made, he will call."

Lynette immediately sends a message to family and friends:

"Got a situation with Lauren and Andy. Working it out with Lauren. Will be huge in news, please do not call or text her phone. Standby."

When Lynette sends a message with "standby" it means for everyone to chill out. This keeps Lauren's phone free of messages from friends asking if she's seen something she is obviously aware of. They learned from the Dallas accident that as long as family and close friends know they are in the inner loop, they will sit tight and when there is something new they will be told the latest.

Lauren heads upstairs to make her bed and take a shower. Hot running water washes the night away while she imagines how awkward this day will be. It's going to be okay, as long as Andy didn't sleep with that chick. And he never would've done that. He'll be so embarrassed. But how could he be so stupid to let photographers catch him?

She comes downstairs and Davis gestures for her to sit next to him at the desk.

"Let's see if the credit card charges give us a clue," he says. After she types in her password and Davis hits a few keystrokes, he moans. "Quite a few charges. Over $4,000 yesterday at bars and stores."

"He's staying at a nice hotel. Blowing off steam will be pricey."

"Um, including $279 at a lingerie store," he slowly says.

"Then there's probably $279 worth of lingerie coming home in a gift bag for me."

Davis looks in disbelief to Frank, who has just walked in the room. They start to discuss different scenarios that could have resulted in a $4,000 spending spree, plus racy photos.

"It's not even nine a.m.," Lauren says. "I'll call him if he doesn't call me soon."

By eleven a.m. they have not heard from Andy but the whole world has learned of his night. They can't take the plane to get him because Cory has it in New Orleans. Even if they could fly to Ft. Lauderdale, they don't want to remove Andy by force. He left a note all but telling her to leave him alone.

Enough. She walks into the living room and calls him. No answer. She sends a text.

"Seeing pictures of you from last night. Please call. You are going to get killed by the press."

By one p.m. there is no reply to Lauren's text or Frank's calls. The tracking feature on Andy's phone remains off. Calls to his hotel room go unanswered. No one has Chase's cell number. Tension in the house builds as they consider the options.

Ryan's voice buzzes from the intercom. "Lauren, Johnny and Michael have come through the hut and will be here shortly."

She punches the confirm button. Now they have come to watch her go through this?

The study is abuzz with Davis, Lynette and Frank all sitting at computers and talking on their phones. Then Johnny stomps into the study. "I'm not waiting on standby. What the hell happened?"

Lauren's shoulders sink. *Angry Captain Control.* She leads Johnny away, towards the kitchen. They stop in a hallway.

"Photographers caught Andy doing something stupid in Ft. Lauderdale."

"Why the hell was he there? Is he on his way back?"

"We don't know if he's coming back. He hasn't called."

Johnny's eyes cross.

Lauren glances over Johnny's shoulder, now noticing Tish has arrived. She's busying herself by arranging a buffet on the kitchen counter. Now they have the catering for a party with the feel of a funeral.

Lauren looks back at Johnny. "Andy left a note," she whispers, leaning closer to him. "He said he wanted a new start and it was time for us to move on."

"He broke up with you?" Johnny loudly says, his hands fly in the air.

Everyone steps out of the study and looks down the hall at Lauren and Johnny.

"No, I don't think…that's not what he meant." Her eyes dart around.

Frank crosses his arms.

"I'll drive down there and get him myself," Johnny says.

"I'm with you," Michael says.

"Let's think about that you guys," Lynette says, her eyes tightening. "The famous ex-boyfriend and his famous, big-muscled friend dragging an adult man home who, at this point, got gob-smacked drunk last night and partied too hard. *Not* a good look."

"Lauren, there's something else we need to think about," Frank says. "It's possible this could be extortion."

"Seriously, Frank?" Michael asks.

"It's possible and Andy may not even realize it's happening," Frank says. "Sometimes this involves alcohol or drugs where someone is kept inebriated and occupied while others spend their money."

"Well, he's with Chase, the guy who partied all the time in high school," Lauren says. She didn't like him then and she sure doesn't like him at the moment.

Davis walks back into the study and everyone follows. He sits at the computer. "Since I last checked, another $1,200 has been spent on three different charges: a liquor store, the hotel boutique and restaurant."

"Andy isn't returning calls but money is flying out the door," Johnny says.

"Did Chase arrange a woman to keep Andy busy while he spends your money?" Michael asks.

"Chase might be taking advantage of Andy's depression," Davis says.

Worry chisels Frank's face. "I want to put a P.I. on the ground immediately."

This is escalating so quickly! Hiring a private investigator to check on Andy the day after he "moved on"? But she needs to know what's happening and she's too recognizable to do it herself. "Do it," she says. "And no one, *please,* no one here *ever* let Andy know I did this!"

Media requests for Lauren's statement are burying Lynette and Lesley arrives to help her. They turn the dining room table into a communications triage center.

Lauren's once peaceful home now operates like a surreal emergency response center. She steps away from the chatter and slowly walks to the quiet living room. A plush chair seems to be inviting her to collapse in it. She does.

Her gaze wanders out the window to the courtyard. Palm trees still blow in the afternoon wind, although not as agitated as yesterday. Their careless movement quickly mesmerizes her, hypnotizing her with simplicity. Lucky palm trees: not a care in the world.

She slowly blinks when she realizes how much her head hurts. There's so much bitter news to swallow from the past twenty-four hours. She found a horrible note she wants to forget. Andy's kissing another girl. He's spending thousands of dollars but not returning anyone's call. She has questioned her trust of him by hiring private investigators to spy on him. She's either stupid or smart. And he's either in danger or making one big ass mistake.

Her phone vibrates with an incoming call, interrupting her thoughts.

It's Andy.

[EIGHTEEN]

Lauren answers Andy's call. "Hey, are you okay?"

"I told you I needed space, remember?" he slurs.

Oh, God. He's drunk.

"Yeah, Andy, I found your note. You know about the pictures, right?"

"I'm not taking any pictures. It's good here. All good. I just want to be left alone. Can you just back off?" he stutters.

"Sure, yeah, but the pictures, honey, they were taken of you and another girl." She hears some rustling with his phone and a woman's voice—maybe a giggle. Lauren leans closer to her phone, like that's going to help her hear more.

"Andy, are you alone?"

A few seconds pass; she struggles to hear what's happening in the background. Is his phone being rubbed on something? Did it drop or get taken away and he's struggling to pick it up?

"Yeah, no more pictures. Got it. All good here." He hangs up the phone.

Her pulse surges. She sits alone, stunned, and tries to recall every word he said, especially the muffled noises in the background. *Quick! Remember everything!* She presses a recording app on her phone and she repeats the conversation. *Remember every detail!* She finishes the recording and can hear her heart pounding. A warm, nauseating mass pulses up her throat. She's not sure if she's mad or scared, if she wants to scream or vomit.

Tish leans into the living room. "Need anything, Lauren?"

"Frank!" Lauren shouts. *"Get Frank!"*

People rush to the living room, her chair instantly surrounded by everyone in her home. She thrusts her phone in the air.

"He called…he just called!" she yells, fumbling with the phone to replay her recording. She hands the phone to Frank, who turns up the volume so Davis and Johnny can hear. She stands, pacing.

"Is he okay or is he just screwing around?" she asks.

Frank lowers the phone. "He's drunk or high, and not alone. That is all this tells us."

She slaps her hands to her face. What a living nightmare! And anyone in the world who wants to make it their business is watching this happen!

"My people should be there by now. Let me call them with this update," Frank says, hurrying out of the room.

"We'll just keep track of the money," Davis says. "I've already called the credit card company and lowered the maximum on the card, just in case."

Lauren's desperate eyes lock with Johnny's. He's helpless to help her. He can't just blow a kiss and make this all go away.

The next hours unfold like a television drama as they try to figure out if the love of Lauren's life is a free man being stupid or a bad boyfriend cheating or a victim being extorted for money. Davis sits at the computer watching the credit card and bank transactions. The private investigative firm now has five spies hanging around the hotel, Frank says, including a young woman playing the part of eager partier.

"And we easily have about ten extra people tracking him for free," Frank says.

"Who are they?" Lauren asks.

"Paparazzi."

Every inch of her despises this unfolding in the public eye but paparazzi photos could be helpful right now.

At least the panicked pounding inside her chest has calmed down since Tish slipped her a sedative. She asks everyone to come in the living room for a minute.

"I just want to be sure we are on the same page," she says, twisting her hands. "My priority is that Andy is safe. I want to make sure he is not being forced to do something he does not want to do."

Everyone nods.

"Only second is the money. If he needs money to figure out his life before he comes home, my money is his to spend even if he spends it stupidly. But my priority: make sure he's safe." Everyone nods.

She leaves the room and heads outside.

It is sunset now, usually Lauren's favorite time of day but there is nothing about this day that she likes. The lazy breeze from earlier is now a chilly January wind. She swears she can hear a helicopter circling near her house. No one has told her but she imagines there are paparazzi sitting outside the hut, waiting for their cars to come and go. Everyone loves a good celebrity cheating boyfriend story. She walks to the double chaise and crawls like a wounded animal onto the soft cushion. She flips over to lie in the chair, shivering in the cold thinking about this horrible day.

Focus. Focus on what is important! Cory has the boys safe in New Orleans and Brittney is safe at Janie's house. She texted each of them earlier and promised to have a longer phone call with each of them later.

Across the pool she notices a light in the studio and sees Johnny and Michael inside at the same time they notice her. They step outside.

"Can we join you?" Johnny asks.

"Plenty of room on this chair now that Andy isn't here," she drily says. Johnny slides on the chaise to her left, putting his arm behind her shoulders while Michael struggles to fit his large body in on her right. "I'm too much man for a double lounge chair with two people already on it," he says, smiling. He nudges her arm. "I guess we aren't going out to dinner tonight." Her head drops. There's a good chance she'll never get to have dinner with Andy again.

The three sit quietly. Johnny and Michael surround her like a powerful, warm blanket. And it weakens her. Tears she's been holding back start to trickle from her eyes. She sniffles, trying to rein them back.

"You guys just missed my priorities speech," she says, sniffling again.

"I know what your priorities are," Johnny says, squeezing her tighter.

"What are you going to do if he slept with her?" Michael asks.

She cringes and looks up at the stars.

"I'm not sure. I'm not even sure what he and I are anymore…" she pauses for a minute as the helicopter buzzes closer, "except that he's my life and I can't be without him."

Lesley has been on the phone most of the day, personally calling those on Lauren's inner-circle list. Many of them have also called Andy and left messages. As Lauren passes through the dining room, Lesley hands her a paper with their comments and suggestions, pointing to her note at the top of the page.

"Christy is about to explode," Lesley says. "She wants to know if you want her here."

"My best friend; she always wants to help," Lauren says, "but she lives across the state. She doesn't need to drive all the way over here."

"Christy may be the silver bullet you fire if you run out of options," Frank says. "She's only an hour or so from Ft. Lauderdale. We may need her to go talk to him if this situation deteriorates."

Lauren glances back at Lesley's notes. There are messages from some celebrities she knows. At least other celebrities can relate to what she's publicly going through.

"We have the first report on what is happening in Ft. Lauderdale this evening," Frank says, leading Lauren to the study where everyone has gathered.

Andy and Chase have left the hotel with two women.

"Lauren, they came from their room," Frank says.

Her eyes go glassy with the thought.

"I've got a charge that just hit," Davis says. "Hotel boutique for $136."

Johnny pounds the desk. "What the hell is in that damn boutique?"

An hour later Frank has the next report: beachside bar; drinks bought for their group plus nearby tables; open affection between Andy and the blonde. Appears mutual. Andy freely walks around the bar to the restroom; he is not under duress. Davis sees the charge appear a few minutes later: $259.

An hour later: they are at dinner at an upscale, rooftop restaurant at another hotel; still the four; still open affection between Andy and the blonde; Andy appears to be drunk.

Two hours later: they are at a club at the new hotel and drinking heavily; the blonde is drunk; Andy is drunk. The female undercover P.I. makes advances to Andy. He does not refuse and kisses her; the blonde with him encourages it. The undercover woman tries to leave with the group but the two women tell her to leave.

"The charge from dinner two hours ago has just posted," Davis says. "Wow: $832."

Darkness now covers Lauren's study, except for the soft glow from computer screens and cell phones. With every update, extortion seems less likely. With every update, the words in his note might be true.

Frank comes in with a new twist: the agents have sent him photos. These are more detailed than paparazzi photos because the investigators' hidden cameras are closer. He hands them only to Lauren. Seeing Andy's drunken face feels like acid in her stomach. He's smiling, laughing and kissing this woman while Lauren aches in pain looking at it.

She throws the papers on the desk.

"Frank, please have your guys make sure he is safe. Don't interfere unless he is in danger," she says, the words falling from her mouth in exhaustion, "and please stay on him."

She leaves her friends, dragging her numb body upstairs to her room. She walks straight to the bed and collapses on it, pulling the side of the comforter around her legs rather than bother to slide under the sheets. Her fingers crawl across the comforter, reaching to snatch the square H pillow; slowly pulling the thought of Andy to her aching chest. This pillow is all she has of Andy right now; all she has.

Morning comes fast, filling Lauren's bedroom with bright sunlight. She's in her bed, alone, but she hears strange breathing.

There's a body on one of the sofas in the sitting area of her bedroom. *Wow.* It's Michael. He must have come up here to check on her and crashed on her sofa. Now, she's worried about him. This drama isn't a good thing for him to see a month before he and Sunny get married. Lauren's no role model for healthy relationships right now.

She walks softly downstairs to her study: the war room. There's a body on the living room sofa and someone else lying on the sectional in the family room. Who claimed the guest house or guest bedrooms? She couldn't have handled yesterday without these good friends.

The study is eerily quiet and so is she. She feels small today. She sits behind her desk; the solid wood and sturdy white leather chair helping her to feel stronger. Several information briefs from the P.I. firm are scattered on the desk. One catches her attention. It's a complete profile of the girl Andy was with. Her hands quiver in uneasy anticipation as she begins to read.

> *Marcia Lawson, age 35, divorced, works at Art Loft, an art gallery at 345 Ocean Drive; drives a Toyota Camry, $10,567 in assets; $69,345 debt; renting apartment on top of clothing store at 73290 Stockton Street; two charges for cocaine possession and distribution, twelve parking tickets, one aggravated assault charge. High school diploma highest education completed.*

She slams the report on the desk and sarcasm loads as her defensive weapon of choice. Look at this, the two of them—just like twins right? Oh, what she could do to her. She should buy that art gallery just to close it down. Or she could buy that clothing store her apartment is over and turn it into a Chinese food restaurant so she always has a constant greasy smell.

Lauren stops her vindictive mind. Andy might be with that woman right now. Her stomach sours.

Part of her wishes Andy was here so she could slap him. The other part wants to sweep him in her arms and forgive him so they can go back to the way they used to be. But he has to come home for her to do either.

Sunday progresses slowly as people come and go. Lynette's husband arrives with clean clothes for her, since she's not leaving until this crisis is over. Frank appears fresh and ready from wherever he found a place to sleep last night. Michael needs to leave and so does Johnny.

"We're supposed to drive up to the cabin today but I can cancel and come back here later," Johnny says.

"No, don't," she says, giving him a hug. "You enjoy your trip to North Carolina with Amie."

"You don't deserve what he's done to you."

"He didn't deserve to be crushed in a car when all he was doing was riding with me."

His eyes narrow. "That's an excuse and you know it."

She looks down. *You're full of those.*

The morning passes quietly, but the afternoon heats up as activity in Ft. Lauderdale generates a new batch of P.I. reports.

1 p.m.: Chase and Andy check out of the hotel; the two women have accompanied them; Chase and Andy part ways. Andy leaves in his vehicle with Lawson and drives to 73290 Stockton Street.

"They spent the night together?" Lauren asks Frank.

"I don't think they've been apart since the story broke Friday night."

She clutches her stomach. And she keeps clutching her stomach every time a new report rolls in.

3 p.m.: Andy remains at 73290 Stockton Street

5 p.m.: Andy remains at 73290 Stockton Street

7 p.m.: Andy remains at 73290 Stockton Street

9 p.m.: Andy remains at 73290 Stockton Street

Even though Andy told her to back off, she can't wait any longer. She calls him. He doesn't answer, so she texts:

"Can you call me so we can talk?"

No response.

By 10:30 p.m. Davis, Lynette, Frank and Lauren talk about what to do next.

"The guys on the ground say there are no paparazzi near her apartment yet," Frank says. "This may be a good time to dispatch Christy. Or since Cory is back from New Orleans with the boys, now we have the plane. We could fly down there tonight and confront him before he self-destructs more."

"If no photographers are around, you could do it yourself," Lynette says.

"How can I go to her apartment if I'm not supposed to know where he is?" Lauren asks. "I need information but I don't want him to know I hired spies!"

At 11 p.m. Lynette pulls up a gossip website's photo of Lawson's apartment with the headline "*Love Shack*" and a story about how Andy has moved in with her. With that story went Lauren's chance for a face to face with Andy. Now the world knows where he is.

Lauren stumbles out to the family room; her bones creak as she stretches out on the sofa. *What the hell is next?* Her heartbroken body aches for sleep but she doesn't have the energy to walk upstairs to her bedroom. Right now, it's too much energy to breathe.

Lauren wakes up on the family room sofa, wearing clothes she thinks she's worn for days now. Last she remembers she was trying to think of what to do next. Evidently her body decided for her.

It's Monday morning and the boys should be at school; Cory hasn't sent word about whether they made it or not. She can't imagine what Brittney is feeling right now but she's certain Janie kept her home from school. Brittney has probably called her dad a hundred times. Thankfully, the boys will spend another night with Cory and Brittney will spend another night with Janie. Lauren has no emotional energy for the kids right now.

Lauren, Frank, Davis, Lynette and Tish spend the day waiting for information. They discuss so many options of what to do, Lauren has lost track of what they've done.

After Tish leaves for the day, they settle in the study for their new evening routine: P.I. briefs from Ft. Lauderdale. And the briefs are not good. Andy's still with her, he's still spending money and he's not returning calls.

Lauren's quivering fingers hold one of the photographs taken tonight. Her tears have wet the paper. It's a wonder she has any tears left.

Her mind goes back to a happier time, to a beautiful balcony in New York City. She remembers the views of the busy river and her first long, revealing conversation with Andy. He told her that his life had been full of superficial, easy beauty. Even Brittney, on the night Lauren first met her, said she was surprised her dad wasn't dating another sketchy woman. Maybe Andy is still as immature as he used to be.

She glances down at the tear-stained photo taken tonight. She squints to focus. *Can't be.* Both of them are holding cigarettes. But

Andy doesn't smoke.

Maybe he was never the man she thought he was.

Tuesday arrives and Lauren's group of cheating boyfriend trouble-shooters are back to help her again.

"I know you don't want to hear this, but you have got to protect your assets more than you already have," Davis says.

"I don't need to protect my assets. I just need him home so we can work this out."

"How long do you want to pay for his life with another woman?" Davis blurts.

She coils back. Reality has arrived. Actually, it arrived Friday via the note on her bed. Deal with the truth, or live the rest of your life secluded at home, waiting for his car to pull up the driveway.

"Stop wasting your time calling him," Davis says. "At this point I wouldn't want to talk to him if I were you."

"Maybe try one more time," Tish says.

Lauren looks at them both. Davis has always been right, but Tish has always been so kind. *Maybe one more call?*

She calls him and again, no answer. She leaves another message.

"I still want to talk to you. Will you please call me?"

She sets her phone on the kitchen counter, walks to the breakfast table and buries her head in her hands.

"He's not going to call," Davis says. "So let's talk about moving on…"

Suddenly her phone rings. Frank glances to the counter. "It's Andy!"

Finally! Lauren's chair crashes to the floor in her rush to stand. In three giant steps she has her phone in her hand and bursts though the back door, out by the pool for privacy.

"Hi," she breathlessly answers. It's time for him to do the talking.

"I got your message. Yeah, it's been crazy here," Andy says. It sounds like he's been drinking, though maybe today he's not completely lit.

"You're having a good time in Ft. Lauderdale?" she asks, pretending she has no idea what has happened.

"Yeah, I like it here. I'm gonna stay here awhile."

Her body buckles. "Staying with friends?"

"Yeah, someone."

"So you might not come back…like at all?" Now she sounds mousy.

"Geez, give me a break. I'm tired of always answering questions."

"Andy, I love you, and whatever you are going through, we can figure it out."

"Yeah, you love me."

"And you love me."

"Look, yeah, no… no."

Lauren leans forward. *Did he just tell her he didn't love her?*

"Andy, there's nothing in the world we can't figure out together. You just need to come home so we can talk this out."

"Look, okay, if it gets you to stop bugging me then yeah, I don't love you. Okay?"

She straightens with his verbal hit. "You don't…what?"

There's silence. No background noises; no sound of breathing. No sound at all but there sure is a smell. It's the stench of horrible words.

"I really…" Andy sputters, "I really don't love you. And I don't think I ever really did."

She gasps, loosening her grip on the phone. Shock jolts her, turning her knees to softened butter.

This can't be happening! She's sickened with this conversation. This stupid, stupid conversation!

"Okay, Andy, got it. You're not coming back. I don't agree with you, but…"

"Look," he interrupts.

She talks louder. "I don't know what has changed and why you feel the way you do, but it does not change my love for you. You might not be coming back but you should know…Andy…no matter what you've done and no matter what you've gone through…you will always, *always*…be the love of *my* life."

Then she hangs up on him.

She watches the screen go dark as the call disconnects. Shaking, she's tempted to throw the phone; this horrible phone that produced such a horrible conversation! She stumbles towards their chaise lounge and slowly sits on the edge, sobbing. The weight of her tears pulls her head down, her tears leaving water marks on the cushion.

He doesn't love her and he thinks he never did? The devastating words have stabbed a thousand cuts to her hunched body. Those words…have sliced her soul.

But they're also fighting words. She just spent four days wondering if he was safe. She held on to hope that he would come home. Now he's with another woman and wants to stay with her? *Enough!*

With soft feet and wobbly legs, she stands. With the few ounces of pride she has left, she breathes deeply. She clenches her teeth, steadies herself and then heads for the house.

Frank, Davis, Lynette and Tish have been glued to the window, watching.

Lauren steps inside, holding three fingers in the air.

"Three?" Frank asks.

"Three words," she says. "Cut. Him. Off."

And she leaves the room.

[NINETEEN]

Friends don't let friends suffer and Lauren's people have a plan. Davis moves most of the money from their joint bank account to an account of Lauren's that is solely in her name. He pays the bill then closes the credit card they shared. He calls her lawyer to draw up confidentiality documents that will be presented later for Andy to sign.

Frank calls a locksmith and within an hour all locks in the house are rekeyed. He changes the code to the master security system. Andy's name is removed from the hut's access list.

Lynette has three statements prepared announcing the breakup, ready for Lauren to choose one. Lauren points to the middle statement because it looks the shortest. Lynette will release it after Lauren talks to the kids.

Tish hires movers that will relocate Andy's things to his empty parking spot in the garage until she figures out where to ship them. He will not be allowed back in the house, so anything of his will have to be delivered.

Their work is efficient and quick; emotionally and financially lethal. That leaves Lauren with one thing to do. And when it's done, it brings her team to a standstill when she steps back into the kitchen.

"Shit, you look pale," Davis says, rushing towards her. "How did the call go?"

She plops on a barstool and buries her head in her hands. They surround her, Tish rubbing her back.

"That was, by far, the hardest phone call I've ever made," Lauren whispers, looking up.

Frank's eyes are wide and Davis shakes his head. Lynette has her hands to her face and Tish now slides a glass of water towards her.

"Was Janie at least…nice?" Davis asks.

"She was short with me like she usually is, but polite," Lauren says. "I told her there is no rush for Brittney to move out but at some point, with Andy not here anymore…"

"Oh God, this is so awful," Tish whispers.

"I told her Brittney is always welcome here and I still consider her part of my family. Janie took a few cheap swipes at Andy and I have to say, I didn't disagree. He abandoned me as fast as he abandoned her."

"We have about two hours before Brittney and the boys come home," Frank says.

Lauren buries her head in her hands again. Seeing them will be the worst part of it all.

She heads back up to her bedroom. She's got to calm this itching, this agitation. If she could unzip her skin and remove it to relieve this disgusted feeling she would. Andy has broken up a family. He's with that woman right now. He wants to be with *her*!

She grabs the H pillow from her bed. She punches it and screams, then throws it across the room, only to pick it up again and repeat the punishment. Finally, she crumbles onto the sofa in exhaustion, squeezing the pillow until little pieces of white foam filling ooze out from ripped stitches on the side. Then she hears a soft knock on the door. Aiden, Lee and Brittney are home from school.

The four of them sit on the sofa in her bedroom, Lauren stroking Brittney's soft brown hair.

"It's been a difficult few days, I think, for all of us," Lauren says. "I finally talked with Andy. He's not coming home." She can't even look at the kids; her eyes roll to the floor.

"I don't understand why. Why hasn't he called me to explain? Why is he being such a jerk?" Brittney says. "Now I have to leave here, right,

Lauren? I'll have to move out because *he* has to be such an idiot!"

Lauren strokes Brittney harder to calm her. "At some point in the future, yes, you will have to move out. It would be complicated for you to live here without your dad."

"He's ruined my life—again! He's never been there for me and now this!" Brittney rises in a rage. "I finally had a family, a real family. And now he's taken that away!" she screams, storming out of the room.

Lauren can't rally the strength to follow her.

"We were just working it all out. I was getting used to Brittney being around," Lee says. "Why didn't Andy want to live with us?"

"Oh honey, it's not you. Andy didn't want to be with me." Her arms and legs, her entire body, feels weighted with her words. "Maybe one day I'll know why. Maybe by then, I won't care. Right now, it's just hard. Real hard." She reaches over to give her boys a hug and savors theirs in return.

When the house quiets for sleep, it's just Lauren, Brittney, Aiden and Lee, along with Ryan or whoever is on duty in the office above the garage. Just hours ago this house was set up like a combat zone with people trying to keep track of Andy. Now here they are, just Lauren and the kids knowing Andy will never come home. The house itself is probably breathing a sigh of relief that at least this drama has a conclusion.

She sits up in bed, lights off, clutching the beaten H pillow, watching the clock.

11:58, almost time.

11:59, the end is near.

Finally, midnight.

And the end of the day he said he never loved her.

Tish arrives early to help Lauren get the kids off to school. Lauren stands barefoot in the kitchen, blankly staring at the peanut butter and peanut butter sandwich she just made for Aiden. Tish swoops in, replacing one of the peanut butter sides with a jelly-spread slice of bread.

Lauren shuffles to the window of her study, waving goodbye to the kids. Frank steps in behind her. "Hey. I have a brief from the past evening."

Oh goody. More pain.

"So what did the love of my life do with his slutty new girlfriend last night?" she mumbles, closing the shutters and slumping in her desk chair.

"According to this, Andy and Lawson went for drinks at another beach bar. They were joined by several people at the table. Lawson was friendly to one of the men. Very friendly. She was seen kissing that guy when Andy briefly left the table."

"So she's cheating on Andy already?" Her voice is monotone, her emotions numb.

"That's not all. One of the agents was at the next table and heard the entire episode unfold when Andy's credit card was declined. Andy was livid, paid with another card, and then stormed down to the beach as Lawson chased him. They yelled at each other and for some reason, Andy also yelled at the water. Then, Andy walked back to her apartment and was not seen the rest of the evening."

"Well, I know Andy has his own credit card and plenty of his own money," she says. "He probably didn't like using it. Must be hard for him to realize the millions have dried up."

"There's more," Frank says.

"It seems impossible that there could be more."

"After Andy left the beach, Lawson was joined by two men who are known drug dealers and a purchase ensued. Lawson then returned to the Stockton apartment. So now we have confirmation that drugs are involved."

"That, sadly, explains quite a bit." She slaps her hands to her thighs as she rises from the chair. "Frank, thank you for your tireless work. I know it's only eight a.m. but I have nothing else to look forward to today. I'm going back to bed. Please—get some rest for yourself."

He nods.

Safe in her upstairs bedroom, she tugs the comforter up to her neck, lying on her side and looking out through the sunny windows. If she was a betting woman she'd wager that Andy will call today. It sounds like his new paradise is not perfect and maybe today he will want to come home.

Even though she has been publicly humiliated, officially announced their break up and is moving his daughter out of her house, Lauren would answer the phone if he called. She would grant him access though the hut. She would welcome him back in this bed—well maybe after he answered some questions and passed a sexually transmitted disease exam—but she would take him back. She thinks.

The day drags by, but Andy never calls. She busies herself by returning some messages.

She has a surprisingly pleasant conversation with Oliver and a quick conversation with Doug. She had a hard time ending the long call with Johnny. She calls Michael to change her wedding RSVP from a party of five to a party of three. She chats with her mother and brother and talks with Christy for over an hour. Then she returns some calls to other people she doesn't know very well but whose outreach she appreciated. One of them is Dina Marks.

Lauren met the actress at an awards show party last year and their conversation was natural and friendly. Dina's husband Hugh is also an actor who appeared on a popular television sitcom a couple of years ago. Dina had left Lauren a long voicemail that Lesley passed along.

At the end of their thirty minute conversation, Dina invites Lauren to fly out and spend a few days with her and Hugh at their Utah ranch. Lauren said yes and she can come tomorrow. After being in this house for five days straight she's ready to go somewhere no one expected and spill her heart to someone new.

* * *

Craig and Henry have her plane ready for the early Thursday morning flight, while Cory takes over daily duty with the boys. Frank will be flying with her and will stay in a nearby hotel where Craig and Henry will be.

Lauren can't get out of town fast enough and the departing view of Florida is something she enjoys watching from the plane's window. Her visit with a movie star will probably generate more publicity she doesn't need, but that publicity can't be worse than what she's already had. She rests her head on the leather seat and parses a small smile with another thought.

Unless he disabled his flight tracker app, someone's phone at 73290 Stockton Place just pinged with a notification that her plane is on the move. Maybe, just maybe, it will bother Andy that he does not know where she is going anymore.

Lauren looks back at Frank. "It's time," she says.

"Time for what?"

"Time to stop trailing Andy. Stop the private investigators."

He nods.

It's time to start letting go of the man who let her go.

Dina's wide, warm smile is as gracious as she is a host. Her Utah ranch has spectacular, sweeping views of the mountains near Snow Canyon. Inside the two-story home, vaulted ceilings top the glass walls, which offer views of a snow-covered terrace. On the terrace, a bench is perfectly positioned for anyone to sit and take in amazing view. Hugh welcomes Lauren with a home-cooked meal of chili and cornbread. Their home has a cozy glass-walled sitting room that Dina and Lauren enjoy for hours, talking about love, loss and life. Dina is the ultimate girlfriend's girlfriend, someone much deeper than the characters she has played in her movies.

On Friday, Dina and Lauren venture out in Dina's Jeep to visit a coffee-house she insists is a must-see. With log walls, bear rugs and indie music, it certainly isn't the usual chain coffee shop Lauren is used to, plus the coffee is delicious. When they walk out there is a celebrity videographer hanging near Dina's Jeep.

Dina leans closer to Lauren. "He's always here trying to get shots of me."

His smile is wide and his camera is rolling as they come closer.

"Lauren, Lauren? You over Andy yet?" he yells.

"I'm enjoying a beautiful Utah day in the company of a great, great friend," she says, climbing in Dina's Jeep.

Within the hour, Lauren receives a text from Lynette, who has already seen the video clip online.

"Perfect quote. Peeps going crazy you are with Dina. You look good too."

On Saturday morning, Frank waits at the St. George airport with Craig and Henry to take Lauren home. She hugs Dina and Hugh and offers a reciprocal visit anytime they are near Florida.

* * *

The long flight home gives Lauren plenty of time to rest but once the plane's wheels hit the ground, the uneasy feeling of reality returns. Before getting off the plane she glances at her messages. A text from Christy catches her eye.

"Call me when you can. I have some info on Andy."

As soon as Bill pulls up the Tahoe and Lauren and Frank get in, she returns Christy's call.

"You have a good trip?" Christy asks.

"The best distraction trip ever."

"Good. I'm sorry to bring this back up, but I've got some

information on Andy. I got a call from Cheryl. Do you remember her from high school? Dated Bobby—they married—Bobby is friends with Andy?" Christy asks.

"Yeah, I remember them. You brought them with your group to Plebeian's first concert."

"So Cheryl called me a little while ago. She told me they have Andy. She didn't want to give me details, but she thought someone in your circle should know that Andy is safe with them."

"They have him? That's huge," Lauren says, and repeats the information to Frank while they continue the drive home.

Christy continues, "Cheryl and Bobby live in Port Saint Lucie, not too far from Ft. Lauderdale. Somehow Andy got to them, or they went and got him. That's all she would tell me."

As soon as they hang up, Bill, Frank and Lauren discuss every option that could be applied to every word of Christy and Cheryl's call.

"Something big must have happened and Andy left," Bill guesses.

"Maybe he ran out of money," Frank cracks.

"At least we know he is safe," Lauren says.

And now they know where to send the legal documents.

* * *

Her attorney Pamela pulls up to the portico on Sunday afternoon and Davis opens the door to greet her. She has brought along a colleague, Todd Peppers, a defense attorney in their firm. Lauren steps out from her study and freezes. Todd is over six feet of seriously fit deliciousness, a former professional football player with gelled hair, tanned skin and a wide smile with teeth that light up her foyer. His biceps bulge under the fabric of his smooth wool suit. *Dang. Lucky fabric.* She shakes her head back to reality and welcomes him to her home.

They gather in her study and Pamela pulls out the documents Andy needs to sign.

"It's good that you're doing this, especially these documents that distribute your assets," Pamela says. "Todd will deliver these in person to Andy. This would never be something Todd would normally do as he is our firm's top defense attorney, but…"

Todd interrupts. "It was my idea to deliver them. I want to go see this guy face to face."

Well this certainly is a twist. Perhaps there's nothing wrong with the best-looking attorney she's ever seen knocking on Bobby's door to slap these papers down in front of Andy.

"Okay, so what's next?" Lauren asks.

"I call him right now," Todd says, "and go see him tomorrow."

Lauren watches Davis glancing through the packet. *What would she do without Davis right now?* He nods to Lauren; everything is there.

She gives Andy's number to Todd.

Todd places his phone on Lauren's desk and dials with it on speaker. Every digit he presses thumps in her heart. She isn't ready to hear Andy's voice! She gives Davis an *I-think-I'm-gonna-die* stare.

She holds her breath with every ring until finally, a man answers. But it's not Andy.

"It's Bobby, Bobby!" Lauren whispers. Todd nods.

"Andy?" Todd says.

"Who is this?" Bobby asks.

"You must be Bobby. I'm Todd Peppers and I'm an attorney representing Lauren Logan. She gave me Andy's number. I need to talk with him to arrange a time to meet. I have some legal matters that need finalizing regarding their time together. There is nothing major, more of a formality, but still a necessity given Lauren's high profile."

"Um…okay, let me talk with him. Just a minute," Bobby says.

They all lean in, trying to hear Bobby's muffled words.

"Hello, this is Andy."

Lauren grips her face. Mad or not, her heart still lurches at the sound of his voice. He sounds tired. And sober.

"Hi, Andy, I'm Todd Peppers. I have been asked by Lauren to meet with you to go over some documents." Todd repeats his earlier story.

"I'm a little surprised, I guess. I'm not sure what has to be done," Andy says.

"There are bank accounts, credit cards and some personal matters like your mail."

"Okay, yeah, I guess there are a few things I wasn't thinking about."

Lauren wildly nods, pointing to the phone. *Oh, hell yeah. Quite a few things.*

"I can come by Bobby's house tomorrow morning if that works for you. Say ten a.m.?" Todd says.

"Um, sure. Ten a.m. I'll be here. I'll put Bobby back on to give you the address."

"Oh, that won't be necessary. I know where to go."

"Of course…ten a.m. then. That…works," Andy slowly says.

"Thank you, Andy. I'll see you then." Todd hangs up.

Todd, Pamela and Davis start to talk about tomorrow's arrangements.

Lauren still stares at Todd's phone sitting on her desk. "Do you think he sounded okay?"

"He sounded tired to me," Davis says. "And confused that what he did last weekend is causing your lawyer to show up."

Pamela and Todd start to leave, agreeing that Todd will come back to the house tomorrow afternoon to go through all that Andy has signed. Todd has been assigned the law firm's plane to expedite the trip. As they begin to walk out the door, Lauren pulls Todd back and whispers something.

"Will do," Todd says, and then leaves.

"What was that?" Davis asks.

Lauren looks away. "Just something I need to know."

* * *

Darkness overcomes him.

All he ever wanted in his miserable life was what she gave him.

Now he has no direction; he's lost his path.

Her pain is his pain.

The weight of sadness crushes his body. He sits, crumbled, on the floor.

His arms cradle the open mouth of the porcelain bowl.

A pungent smell fills the room; his vomit spread on the floor.

He can't even throw up right.

He can't do anything, without her.

/ [TWENTY]

Those pesky patches of crabgrass in Lauren's lawn didn't have a chance. Her nervous fingers picked through the weeds early this morning, before she took a shower so long her fingers and toes got pruned. Now, she's sorting the kitchen utensil drawer, even though Tish keeps this drawer color-coded and expertly organized. Lauren's running out of things to do to keep her mind off Todd and his trip to see Andy this morning.

Davis shows up shortly after ten a.m. "Any word yet?"

"The silence is deafening," she says, stacking spoons.

Finally, at ten thirty, Todd calls on his way back to the Ft. Lauderdale airport.

"We're finished. Our meeting went very well. All papers were signed by the hung-over offender," Todd says to Davis and Lauren on speakerphone.

"Can't wait to hear the details. See you soon," Davis says.

Within a few hours, Todd arrives and they gather in her study.

"When I got there, Bobby greeted me and the three of us sat at the dining room table," Todd says. "Andy asked me to give all papers to Bobby first. It was clear Andy was weak or recovering from one bad hangover.

"I started with the bank account and pointed out Andy didn't need to close the account because you had moved your money from it and the paperwork removes your name from the old account. Andy hid his face in his hands, shaking his head after he saw the balance you had left."

"Did you think $200,000 was enough?" Lauren asks.

"More than enough," Todd says. "Andy did not have an address to provide for mail forwarding. He understood when I told him to contact me, not you, for any matters going forward, including when he is interested in claiming his clothing and personal property."

"As for the confidentiality agreement, Andy did not understand why he had to sign it. I explained that you wanted to protect the private matters the two of you shared together by making sure that neither of you would profit nor sell the story about your personal lives. He signed it and insisted he would never tell anyone about your time together."

"That's reassuring," Lauren says.

"He kept his emotions in check until the last item," Todd says. "When I handed him a copy of the college tuition plan you purchased for Brittney, he got emotional. I told him that both he and his ex-wife were being provided copies of the documents and you had only one request: that you would be able to tell Brittney first. He couldn't even look at me when I told him that you considered Brittney part of your family, and even though you knew he had some college savings for her, you want to be sure she has every opportunity for the best future."

"Overall, what was his state of mind?" Davis asks.

"Shy, embarrassed and reduced."

With business finished, Todd gets up to leave.

"Thank you for everything," Lauren says, shaking his hand. "Um… one last thing. Were you able to notice…"

"Yes, I did look," Todd says. "I'm sorry, Lauren. He was not wearing the ring."

Her head drops along with any hope she had left in her heart. All she sees are Todd and Davis's feet as they leave. As she closes the door behind them, she realizes a chapter of her life has been closed too.

The calm, running water in the bathroom sink is the only soothing sound in her upside-down world. The soft glow from a night-light is just enough for her to see her empty reflection in the mirror. She stands at Andy's sink, washing her hands with his soap, breathing in his familiar spicy leather, comfortable smell. One tug. Two tugs. Finally three tugs at her right-hand ring and the soapy bubbles finally loosen it from the finger that does not want to let it go. Water keeps running as she holds up the silver ring and remembers happier times. Promising times. Until such time—but it ended too soon. Now Andy isn't wearing his ring so she won't wear hers, even though she wants to.

She's nowhere close to letting him go. She lies in bed clutching the H pillow, the smell of Andy's soap still fresh on her hands.

Why? What? Where did they go wrong? It was Dallas and the stupid accident. Look at the damage one drunk driver can cause.

She rolls over in bed, so empty without Andy. Her skin aches for his hands to touch her the way he used to every night, before they fell asleep. He'd be giving her that wide, burning smile right about now when he would roll over, wanting her. But he doesn't want her anymore.

He left the blonde but still hasn't come back. He hasn't even tried to call. There was a big opening today with Todd's visit and he could have said something. Even easier: he could have been wearing his ring.

He meant what he wrote in the note about moving on. It wasn't the alcohol talking when he told her he didn't love her. Johnny warned her not to play with fire and she got totally burned. She failed to win the heart of her high school crush.

Now she's left to face her fears alone. Andy won't be by her side. There are no sunglasses big enough to hide the violating stares now. Fans everywhere will be watching her and how she handles this.

She pushes her feet to the bottom of her cold sheets, lying in the middle of the bed. Doubtful she'll get any sleep tonight, even though she should. Tomorrow is a big day. It's the beginning of her new life.

* * *

The smell of jet fuel fills the Tahoe when Bill opens her door.

"You're late!" Oliver yells out over the idling engines. She squints in the bright morning sunlight and then follows him on board her plane. Johnny, Michael, Doug and Davis have each taken a seat. Oliver plops down in hers.

She stands over him, filled with enough anger to fuel this flight to California. "I'm in no mood to fight for my favorite seat on my own damn plane."

Oliver lowers his eyes, gets up and slowly saunters to the back.

They are off to Los Angeles and a long-scheduled meeting with Thom Stewart and their record company, already laying the groundwork for Plebeian's third album and next tour. It will be a full day of meetings and tonight, an intimate dinner at their record company president's Malibu home. Though it feels good to be back with the guys, it's hard to ignore the lingering ache in her heart. Plus the swelling of her eyes is hard even for sunglasses to conceal.

When they land at the executive airport, a mob of photographers gathers like hungry wild animals smelling their next meal.

"Have you talked with Andy, Lauren?"

"Is Andy still with his girlfriend?"

"Lauren! Johnny! Will you get back together now?"

Questions are hurled at her like stones, becoming difficult to ignore as they quickly walk to their waiting cars. Suddenly, someone's arm protectively wraps around her shoulders. Oliver pulls her closer and she leans against his tall frame for shelter. Frank pushes people back. Michael fists his hands. Doug opens his mouth like he might start yelling. And Johnny seems to be one angry breath away from a full Tasmanian devil death spin. It's loud and tense but they find their drivers and head to the meeting without doing something that will get them sued.

Safe at the Platinum Plate offices, the guys loosen up. They are not far apart on the vision for their third album. Davis seems close to agreeing to a comprehensive 360 deal on it too, covering the record, tour and another television concert; a deal more attractive thanks to Lauren. It seems Andy's affair has made Plebeian even more popular. Every time a crisis or accident happens in her life, record sales go up. Lauren slumps in a chair, listening to this conference room of important people. She's an emotional mess and their marketing trophy.

"This next tour really should be a world tour," Thom suggests to the group.

Lauren stiffens.

"Let's do it," Oliver says.

"Already?" Lauren whispers to Johnny.

"Not this year, but by next year we should," Johnny says, patting her leg.

"I'm not sure I can do it then either," she mumbles.

"Your cool sunglasses fit in your suitcase; you'll be fine," Oliver says, leaning over.

"Day after day overseas; I'm not sure I can keep it together that long," she whispers. "What happens when we're in, like, Bangladesh and I freeze again?"

"Easy," Oliver whispers. "We won't go to Bangladesh."

She has nothing but a stare to throw at Oliver. She wants no part of this conversation, no part of a world tour. She wants no part of anything right now.

* * *

Lauren gazes vacantly out the car window, taking little notice of the beautiful sandstone canyons on the drive to Malibu. Coastal scrub bushes cling to steep hills, while the Pacific Ocean crashes into the sandy beaches below. To her, it's a blur.

They are on their way to dinner at Robert Burgess's Malibu beach home. Robert is president of their record company and a producer of several hit songs. He's been involved with Plebeian since their beginning. He invited the band to join a group of fifteen guests for a private dinner. Lauren would rather be in a room with a thousand people and not be noticed than sitting at a table with fifteen people looking her over.

Frank drives up through the open iron gates to the tall glass front of the Burgess' home. Even the bushes look stylish nestled against the home's contemporary, no-expense-spared architecture. *Andy would have loved to see this design.*

All eyes turn as they make their entrance: two executives from the record company, some people she doesn't know, Robert's blond-haired, college-age son Max and three famous faces she recognizes: a movie actress, a TV actor and a director. Lauren can feel the drag of their stares following her while Robert gives them a brief tour of the downstairs area. *Stop. Looking.*

When dinner is ready, the guests wander around the table searching for their name cards, each nestled in a gold pinecone at each place setting. Lauren quickly finds her seat. Good: Doug is sitting to her left. She doesn't have to worry about talking to him because he doesn't talk. Across from her is one of the record company executives. Good: she already knows Shane Mitchell. To her right is Josh Spencer, the TV actor she recognized. He's cute, about her age with loosely curled brown hair that matches the vibrancy of his smile. He's recently divorced, she thinks, and she remembers he was hilarious in his TV roles.

She pulls out her chair when Josh extends his hand.

"Josh Spencer," he says with a contagious smile.

"Lauren Logan," she says, shaking his hand. *What a fun smile.* His energetic conversation draws her out of her "pity-me" shell as they discuss Plebeian's music, his acting and the pros and cons of California versus Florida. They barely pause long enough to eat.

After dinner everyone steps out to the expansive pool terrace for drinks and the evening beach view, and within minutes Josh and

Lauren have worked their way back to each other.

Lauren's new self-assigned security team is with her. Michael and Johnny are watching their emotionally wounded lead singer closely and seem to be watching Josh even closer. They make a foursome sitting on the teak chairs talking about amazing swimming pools, the coarseness of beach sand and the perils of fame and love. Lauren pauses to take in the view of the ocean and the sound of the waves, everything so beautiful, so comfortable and so calm.

"Here I am enjoying this fine evening on the edge of the Pacific Ocean while Andy is recovering from his binge drinking week somewhere near the Atlantic," she blurts, forgetting that Josh is there.

Josh raises his glass. "And you clearly have the better deal, and better company."

The surprisingly wonderful evening even has Oliver smiling, especially once Robert breaks out his Arturo Fuente OpusX cigars and A.H. Hirsch Reserve bourbon.

At the end of the evening, their group begins to leave. Johnny politely smiles his goodbye and then lays his arm on Lauren's shoulder to steer her towards the door. A few steps later, she twists away from him to say goodbye to Josh.

"I would love to spend more time with you next time you come to L.A., maybe even take you up the coast for a bonfire," Josh whispers. "I know the timing for me to ask this is bad."

Lauren smiles. "My timing for everything is bad." And she gives him her number.

On the car ride back to the hotel, the guys are complaining about the dainty food and how they're still hungry. Lauren's still hungry too but her mind keeps replaying her conversations with Josh. Just a week ago she was punching a pillow when Andy said he didn't love her and tonight, she's giving her phone number to a cute actor. What a week.

* * *

A Tuesday evening is rarely a busy night at a shopping mall. Still, Frank cautiously eyes the few other shoppers in the Tampa Louis Vuitton store.

"We'll take two," Lauren says with a smile, handing her credit card to the grinning saleswoman. But the biggest smile in the store is now on Brittney's face.

"Really? I get one?" Brittney says, throwing her arms around Lauren. "Thank you so much!"

Lauren pulls her closer, cherishing Brittney's embrace. This evening is about more than spending money and telling Brittney about her college fund. It's Lauren's attempt to start a new relationship with the daughter she used to have.

"Well, every girl should have a Neverfull bag," Lauren says, signing the receipt. "And now we match."

Brittney is already dumping the contents of her purse into her new bag. Her pink skater skirt really doesn't match her yellow pixie denim jacket but anything matches the iconic monogram print of a classic Louis bag.

"Guess you don't need me to run this package out to the car," Frank says, smiling.

Together they walk to a colorful, boisterous restaurant towards the back of the mall, across from the City Grille steakhouse where Andy and Lauren had their first date. They take their seats and thankfully, the restaurant is loud so they can't be overheard.

Lauren reaches across the table to hold Brittney's hands. "I know your mom and dad had planned to send you to college, but I have added to that. Whether you want to go out-of-state, or grad school; even medical or law school, I've set up a fund so you can reach your dreams."

Brittney squeezes her hands. "I don't know why you are still so nice to me, after what my dad did."

"Because you were part of my family, even briefly, and I will always think of you as family."

"Thank you, Lauren. Even if you never spent a dime on me, you were the best family I ever had," Brittney says.

Lauren swallows hard. Truth is, Brittney, Andy and her boys were the best family she ever had too.

"You know my dad is back in town, right?"

Lauren nods. "His things have been moved but I didn't ask Tish where they went."

"He's renting a studio apartment downtown. I've stayed at his place a couple nights. He's back at work, trying to get his act together."

This news peaks Lauren's interest, but she tries not to show it. "I've heard that from a few mutual friends. Their conversation with him seems to be the same: he's reflective, he's apologetic, he's hopeful for the future."

"He is. He's very quiet right now," Brittney says. "He's just not right, Lauren. He's so messed up without you."

"Well, I'm..." *Watch what you say to a teenage girl, eager to repeat any story.* "I'm messed up without him, but I can't make a man want to be with me. He chose to leave and hasn't tried to come back. He hasn't even called. It's a pretty clear message."

Brittney starts to react but her phone rings. "Speak of the devil. It's my dad."

Lauren stares at Brittney's ringing phone. This is the closest she has gotten to Andy since hearing his voice over Todd's phone! Her heart beats faster and the call isn't even for her. "You should answer it."

Brittney nods, answering.

"Hey, Dad. No, I'm not home. I'm at the mall having dinner with a friend...I know it's a weeknight. I've got it covered...It doesn't matter who I'm with...Why do you care, anyway?...I don't know when I'm coming home but sure, I can call you later. I gotta go."

Their food arrives and they dive into their salads, picking up their conversation. Within minutes her phone rings again.

"It's my mom."

Lauren nods that she better take it.

"Hey, Mom…Really? He called you asking who I was with? Why is he trying to be super dad all of a sudden anyway?…You told him! You told him I'm with Lauren? Crap, Mom, now he'll probably come up here or something. Let me go so we can finish and get out of here. Bye."

And Brittney hangs up.

Lauren sits straight; her head to one side, hoping Brittney will tell her the part of the conversation she couldn't hear.

"I can't believe this," Brittney says, chomping on a forkful of romaine lettuce. "After I talked with my dad he called my mom demanding to know why I was at the mall on a school night. My mom just came right out and told him that I was with you! He had lots of questions and you know my mom, she doesn't have the patience for anything not about her.

"Seriously, if we don't leave soon I wouldn't be surprised to see him walk in here to talk with you."

Lauren shakes her head. "Why would Andy want to come to a public place to talk with me?"

"Because he can't get to you otherwise. You don't go to places where he can run into you. He can't get back to the house. And he's probably scared to death to call you. If he runs into you in public, he can break the ice, get back on your mind."

Lauren shakes her head. Sweet Brittney; she's a hopeless romantic. "I don't think that's what he'd want to do. He's had plenty of chances to send a message."

They finish their salads and Lauren pays the check. Then arm-in-arm they follow Frank out of the restaurant. Lauren glances over at the steakhouse to the left. This is the same valet area where she and Andy made their first steps out to Franz's snapping camera on the night of their first date. That seems like a lifetime ago; a happier lifetime ago.

* * *

On Friday, Craig and Henry have Lauren's plane ready for her weekend trip to L.A. First up will be lunch with Dina, who has invited her to see the set of the new movie she just started shooting, and then Lauren is taking Josh up on his offer for dinner at his house and then a beach bonfire with his friends. There's a tiny patch of warming in her heart, and a little bit of nerves in her stomach, about seeing Josh.

"Anything you need while you're gone?" Davis asks, stopping her and Frank as they leave the house.

"Yes, there is," Lauren says, grinning. "I want a revenge car."

"A revenge car?"

"You bet. Something fast, sporty, built for two. You know… something on behalf of all girls who have been pushed aside by their boyfriends," she says. "Not red," she clarifies with a pointed finger. She swings her Louis Vuitton purse over her shoulder.

"You know my tastes. You have two days!" She steps into the Tahoe. "And under $300,000, please," she says with a smile before closing the door, his face full of excitement.

* * *

After her lunch and set tour with Dina, Lauren gets ready for dinner with Josh.

Frank pulls up to Josh's house, a 1980's California ranch home nestled under the oaks and palm trees of Hollywood Hills. Josh greets them at the door wearing a big smile and a dorky apron with a picture of a squirrel holding a baseball bat that reads *Be A Man: Protect Your Nuts.*

He's got the grill lit in the backyard and while they are cooking marinated chicken he tells her more about his pool renovation ideas that they talked about at Robert Burgess's party. When they head inside, she kicks off her heeled sandals, standing barefoot in his kitchen and tossing a salad while he slices the chicken.

"Do you mind if I pick these out?" she asks, holding up a sliced cucumber.

"Nah! I don't like cucumbers either!" he says, smiling. "I got them because that's what the recipe told me to do."

So sweet.

They sit down at the kitchen table and begin their meal by toasting with a sparkling lemonade drink he's made with white wine. While they sit in the kitchen nook, Frank has tried to become as invisible as possible in the living room.

"You sure you don't want anything?" Josh yells to Frank.

"No, I'm good here eating my peanut butter and peanut butter sandwich." Now Lauren has to explain to Josh how she couldn't think straight one morning during the worst of her Andy stupor and forgot one side of jelly on a sandwich.

After dinner, the three of them start the drive to meet Josh's friends. All the way up the coast there are slices of beach where people claim bonfire spots. About thirty minutes into the drive Frank pulls into the hilltop parking lot of Bryson Beach.

"We've come here for years, since high school," Josh says, unpacking their chairs and blankets. His friends already have the fire ring roaring and get up to meet Lauren. Tonight's agenda is simple: just sit, talk, listen to music and watch the sparks from the fire dance up in the sky.

There are two other groups on the beach with similar set-ups; it's very communal and casual. It doesn't take long for one of Plebeian's songs to come on and everyone looks at Lauren, trying to get her to sing along. A couple of people are dancing while a few others get up to chase each other over some failed bet. Lauren finds herself alone with Josh, who is leaning in poking at the fire. She doesn't want a boyfriend right now; she's not ready for romance. But Josh has been amazingly fun company. He's easy to look at too.

Her unfiltered thoughts slip to her mouth and she blurts, "You know right now, under these stars, in the light of this fire, you are the cutest guy on the planet."

Josh drops his stick and looks at her. "And you know, right now, under these stars, even knowing you have a broken heart, I have to say, you are the most beautiful woman in the universe."

Their smiles burn hotter than the bonfire. Maybe there could be a next guy after Andy.

Saying goodbye at Josh's house feels bittersweet; she's not sure when she'll be back in California, but now she thinks she'll make it soon.

Josh lays his hands on her shoulders and kisses her cheek. Then he blurts out, "Hey are you going to change my contact in your phone to cutest guy on the planet?"

"Of course!" she answers, pulling away from their warm goodbye.

Soft music from a local jazz station has been the only sound in the car since Frank and Lauren left Josh's house. Frank merges onto the freeway heading for their L.A. hotel.

"What time will the plane be ready?" Lauren asks.

"Seven a.m. Is that still okay?"

She nods. Her eyes have been glued out the window, watching cars pass and the rest of the normal world go by. Her mind is a mush of rambling thoughts.

Andy. Home. Andy's not home. California. Josh. Bonfire. Fire… cigarettes.

"Frank, whatever happened with those cigarettes Tish found in front of the house a few months ago?"

He glances at her. "We fixed the cameras and haven't seen anything since. I had her pick up the cigarette butts and I kept them, just in case."

So he thought it was fishy too?

She looks to her lap. "Did you ever think it was Andy?"

"No. One, because he doesn't smoke. And two, because that week he was alone in the house. If he was sneaking a smoke, he would have likely lit up in the house, not on the curb."

"But there was a picture of him when he was…you know…in Ft. Lauderdale. They both had cigarettes."

"I think after Andy left he did a lot of things he doesn't normally do. Smoking might be the least serious of his infractions. But when he was with you, he didn't smoke. Tish would have smelled it in the house and on his laundry, the cameras would have caught him as he walked outside and you would have known from his breath."

"Who do you think it was?"

"Probably the yard crew. If it was a fan or photographer who had found your house, they haven't been back. Ryan and I have been watching."

"Okay, thanks. Good to know." That whole cigarette thing never settled well with her. Who stood there long enough to have a few smokes? It's hard for her to come to terms with things sometimes, especially things that are unfinished.

But she is coming to terms about one thing.

Tomorrow she begins another week. And day by day, minute by minute, she's peeling the layers of her heart away from Andy.

* * *

He pulls into his preferred parking spot at the wholesale florist warehouse.

He has the best view of the Northrop landing strip from here.

According to the plane tracking app on his phone, she will be landing soon.

The familiar black Tahoe has just arrived, making the left turn towards the airport gate.

He narrows his eyes with concern, seeing something new. Behind the Tahoe is a yellow Ferrari, which also makes the turn. Both cars are granted access to the tarmac; both of them pull closer to her arriving plane.

His heart beats faster when he sees her running down the steps of the plane.

She must be seeing the Ferrari for the first time; she's jumping around, now getting into it. His mouth dries as he feels her excitement, watching her drive up and down the runway.

The Ferrari leaves the gate and reaches the corner, ready to turn.

He sits up straighter so he can see her better.

She looks beautiful.

For the first time in a while, she is smiling.

She takes a sharp right turn towards her home. The Tahoe carrying her luggage follows.

The deep sound of his car engine starts up and he quickly backs up from his surveillance spot, driving fast through the warehouse parking lot.

He makes a rapid left turn to follow her in his blue BMW.

[TWENTY-ONE]

Tish struggles with a delivery at the front door. "For you!" she exclaims to Lauren, barely able to hold a large gold vase bursting with at least six dozen red roses.

"That's huge!" Lauren says, coming around from the kitchen. She helps Tish place the vase on the oval breakfast table. "They take up most of the table!"

Tish examines the flowers while Lauren pulls out the card.

Until our next fire.
From,
The cutest guy on the planet

"Josh!" Lauren says, with one hand on her hip and the other waving the card in the air. She folds the card writing side out to make the display perfect.

"Some weddings don't have that many roses!" Tish says.

Frank's voice comes across the intercom.

"Tish, Lara has come through the hut and will be here shortly." Tish presses the confirm button and heads again to the front door. Lauren has been waiting to see what her stylist is bringing for her to wear next week.

Next Thursday, Plebeian will debut their new single during Daytime, a Boston-based syndicated talk show. The band normally does all interviews together, but the host wants to interview Lauren first about her recent challenges, including her breakup with Andy. Lauren said no at first, but the guys thought it will be good for their fans to hear from her directly. She reluctantly agreed.

Lara wheels in a wardrobe cart and sets up a mini boutique in the living room. As Lauren walks through the kitchen to meet her, she passes by the roses and thinks about Josh. Maybe he'd like to come with their group next Thursday for that interview. She'll think more about it on Friday, when she will have hours alone driving in the car to visit Cal and Christy.

Lauren steps into the living room and starts to look over the beautiful clothes that Lara has brought.

* * *

"It's road trip Friday!" Lauren says to Frank, playfully punching his arm. "Christy's house or bust!"

Frank has just backed out her new Ferrari 458 Italia coupe from the garage to the auto courtyard. "Davis made the perfect revenge car choice, don't you think? Yellow makes me happy," she says, walking around her sweet new ride.

"I really want you to reconsider and let me drive you," Frank says.

"We've talked about this ten times! I want to drive and I'll be fine. You'd be bored once I got to Christy and Cal's. It's an easy interstate drive to Cocoa Beach, and I promise we won't go anywhere once I get there."

"I need you to keep your phone's tracking feature *on*," Frank says.

"Deal! And I'll call you when I head back on Sunday. I won't pull an Andy Hayden here. I *will* come back," she says, smirking.

During the two hour drive, she clears her mind as her car speeds down the turnpike. And she makes a phone call. Josh accepts her invitation to join her and the band in Boston.

When she arrives at Christy's house, both Christy and her husband Cal bolt out of their one-story classic Florida home.

"Hot ride!" Cal yells, already taking a seat behind the wheel.

"Hot mama!" Christy yells as Lauren slides in the passenger seat. Cal pulls away to take a lap around the neighborhood.

Lauren laughs, thinking of Frank at home, watching the blinking light of her tracking app go round and round in circles.

Back at Christy's, Lauren plops her suitcase on the guest bed, digs out a black t-shirt and her favorite pair of denim cut-off shorts. She abandons her shoes and quickly changes.

"Good to see you getting comfortable!" Christy says, laying an arm around Lauren's shoulders as they step into the kitchen.

"I have so much to tell you," Lauren says. Heck, just bringing Christy up to speed on everything Josh will take all night!

Cal has made himself scarce, evidently waiting in his den for someone from work to drop by. Christy and Lauren busy themselves in the kitchen, watching a show from the family room TV while ripping lettuce for a salad and seasoning steaks to grill.

Lauren hears Cal opening the door for his friend but she's not interested in going to meet anyone. She's more interested in this hysterical commercial on television.

"You missed it, Christy!" Lauren yells, running from the kitchen, grabbing the controller to play it back. "This is one of the funniest ads I've ever seen!" She quickly looks back to be sure Christy can see it, and freezes.

Hazelnut-olive eyes.

Straight brown hair.

Thin nose.

Andy is standing in the kitchen.

The TV controller falls from her hands and crashes to the floor.

Christy leaps forward. "I know what you're thinking but he just wanted to talk to you and we thought this was a good time…"

This…was planned?

Rage boils in her veins. "You thought *this* was a *good idea*?" Lauren screams.

Andy steps forward, his eyes desperate. "I just wanted to talk to you."

Lauren focuses her rage on Christy.

"This? You planned this?" she screams, her face hot with anger, her finger pointing like a laser at Christy. "*This* was supposed to be safe for me! *He* does not get to come to *my* friend's house!"

Cal steps towards her. "Calm down and listen for a minute!"

She spins to face him.

"Calm down? You want me to calm down when you brought the man who *broke up* with me and then *ruined my life* to…what…tell me what?" she screams, waving clenched fists.

"I need to talk to you," Andy says, still behind the kitchen counter with a terrified Christy behind him. Lauren ignores him and continues yelling at Cal.

"*He* does not get to decide when *he* gets to talk to me after *he* ruined my life!"

"Stop, please and listen," Cal yells.

"*No!*" Lauren yells. "I don't have to listen to anything." Sweat starts to flow from her face she's so hot with anger. "This was supposed to be *safe*! I was supposed to be *safe here*!"

"Lauren, I have to talk to you," Andy pleads.

"Let it go, Andy," Christy says, pulling his arm. "This isn't working."

Lauren stomps closer to the kitchen, still focused on Cal.

"*You* set a trap for me," she points in his face, "and I don't have to stand here and talk to *anybody*." She scrambles to reach over the counter and grab her purse.

Cal grabs it at the same time, tugging it back.

"I knew you'd want to leave so I took it…I took your key…I took your key fob so you can't!" Cal yells.

Lauren stands taller as her spine stiffens with rage.

"*You* went in my purse and took the fob to my car? My brand *new* car? How could you!?"

Cal yanks her purse while Lauren pulls the other side. Her anger crests and one hand lets go, slapping Cal across the face.

"Stop!" Christy screams. Andy tries to separate them.

Cal and Lauren both let go of her purse and it drops to the floor with a thud. Lauren stands back, glaring at the three of them.

Then, like a cornered animal, she runs. She darts around the corner, running straight for the front door and bursting outside.

"Lauren! Don't! Please stop!" Andy cries out but she keeps running, down the driveway, past her car and onto the street. Andy runs after her, with Cal behind him.

"Lauren! Please stop!" Andy calls.

"Andy, run faster!" Cal yells.

Her bare feet hit the pavement hard, sprinting with super-human, wronged-woman speed. Her quick start is the only reason Andy hasn't caught her yet.

"Lauren! Please! Lauren, please stop!" Andy yells.

She glances back. *Shit!* Andy is closing in fast and Cal not far behind him. No way in hell they're catching her. She cuts left, running off the street into a wooded conservation area. Sticks and cypress tree stubs slice her feet as she runs farther and farther into the scrubby woods. Bushes and branches are breaking behind her as Andy follows her off-road.

"Lauren! You've got to stop! Lauren! You're going to get hurt! Please!" Andy pleads.

Anger and betrayal fuel her speed and she moves faster, darting around some trees. She quickly looks behind her. *She did it!* She outran Andy.

She slows down a little and continues turning around trees, ducking under smaller branches that keep hitting her face and snarling her hair. Finally, she's deep in the woods and hears nothing behind her.

Safe behind a large tree, she stops. She awkwardly squats down, exhausted.

Her chest heaves; she can't feel her feet. Her ankle is swollen; twisted from the uneven ground. Her head falls into her hands and she starts to cry, deep from her stomach and so hard it hurts. *What just happened?* She was safe with her best friend and then Andy was there. *What did she just do? Why did she run away?*

She's barefoot and dirty, crying and hurting. *Is this rock bottom? Is this what it looks and feels like when you have no options? What the hell now?*

Her thighs begin to burn so she pushes to her feet and feels something hard in her pocket. Her phone! She pulls out this glorious find, but who can she call? Her best friend just betrayed her. What if she calls home and they all say she should stay here and talk to Andy? Who is on her side? Did everyone know Andy was coming?

Then she remembers: the phone could betray her too. The tracking app is on! She punches the app to disable it and in anger she turns off every other setting that allows her phone to reveal where she is. She'll figure out her own way home because she sure as hell isn't going back to Christy's.

"Lauren?" she hears Andy's voice calling nearby.

"Did you check over here yet?" she hears Cal yell. She stands still, careful not to reveal her position. Then, the telephone assault begins.

Christy calls first and leaves a voicemail. She wants Lauren to come back to the house. She's very sorry, please just come back. Next is Andy with a call, voicemail, then text. Lauren deletes his text and erases his voicemail without even listening to it. It's a little too late for him to call her now.

Daylight is dimming and nasty bugs are starting to bite. It's time to figure out what to do. There have been no sounds from Andy or Cal for awhile, so it's probably safe to get moving. She takes a step forward but feels like she stepped in water. She looks down. Blood covers her feet. Her stomach retches and she feels dizzy. *Shit!* Now she needs to hurry. She sees lights in the distance and hobbles towards them to a shopping center behind Christy's neighborhood. Standing at the edge of the trees, she drafts her plan. She needs to get some help for her feet but she doesn't want to be noticed and she has no money. There's no one nearby to call. Once she stops the bleeding she'll call Frank or someone safe. At least she *thinks* Frank is safe.

Options for help in the shopping center seem to be a grocery store or a sports restaurant. The grocery store sure isn't ideal. Walking in the sliding front doors with a pair of bloody feet will certainly catch the attention of shoppers in check-out lines. Looks like the best she can do is the sports restaurant. If she slips in the side door for take-out orders and asks the manager for help, only employees in the back will see her.

She slowly limps across the parking lot, keeping her head down and stepping in grass medians to keep her bloody footprints from leaving a creepy trail. She walks a little too close to a white SUV parked at the end of a row, just as a young woman approaches the car with a cart of groceries. "Do you need help?" the woman asks.

"I'm heading that way, I'm fine." Lauren points to the restaurant.

The woman leaves her cart and comes closer. "Oh, you need help now, I think." Placing her hands on Lauren's shoulders, she leads her back to her SUV. She sits Lauren down in the front passenger seat, with Lauren's legs towards the pavement and hands her a bottle of water.

Lauren pours the water over her feet. "Thank you. I appreciate it." She pulls back her stringy, sweaty hair.

The woman recognizes Lauren instantly. "Oh, I think I know you."

Lauren gives a surrendering smile. "There's a chance you might. I've had…I've had a really bad night."

The woman's generosity and kindness unfolds as she wraps Lauren's feet in paper towels and offers her a beer, all freshly bought from the store. They sit inside her car with the windows down and Lauren tells her why she's in the condition she's in. Her name is Susan and she and her husband Brad have lived here for years and actually attended Plebeian's concert last year in Miami.

"My husband is probably your number one fan," Susan says, smiling.

"He might not be anymore since it looks like I'm keeping you from your dinner," Lauren says, pointing to groceries in the back of the SUV.

"I'll sit with you for as long as you need," Susan says.

While they talk, Lauren's phone comes alive with a second wave of calls, none that she answers. Davis calls first, so now she knows Christy, Andy and Cal are worried enough to call people at home. Lynette calls. Tish calls. Lauren's mom calls. About ten minutes later comes the band: Johnny, then Michael, Oliver and Doug. Lauren can only imagine how mad Johnny is but right now, she's not in the mood to talk to any of them.

"You need to let someone know you're okay," Susan says.

It's been an hour since they met and now Susan's husband is calling her. She answers the phone.

"Hey, honey. I'm still at the store. I stopped to help someone. I'm fine, really, but not sure when I'll be home," she tells her husband Brad. Within ten minutes Brad arrives to find his wife and pulls up alongside her car. She gestures for him to sit in the back seat.

"Hi, honey. So is everything okay?" Brad asks, getting into the back seat.

"I was just helping, um, Lauren here with a little problem," Susan says. Lauren turns to face him.

He lets out a gasping yelp. It's only the lead singer of his favorite band, dirty and bleeding, in the front seat of his wife's SUV, drinking beer.

"Wow, um, hi," he says. "Okay, so what happened?" Susan gives him the quick version of the story.

Lauren's phone rings again and of all the calls, this one she should answer. She takes too long to decide and it goes straight to voicemail.

"Listen, I'm almost already to Cocoa. I know you are not answering calls but you have got to talk to me. You have got to let me know if you are okay and how I can help. Tell me where you are, please."

"Who's that?" asks Brad.

"Frank, my head of security. I had begged him to let me come here alone and now I screwed up the one time I was without help," she says, her head hanging down.

Lauren has screamed at her best friend, hit her best friend's husband, cut up her own feet, ignored the worried people who love her and run away from the man she still loves.

"You have to swallow your pride and let your friends help you," Brad says. "Even if we drove you all the way home now you will have to face them sometime."

Susan nods. "You need help now."

"Give me Christy's address. I will go there now and talk to them," Brad says.

"I don't know…" Lauren says.

"It's important that they know you are okay," he says.

She looks at her lap; her shoulders hunched. *There's no choice.* She gives him the address.

It seems like Brad is only gone a few minutes when he calls from Christy's house. He told them Lauren was hurt but safe with his wife and scared to come back.

"They want you back, Lauren," Brad says over the phone. "Andy wants you back."

And if Lauren is honest with herself, those last four words are what she wants to hear most in the world.

[TWENTY-TWO]

Susan's headlights sweep the road as she takes the final turn towards Christy and Cal's house. Lauren stares at the bumpy asphalt; her feet twitch remembering the painful run. Already she's changing her mind about going back. If her feet didn't hurt so badly, she'd be tempted to jump out of the SUV and run away again.

Susan slowly turns up the driveway. Lauren's heart pounds as fast as Andy runs towards them.

He opens Lauren's door. His eyes look hollow and his face dirty, like hers. He looks at Lauren's feet as she tries to get out and without saying a word, his arm slides under her legs, lifting her up. *Damn it: he's touching her!* She has no choice; he's already carrying her to the house. Her arms wrap around his neck for balance. She's tired, embarrassed and mad, yet she instinctively rests her head on his shoulder.

"Hurry! Take her to our bathroom," Cal says to Andy. Christy waits by the tub with running water, towels and bandages. Andy carefully sets Lauren down and Christy moves in. Lauren peels off the paper towels, allowing the blood to flow free in the running water. She and Christy both work to clean and bandage her feet.

"Go get her a change of clothes—something from her suitcase!" Christy says to Andy.

Growing tears in Lauren's eyes make Christy look blurry in the bright bathroom light. "I shouldn't have freaked out like that," Lauren softly says. "But you broke my trust, Christy. You should have never arranged an ambush like that."

Christy pulls her closer and wraps her in a warm, clean towel. "I will never forgive myself. I am so sorry," she says. "I always try to do what's best for you and I thought this would be helpful. It was a huge mistake."

In seconds Andy returns with another pair of shorts and a t-shirt. Lauren sits on the edge of the tub and changes out of the dirty ones she's wearing. She feels his eyes gliding across her body as she changes. Let him look.

She tries to stand at the same time Christy and Andy both say she shouldn't, but the sharp pain in her feet is the final voice. Andy sweeps her in his arms and carries her to the living room sofa. As he bends to put her down, for a second they are eye to eye. Her anger seeps from her expression. He releases his arm from under her leg and steps back.

Brad and Susan are talking with Cal, while Christy rushes to the laundry room with dirty, bloody towels. The loud pounding on the front door announces Frank and Ryan's arrival.

Frank's wide eyes are frantic until he sees Lauren on the sofa. He rushes over. "You are okay now? Physically okay?"

She nods, officially embarrassed.

"I…I'd like my purse, please," she murmurs. Andy dashes into the kitchen to bring it. She looks inside.

"I put your key fob back in," Cal says. She nods.

Everyone stands, watching her.

"Um, Brad and Susan, thank you for your help tonight," she says. "You helped a total stranger without reservation and that…that is something I won't forget."

Susan comes closer, bending down. "You have good friends, Lauren. Swallow the fear and bring up the trust." Lauren gives Susan and Brad hugs from her seated position on the couch and then Cal sees them out the door.

She knows what she has to do next.

"Cal," she whispers. He stuffs his hands in his jeans pockets and steps closer to her. "I'm really sorry that I hit you. I should have never, ever done that and I'm really sorry."

He sits down beside her and wraps his arm around her shoulders. "Didn't hurt." They both smile.

She looks up at Frank, whose expression reads: *you hit Cal?* Somehow, apologizing to Frank seems the hardest of all.

"I know you will take it personally, what I did tonight, because you feel responsible for me and my safety." Frank smiles and nods. "You, and your advice, had nothing to do with my bad choices. You are not a bad security person because I made a really bad decision."

He nods. "We can stay here with you, take you home now, or we can come back in the morning and take you home then."

"Well…it's already morning," she says, smiling. "You just drove a long way and I don't want to make you drive back right now. Why don't you guys get a hotel room so you can get some rest."

"We need to take you to a doctor in the morning," Frank says.

Lauren nods.

Frank turns to leave, giving a long, uncertain glare towards Andy. Frank and Ryan walk out the door but Lauren knows they won't go far. They'll probably sleep in the Tahoe or whatever car they drove. And their vehicle is likely blocking hers on the driveway.

Christy gives Lauren a fluffy blanket and an extra pillow. "Unless you need anything else, I think Cal and I will go make some calls to bring everyone up to speed."

The sound of their bedroom door closing brings the house to complete silence; so quiet it hurts Lauren's ears. Andy remains standing by the side of the sofa.

They're alone.

She can't run away and she's already yelled. Her options to resist his presence have disappeared.

He turns off some lights. "Is there anything you need?" he softly asks.

It seems ages ago that he tried to comfort her like this, back when

Cory was caught cheating. Andy ordered room service chocolate and wine and they relaxed in a bubbly hot tub. She felt safe. Free. They made love for the first of many times.

Now she can't even look at him. She moves her legs to stretch out on the sofa, facing the front door. The wall to her right is the only thing standing between Christy's bedroom and them right now. She pulls her purse closer, feeling more powerful knowing it's next to her.

Andy sits on the floor beside the sofa, close enough that she could reach out and touch his hair, if she wanted to. She stiffens and pulls the blanket closer to her face, still looking straight ahead at the door.

"I wanted to tell you what happened. I wanted to explain what *has* happened," he somberly says.

Lauren blinks hard and breathes in a huge sniffle.

Ready or not, she is about to hear everything she wants to know.

He breathes in deep.

"I felt like I had no choice when I left the house that Friday. For months it had been building; the old feelings of helplessness and doubt in myself. I felt lost. Confused. Trapped. Everything between us had changed and I knew I was bringing you down. I thought you, Brittney and the boys would be better off without me.

"Earlier that day I had talked with Chase and he asked me to come to Ft. Lauderdale for awhile. It was spontaneous and I felt so alive when I left, so free. The best I had felt in months. I got to the hotel where Chase was staying and two women he invited were already there, Courtney and Marcia."

Lauren bristles. He just pronounced Marcia as *Mar-see-ya*. What—that girl is so special she can't pronounce her name the way it's spelled?

"My pain went away as fast as I drank. This was a fresh start and I...I just couldn't stop. I had no idea photographers were taking pictures. Night turned to day and I was so confused. I got your text about the pictures but didn't know what you were talking about."

Lauren realizes that Christy and Cal have stopped talking in their room. Bet their ears are pressed against the wall, trying to hear Andy's quiet confession. And oddly, Lauren wants to hear more too.

"On Saturday night, we partied at another hotel and danced at bars on the beach," he says, this part of the story familiar to Lauren from the private investigator's reports. "In the bathroom of the beach bar that night, I started taking some pills. The feeling…I felt invincible.

"And I was never alone. Marcia stayed with me. She was always drunk or high and she shared everything with me. I checked out of the hotel and stayed at her place. You kept texting and I was so confused. It was like you were a mother and this other girl was my lover."

Bile rises in Lauren's throat.

"Since the accident I felt like you were crushing me. I know you were trying to help me but over time, I felt like a child who couldn't do anything for himself. I've had that worthless feeling before and I couldn't deal with it again. I just wanted you to stop bugging me."

Interesting. Was he so damn drunk he forgot the conversation where he said he never loved her?

"I got so angry one night when my credit card didn't go through. I was so mad when I realized you wouldn't pay for me anymore. That's how upside down I was. You were a mother that was supposed to pay for me and you cut me off."

Lauren remains still, one hand clutching her purse and the other the fluffy blanket. Her heart feels like it is beating with acid; every pump a burning irritation.

"I was mad, really mad, and I was on the beach. I didn't want to remember you anymore. I was so mad I took off my ring, *our* ring. I took it off and…"

She feels his eyes scanning her, looking for a reaction. No way will she give him one. She stares forward; her breath feels caught up in her heartbeat.

"And I…I threw the ring in the ocean."

"No!" Her blurt is uncontrollable. Their ring? *Gone?* This hurts more than any other disgusting thing he has said so far.

He continues, "I was starting to hurt but still felt so excited. I'm not sure what I was taking but Marcia kept giving them to me. Then one morning before she went to work she told me she needed more money. She left and I remember rolling around the bed alone and wondering where I was and what I had done. And then something, something…" His voice trails off as he takes a hard swallow.

"My phone. My phone made a noise. It was the alert from my plane tracker app. I got up and saw that your plane was on the move. I tried to figure out where you were going. I followed that blinking dot all morning, wondering why you were flying northwest. I started thinking about you, wondering about you."

Well, lace up the running shoes and run a virtual victory lap. That was exactly what she hoped would happen when she flew to Utah to see Dina.

"That day all I did was sit at the computer and try to get information on you. I was going crazy thinking about you, Brittney, the boys, the beautiful life I had run from. I didn't eat or shower, I felt my body craving a drink but I didn't have one. I needed to focus. I had to figure out where you were. Then, Marcia came home drunk."

Lauren fists her hands. Could this horrible story get any worse?

"She brought home another guy and wanted the three of us to…" His voice trails off again.

Her teeth grind. It just got worse.

"Right in front of me she took off her clothes and his too. They went at it…right in the bed in front of me. She laughed; she didn't care. I didn't want that. I didn't want her. I…I pulled my things together and walked out the door.

"I drove, I'm not sure where. I think I was trying to head home but I was tired and dizzy, so I stopped at some cheap motel. It was so gross, so dirty and I was getting sick. I just wanted a drink and I was so sick. By morning I could hardly move and didn't know who to call. I knew you were gone somewhere out west and I was too scared to call you or Frank. I figured by then, you had moved on. Then I remembered Bobby lived near Ft. Lauderdale. I asked him for help.

"Bobby and Cheryl took me to their house. That was Friday and I think Cheryl called Christy the next day.

"I was detoxing. It was horrible. They sent their daughter away to Cheryl's mom for the weekend. I don't know what I had been taking but getting rid of it was awful.

"By Sunday I was starting to feel a little better and I showered and shaved for the first time in days. Then your lawyer called. And of course when he arrived he was the biggest, smartest, best looking lawyer."

She grins with her head buried in the fluffy blanket. *The "Todd Peppers Maneuver" for the win.*

"The forms, the papers; I just about died knowing that it was final with you. I was so sick with myself for breaking it off. I ruined everything we had ever had.

"Bobby encouraged me to get some help, so we flew to Dallas to see Dr. Tobias. He's the only doctor I trust and I knew my problems started from the accident. Tobias told me physically I'm fine but emotionally…" He shakes his head. "He referred me to a psychologist. I had been afraid to see one before. But now, I knew I had no choice. As we worked on my issues, he suggested one way to reconnect with you was from the outside in; like a circle with you in the middle. Talk to people not closest to you and work up my confidence. All I wanted was to talk to you. I wanted to tell you I made a mistake…" He stops again to gather his words, "and when Christy said you'd be here I thought I could…I thought *we* could…"

"Enough," Lauren says. "This…this is enough for one night. This is enough for one lifetime."

She stretches flat to lie down with throbbing feet and an overwhelmed brain.

Andy gets up from the floor and quietly walks into the kitchen to get a drink. He comes back with some pillows he grabbed from the family room.

Without a word, he places the pillows on the floor beside her sofa. He lies down on the carpeted floor with a dirty face and no blanket.

He says nothing else the rest of the night.

[TWENTY-THREE]

Andy

The rising sun brightens Christy and Cal's living room. Andy squints and rolls over on his stomach. His back aches from sleeping on the floor but he doesn't care; he'd sleep on cold concrete if it meant he was next to Lauren again. He pulls the blanket closer to his face when he suddenly realizes he didn't go to sleep with a blanket. This is Lauren's!

He sits up fast and looks at the couch. Lauren is gone. He scrambles to his feet and runs to the guest room, but her suitcase isn't there. Panicked, he runs to the front door. It's unlocked. He opens the door and dashes outside. Lauren's bright yellow car is gone.

He raises his hands in frustration. The woman he loves more than life itself has left him. Somehow, she's gotten away on feet she can't even walk on. He deserves it. His mistakes have left a hole in his heart larger than the empty space in this driveway. The bad choices he's made were reflected last night in a bath tub of watery blood. He screws up every step forward and now Lauren has left before he's even had a chance to apologize.

He walks back inside and softly knocks on Christy and Cal's door.

"She left?" a surprised, sleepy Christy says.

"Don't wait, Andy. Call her now," Cal says, getting out of bed. "Don't let this drag out. Call her now and make sure she's okay."

Andy sits on the sofa to make the call. "There's no way she'll answer," he says, putting the phone to his ear.

"Hi," Lauren answers.

His face brightens. "Lauren, hi, um, you aren't here. Are you okay?" he asks, feeling instantly stupid.

"I'm fine."

"Oh good, okay, I'm glad you're okay. Do I need to call Frank?"

"No need. He's driving me and Ryan's trying to catch us."

"You'll see a doctor today?"

"That's my plan."

"Would it be…if it is okay with you…can I call you later to check on you?"

There's a long pause.

"If you call and I'm available, maybe."

"I'd like to do that. I…um…I just want you to be okay."

"I'll be fine. Bye."

He hangs his head down, even though it's a victory that she even answered the phone. Still, it's a defeat that she left him. He squeezes the cushions of the sofa, the very spot where he told her all the ugly details last night. He feels naked from his confessions, exposed by his stupidity and humbled by the thought of the epic apology that he still owes her.

"Andy?" Christy calls from the kitchen. "Did you see this?"

He walks to the kitchen counter and stands over a note.

Andy,

Until such time?
I guess you decided it was time.

Lauren

On the paper, she's drawn a circle. His eyes fill with tears seeing what she placed inside of it. It's her silver ring. With shaking fingers, he picks it up. She had her ring with her? She was carrying it all this time?

"Maybe that's why she fought me over her purse," Cal says, coming up behind Andy. "She must have had the ring inside it."

"She didn't want to let me go; she was still holding on to me," Andy sadly says. "Until she heard what I had to say last night." He twirls the tiny ring on the ends of his fingers; one surviving ring from a promising set of two.

"You've got a long road ahead of you, buddy," Cal says, patting Andy on the back. "And her returning this ring is not a good sign."

Andy clutches the ring in his fist.

"There's no fast fix for the mess I've made. And returning this ring may be a bad sign but over there—that isn't," he says, pointing to the living room floor.

Cal looks over Andy's shoulder.

"That's a blanket on the floor where you were sleeping, Andy."

"Exactly," Andy says. "And it's the only good sign I've got."

Lauren

Frank pulls the Ferrari into the auto courtyard, where Tish is pacing. "Let's get you inside," she says, gently helping Lauren out of the car.

Lauren latches on to Tish's hand, grimacing with each step towards the house. Her grimace escalates to an outright scowl an hour later when the doctor sticks a needle in each foot during this Saturday morning emergency house call.

The medical result of running barefoot in the woods: four stitches in her left foot; five in her right; plus a sore arm from a tetanus shot. Her right ankle is sprained and healing the multiple scratches and cuts will probably cause the most irritation, the doctor says. He gives her a pair of crutches and tells her she should be fine to travel to Boston later in the week, as long as she stays off her feet for the next few days.

After the doctor leaves, Lauren lies on her family room sofa, staring at the ceiling as images of last night replay in her mind. There's so much to remember: Andy's face, his hair, the feel of his arms holding her. But there's so much to forget too: her slap, her run, his disgusting confession. She was just pulling her emotions away from Andy and his sudden reemergence is like a plunger sucking her back.

When she wakes up from a quick nap, she makes a few calls. First on her list: Josh. He was supposed to be busy filming a TV pilot today so she sends a text:

"Bad night last night. Home now. Went running in the woods barefoot and hurt my feet; Andy chasing me. Not a good night."

Minutes later, Josh calls. "So was he hiding in the woods and you just stumbled across him, barefoot, carrying a little red basket or something?"

Good one. "Red hood," she says, smiling. "I should have been wearing a little red hood. That would have been a better story. Nine stitches in my feet and a sprained ankle."

"You are totally not kidding! Oh my God, are you okay?"

"Physically, not so much. Mentally, not so much either. So basically, not so much."

"Hey, I need to get back on set right now. I want to talk longer but I have to run—sorry for the pun. Call you later?"

"That'd be great," she says, ending a call that has lifted her spirits.

Next on her list: Captain Control.

"I've been waiting for your call," Johnny answers.

Yeah, she figured. "I've got nine stitches in my feet and I'm in no mood for lectures."

"No lecture from me, as long as you are okay and Andy stays away from you. But will you be able to go to Boston?"

"I'll be fine. Just need to stay off my feet for a few days."

"You sound foul."

"Pretty much. I'm tired, hurt, mad…the list goes on."

"Oliver made up a name for what you did last night."

Oh Lord.

"He calls it Bangladesh-ing, defined as the act of freaking out as if you were on world tour in Bangladesh."

Everyone seems to be having so much fun with this.

"No more Bangladeshing, okay?" Johnny asks.

No promises. She uncovered a surprising layer of emotion in last night's rage-fueled run; a level of anger she never knew she had. She used to worry about freezing on stage and now she has the opposite problem. What happens when her gut tells her to run when they are in the middle of a world tour?

"Getting my best friend to stop arranging ambushes would help. And maybe dating a guy that I don't want to run away from would be good too."

"What are you going to do about Andy?"

Lauren quiets.

"I'm not sure what to do next."

The day passes slowly and the peace and quiet gives Lauren time to think. It is early afternoon when peace gives way to Frank rushing into the house, holding his phone.

"Andy's at the hut."

Lauren shimmies to quickly sit up from the couch. "Here, now?"

He nods.

Tish leans over the kitchen counter. "What are you going to do?"

"Andy asked if he could call me later today, but showing up here is a huge surprise." She quickly weighs the options. Turn him away? Or maybe approach this carefree and witty like Josh or Oliver have. After all, being uptight has given her nothing but a bloodied pair of feet. And, at the moment, she's kind of hungry.

"Well, ask the guard…if Andy has brought any food."

Frank looks at her like she's lost her mind and gets back on the phone. He gets the answer. "The guard says no, Andy has no food but he does have a gift."

"A nice gift?"

"The guard thinks you'll like it," Frank says, picking up on her indifference.

"Then…he can bring me my nice gift."

Frank gives permission to open the gate.

Lauren mumbles, "This gift better not be $279 worth of used lingerie."

Within minutes, Tish opens the front door. Since Lauren lies immobile on the couch she has to wait for him to come to her. But she can overhear their greeting.

"Oh, Andy," Tish says. There's a pause, which probably means they're hugging.

"I've missed you so much, Tish," Andy says. "I hope you've been okay."

"I have missed you immensely but what you have done makes me angrier than the sea in a hurricane."

"I'm going to make things right, Tish. For you, the kids and especially Lauren."

"I would hope so," Tish says. "She's resting in the family room."

Lauren's heart thumps with uneasy anticipation as she hears their conversation coming closer. Suddenly, he walks around the corner and a rush of emotions smacks her. The look of his eyes, his hair, his face. *Andy.* Her love, her old lover, standing here in the room they used to share. She doesn't want to joke around anymore.

He shyly smiles.

"Hi," he says, looking showered and changed from the last time she saw him. He moves closer to sit on the other side of the couch, holding a gorgeous bouquet of flowers. "How are your feet? Did a doctor come?"

"Sore, yes and nine stitches total."

"I brought these for you to brighten your day." He extends the bouquet of purple irises and violet roses.

"They're lovely, thank you. Hey, Tish? Can you place these in some water? Maybe put them over here by the TV since there's no room on the breakfast table."

Andy looks to the table, where the massive rose arrangement from Josh sits. His eyes widen and flick back to Lauren. She smiles. *Yeah, buddy, flowers from someone not you.* Maybe just a little bit of sarcasm has its place.

He quickly recovers. "You must have left early this morning. Have you gotten much rest today?"

"Andy, you can't come over here and pretend…you can't pretend that we are even friends."

He sits up straight. "We may not be friends now, but I plan to work every minute of every day to change that."

"Look, I'm tired," she says. "You should leave because all I want to do is rest."

"I'd like to stay."

She ignores him and stretches out for a nap.

When she wakes up, Andy is still sitting on the other side of sectional sofa.

"How was your nap?" he quietly asks.

She squints. Why didn't he leave?

"Hey, Lauren," Tish says, leaning over the sofa. "I have to go now but Frank's still here."

"Thanks for coming so early this morning, Tish," she says. "I'll be fine. I'll get Frank and Ryan to help me up the stairs and I'll be good for the night."

Andy leans forward. "Lauren, I can help you."

She glares, not sure why he's still here. And she's not sure why she hasn't forced him out. They keep looking at each other; absorbing each other. Andy must be trying to figure out where he stands. She's trying to decide if she can still stand him.

But right now, she has a more pressing issue: she's been drinking too much water. She gets up, fumbling with her crutches as she hobbles across the room towards the bathroom. Then her phone pings with an incoming text. And she left her phone right next to Andy's curious eyes.

When she's finished, she hobbles back and sits down, noticing the new message from the contact, cutest guy on the planet.

"My schedule has freed up; I can come and visit you Tuesday. I'll do my part to help you feel better!"

Wow! She smiles and types a reply to Josh while Andy sits and watches her.

Frank comes down from the office. "Want me to call Wes at the deli to bring some dinner?" he asks. Lauren nods. "You staying too?" he asks Andy.

"I'd like to," Andy says.

Fifteen minutes later, Wes arrives at the front door. He walks into the kitchen and does a double take when he sees Andy. "Wow, hey, I thought I saw your usual sandwich order here but I didn't expect…I mean…you are here?"

"I'm lucky to be here," Andy says, glancing at Lauren.

Wes sets up their turkey melts on the table, making several irritated glances towards Andy. Lauren shuffles over with her crutches, smiling. Even the deli guy looks like he's on her side.

"Sorry to see you've hurt your feet," Wes says, pointing to her crutches. "These red roses though, wow, they are really nice."

"Thanks. It's a nice feeling to get flowers from a man."

"Good tip to remember. As always, if you need anything, just call!" Wes says, heading out the front door.

Andy sits down, the roses and greeting card now in front of his face. "Cutest guy on the planet, huh? He sounds very confident in himself."

"Oh no, no…" she says, slowing opening the wax paper wrapping of her sandwich. "He would never say that about himself. Cutest guy on the planet is my nickname for him."

Andy still lives on this planet.

They eat in silence.

The sun has set on one crazy day. It started with open wounds on the other side of the state and is ending with her at home healing. Oddly, Andy has been with her at both ends of the day.

"I'm going to bed, so it's time for you to leave," she says.

"Let me at least get you upstairs." He moves towards her, slipping his arm under her legs. She bristles with his touch but doesn't resist. She can't. His touch makes her limp. *Damn this connection to him. Stop it! He hurt you!* He carries her into the bedroom and gently lowers her on the bed. As he stands his eyes rapidly explore the room. "A pillow is missing."

"No man with an H initial was interested in this territory anymore. That pillow, like me, did not survive the last few weeks very well."

She pulls back her blanket and pushes her bandaged feet under the soft sheets to stretch out in bed, the bed she and Andy used to share. Now he's an awkward, unwelcomed guest standing next to it.

"I thought I'd just sit here on the sofa until you go to sleep."

"That's where Michael slept," she says quietly. "He kept an eye on me during the drama. This was…this whole house was…quite a war zone while we figured out what the hell you were doing."

"I want to know what you went through," he says softly.

"Look, I am not ready to talk," she snaps.

He glances down and then back up. "What if we went away—just the two of us? Somewhere we can talk. Somewhere we can sit like this but talk about what happened and figure out if ending this was really the best idea."

Her knowledge of events just upended. Did he forget he ended this? She's got the damn note right here in the bedside table if he needs to be reminded. Actually, a meeting later could be her chance to tell him what happened and how she really feels now. That is, if she can figure out how she really feels.

"You mean like a retreat?"

"Yes, exactly. A retreat where we have a few days together to talk."

The air feels heavier with every second of her silence. She rolls over to her stomach and turns her head his direction. She slowly blinks, her body demanding rest from that stupid run of hers, little sleep last night, a long drive and very little sleep today.

What the hell.

"If you put it all together and tell me where to go, I'll be there."

Andy

Andy can't believe what he just heard. He puts his hands to his face in silent celebration. She agreed? He's racked up more victories than he could've imagined from a day that started with such devastation. She let him through the hut and inside the house. She didn't throw the flowers back at him. He stayed long enough to have dinner with her and to get her safely in bed. And now she's agreed to go away with him to talk? He doesn't want to press his luck; this probably is a good time for him to leave.

"Great, perfect. I'll get with Frank to pull all the details together," he says, getting up from the sofa and heading towards the bedroom door. "I'm glad you are safe at home now. Hopefully you can get a good rest tonight." He looks back at the bed.

She's quiet again. Very quiet.

He stands at the door for a moment. *What's she thinking?* Is she changing her mind about the retreat? Does she want him to stay? Could she maybe, just maybe, want him to join her in bed? The hopeful thought of crawling into that bed races through his body. His heart beats harder.

"Lauren?" he softly asks, stepping closer to the bed.

He sees the side of her head and her beautiful, sleeping face.

He smiles. *My baby.* Thank goodness she's safe and on the way to healing. He reaches down and pulls the blanket over her, returning the loving gesture she made to him last night.

It's hard for him to stand here, outside the bed. He'd rather be in there with her, comforting her, pleasuring her. He craves that feeling when her hair tickles his body and hearing those groans of pleasure he can get her to make. He has to do everything right to get back in this bed; no more mistakes.

Andy looks around the bedroom, gathering memories. He slowly steps away, torn with each step, knowing he's leaving Lauren behind. Walking down the dark stairs, he remembers all the happy times in this home: the kids, the laughs, the food, the love.

"Frank?" Andy says, pressing the button by the security panel at the front door.

"Yes, Andy?" Frank answers, still here, still working. Andy knows Frank would never leave him alone with Lauren. Not right now.

"Lauren is asleep upstairs and I'm heading out the front door now. You should lock it behind me."

"Of course. Good night, Andy."

"Have a nice evening, Frank."

Andy stands alone in the dark foyer, taking one last look at his former home. This king wants his castle back and he knows there are two things he must do.

The first: deliver the biggest apology in his life.

The second: get rid of the cutest guy on the planet.

[TWENTY-FOUR]

Lauren

"Welcome to Florida!" Lauren says with a big smile spread across her face. She leans against the open glass doors of her home.

Josh Spencer has arrived.

"Love to be here!" he exclaims, stepping out of the Tahoe. "Beautiful home!"

He greets Lauren with a warm kiss on the cheek, squeezing her shoulders. Bill follows them inside, carrying his suitcase.

"Upstairs in the guest suite will be great. Thanks, Bill," she says, turning back to get a good look at her visitor.

Josh smiles. "Glad to see your crutches are gone, but what the hell are those?" He laughs and points to Lauren's feet.

"These are my fast feet," she says, wiggling red slippers shaped like race cars—four fuzzy wheels sticking out of each foot. "Oliver bought them for me, you know, to help me go fast if I need to run away from something again."

"They look comfy," Josh says. "I want a pair!"

"He got a pair for everyone, including you. The guys are back in the studio right now."

After a quick tour of downstairs, Lauren and Josh head to the studio. The band is finishing rehearsals for the Daytime single debut.

They fly to Boston tomorrow to prepare for the show's taping on Thursday afternoon.

"You're still coming with us to Boston, right?" Lauren asks Josh as they walk beside the pool to the studio.

"My schedule is cleared. I'm happy to be your escort."

The day is filled with business and pleasure. Plebeian rehearses for most of the morning, while Josh watches. It doesn't take long for Josh to learn the words to their new song. By the end of rehearsals, he's singing with Lauren, trying to throw her off.

In the afternoon, Lara arrives. She's brought some new wardrobe options, since the high-heel sandals they chose last week are now out and wearing fuzzy car slippers isn't an option. Josh involves himself with the selection, playfully giving a name to each style boot as they look over Lara's options in the living room. Everyone decides on "Two to Tango", a name Josh gives a black wedge boot. He thinks even with Lauren's hurt feet they'd be comfortable enough for her to dance in.

Later that afternoon, Oliver, Doug and Michael head out for the day. Johnny walks her out of the studio.

"See you tomorrow," he says to Lauren, giving a quick nod to Josh. Johnny leans closer to Lauren. "You sure being alone with Josh is a good idea?"

Captain Control. It never ends.

"Eating dinner now is a good idea and I can't have dinner with my guest if you are still here," she says, winking.

Johnny gives a hesitant smile, turns and slowly leaves through the back iron gates.

Tish has already placed dinner on the table and is waving her goodbye. After enjoying a Spanish-inspired feast of paella, Josh and Lauren take their sangria poolside to enjoy the outside air. Flames from the gas fire bowls make a dancing reflection on the pool water while swing jazz music plays on the stereo. They settle at the outdoor table, talking about his pool project and that great bonfire on the beach.

Josh's smile lights up the lanai as bright as the dancing flames from the fire bowls. His head of loose, messy curls looks as off-beat as his fun personality. He dropped everything to come here—to fly to Boston with her tomorrow. The fact that he went out of his way to be with her makes her happy, *Josh* makes her happy. Then why can't she stop looking across the pool at the damn empty chaise lounge chair?

Her mind goes back to Andy, always Andy. They haven't spoken since she agreed to go on the retreat. Every hour she wonders what he's planning. And now she's more frustrated that she's thinking about him while trying to enjoy the company of another man.

* * *

Backstage on the Daytime set, so far the only drama has been Doug forgetting to pack his favorite drumsticks and Oliver smelling like he's been drinking again. Until Lynette steps into Lauren's dressing room.

"We have a situation," Lynette says.

"Oh good grief." Lauren drops her lipstick tube. "Please don't tell me Josh is out there kissing random women. We're not even a couple yet!"

"Luckily, no lips gone wild. Just a yapping mouth situation."

Lynette explains that there's a rumor circulating that Lauren hurt her feet doing something related to Andy. It probably came from one of the personal shoppers that were providing boots to Lara.

"I don't think Lara is gossiping, but in the process of asking stores and boutiques for stylish boots that can cover foot bandages…" Lynette says.

"And they all know she's my stylist…" Lauren adds.

"That's how the rumors start. Be prepared. The host will ask you about this."

Lauren nods, looking up at the television monitor in the dressing room. The taping has already begun and the first guest, an actor promoting a new movie, is being interviewed. Even though this program won't be shown until the next day, what Lauren says could become public once the audience leaves.

Josh had opted to stay backstage. He pokes his head inside Lauren's dressing room. "They're coming for you," he says, smiling. Together they walk down the hall, waiting as the producer counts down the last few seconds until Lauren's segment.

"You look killer. Go knock 'em dead," Josh whispers, crossing his eyes.

What a goof. She fiddles with the long cuffs on her white button-down shirt. Over it, she wears a crisp, cropped black military jacket coupled with tight black pants and her "Two to Tango" boots. But she's missing a trademark accessory: her sunglasses. They'd be overkill for an interview like this. Besides, it's not like they're playing *Closer*. As long as the audience keeps their hands out of their pants, she has a shot at getting through this. She can hear her introduction:

…We feel like we've been along with her on this journey, from average mom to front woman of a multi-platinum band. We've been through her divorce, her recovery from a serious car accident and her fairy tale romance, one that would come to a surprising, shocking end. We can't wait to hear her story. Please welcome for the first time, Lauren Logan!

Josh pokes her in the back, making her walk out with a smirking smile that she didn't intend to have. She waves to the crowd, hugs the host and takes the hot seat.

They begin talking about the reveal of the band, though not for long since that's been discussed in other interviews. The host asks about the Dallas accident as a photo of Lauren's crushed Suburban appears on the screen behind her. And then she asks about Andy.

Lauren acknowledges the obvious, that they are not together anymore.

The host wants to know about Lauren's days with Dina in Utah. *How funny: everybody loves a celebrity rescuing a celebrity story.*

The men of Plebeian sitting in the front row are an obvious target for questions. Johnny and Michael are attentive, Oliver looks bored and Doug looks horrified that he might be asked something.

"Surely some of you have advice for Lauren," the host says to them.

"Nobody's life is perfect," Johnny says, "and all of us have helped each other at one time or another."

Lauren smirks at Johnny's awesome non-answer. If she wasn't on TV right now, she'd be tempted to blow Johnny a celebratory kiss.

The host turns back to Lauren. "Have you seen Andy since that weekend?"

"I did see him recently and he told me what happened and why."

"We've heard a rumor this week that Andy tried to get back with you but you did something that hurt your feet. Did that happen?"

"He didn't try to get back with me, and yes, I hurt my feet. I should have worn shoes when I went in the woods near my friend's home. I had to get nine stitches and the cuts are still healing. My injury is harder to explain than it is entertaining to hear about."

Ha! That non-answer just beat Johnny's.

After a few more questions, the host swoops in for the big one. "Do you still love Andy?"

Lauren straightens. *Oh, she's got her answer ready.*

"There is no doubt that Andy is the love of my life. He's *the* guy. But, I know that the love of your life may not be the person you are supposed to be with. Because the love of your life may lie to you, may hit you, may steal from you, may cheat on you…there are many things the love of your life may do that doesn't make it right for you to stay with them."

"Do you think you'd take Andy back?"

"That's not even on the table right now. We've decided to have a retreat and talk through things."

Her face lights up. "A retreat? Like a team building meeting for two?"

"Not quite team building, but a neutral location, nothing on the agenda except us."

"And what's next for you?"

"Well…I do have a date tonight," Lauren says, curling her

shoulders. The surprised audience applauds.

"I think I saw your date in the green room backstage!" the host excitedly says. "We'll have to convince him to come out later."

When the interview is over, during the commercial break the host convinces Josh to come out and sit next to her to watch Plebeian's performance. As he takes his seat, the audience cheers. Lauren peers out from behind a backstage partition. *Interesting.* People must like the idea of her and Josh together.

After their performance, the show's closing music plays as the five of them stand with the host, waving their goodbyes to the audience's applause. Lauren feels bolder and takes a closer look at the audience while she waves, absorbing the energy from this happy crowd. It's mostly women out there, except for one particularly grumpy-looking man. He was probably dragged to the show by his wife. He looks familiar, but everyone stands and she loses his face in the crowd.

While the applause and music continues, the host suddenly calls out to Josh in the front row. "Where are you taking Lauren for dinner?"

"I was thinking your house. How's seven?" he says and the audience breaks out in laughter.

The dinner date isn't really a one-on-one date. It is a "Josh coming with all fifteen of them" type of date. Plebeian has a private room reserved at a historic restaurant in downtown Boston, where classic New England dishes of oysters, clams and lobsters are endlessly served.

Paparazzi gather outside as the group begins to leave. A frenzy of flashbulbs turns the night as bright as day when Josh harmlessly slips his hand on Lauren's waist to help her into the car. It doesn't take long for that to make headlines:

Andy Who?
She's Moving up to Hollywood
Meet JoLauren

By the time the photos hit the gossip sites, Josh and Lauren are already back in her hotel suite talking about why they'll never be a couple.

"Andy has your heart," Josh says, "real, real bad."

Bingo. "That's my biggest problem. Stupid heart."

Their conversation deepens and Josh finally opens up and tells Lauren about his divorce. Turns out both of them are still in love with the loves that left them.

"What a prize you are for someone," she gushes, poking his ribs. "You need someone who can handle you though." He laughs. Even though her time with Josh was brief, she knows he's a handful, playfully interjecting himself everywhere. She's not sure she has the patience for that. What she is sure of is one time she did have the guy that was perfect for her. Now she has to figure out if he is the guy she thought he was and if she wants him back.

"You need to give me the inside scoop about this retreat," Josh says as they hug each other goodnight. "Listen to what he says but also tell him what you felt. It's good for him to be scared." He backs away with a silly smile. "Hey, do I get to keep the title of cutest guy on the planet?"

"You're the cutest guy on the planet forever." She laughs at him as he walks backwards down the hall to his room. Then she quickly leans into the hotel hallway "Until a spaceship from Mars arrives with some hot new men!" And she shuts the door before he can debate her.

Lauren leans against the door, smiling. Tonight she may have closed the door on a potential romance but she knows she has gained a valuable friend.

* * *

On the early morning flight back to Tampa, chatter fills the plane's cabin. Lauren sits quietly, twisting her hands.

"You okay?" Johnny whispers, sitting beside her.

"Huh? Yeah. Fine," she says. "I was just trying to remember something. Someone."

"Who?"

"In the audience yesterday, I thought I saw someone I knew."

"Can't put a name to a face?"

"Yeah, but I don't know anyone who lives in Boston so it's been driving me crazy."

"I didn't see anyone we know. But I'm sure Frank can get an audience list if it's bothering you."

She shakes her head. "Nah…it's no big deal."

She leans back in the seat, still twisting her hands. The bigger deal is Andy and if he has seen the pictures of her and Josh from last night. If he has, he probably figured out Josh sent those roses.

Plebeian's episode of Daytime will be broadcast soon in some syndicated markets, but it won't air on the Tampa station until four p.m. Since she talked about Andy in the interview, should she tell him what she said before it airs this afternoon? But that would be a very awkward call. And a text would be even worse.

Then she remembers a perfect way to send Andy a message. It's a time-tested, not always accurate, but 100% guaranteed-to-be-delivered messenger: a teenage girl.

* * *

The hum of ink cartridges plays in a rhythmic pattern, back and forth, back and forth, as the paper is pulled lower. Line by line the printer slowly produces its product. The paper releases, emerging with its image.

He picks up the paper and looks at it carefully.

This image is larger than the one on his computer screen.

He cautiously places the paper's left edge in a three-hole punch and slowly presses down, enjoying the sound of crunching paper giving way to the forcing press of the metal rods.

He unsnaps the clamps of a binder.

This photo will go on top.

This photo deserves his full attention.

He gently threads the paper through the clamps, placing the new photo of Josh Spencer over the worn and defaced photo of Johnny Fulton.

He snaps the binder clamps closed.

[TWENTY-FIVE]

"Hi, Lauren! Hold on…" Brittney says, the loud chatter of talking teenagers in the background. Sounds like the cafeteria. It's Friday and Lauren knew she'd be at school but assumed she'd have to leave a message.

"…there; can you hear me?" Brittney asks.

"Yes—can you talk now?" Lauren asks, sitting at the desk in her study.

"Sure! I've got Kayla blocking the view of the AP so I can use my phone. I'm at lunch," she says. "Hey! I loved the Daytime interview!"

What? It's only noon in Tampa. The episode airs at four p.m. and she is at school.

"You saw it already?" Lauren asks. "How?"

"I just got to school. I stayed home with dad this morning to watch it. He figured out a way to see it online."

Guess Lauren doesn't need to worry about preparing Andy.

"So what was your dad's reaction?"

"You know my dad; he thinks you are so pretty—he loved your outfit and the song. He was nervous because he really doesn't know what you think of him now. Don't tell him I told you this, but he didn't like the Josh guy. He was thinking of letting me stay home all day but he was leaving to go out of town so he said I had to go to school."

Andy's out of town?

"Where was he going?"

"Mexico. Didn't he tell you? Cabo San Lucas. He's been planning your retreat!"

Cabo? "We, um, really haven't talked about it. I know he's been working with Frank on the details for next weekend but I haven't asked any questions. Yet."

"Oh, he's been working on it non-stop! Wait until you see the resort he picked. He showed me the pictures online. It's beautiful! The beach, the spa, the pool; you're going to love it."

Lauren swivels in her desk chair. *No, she can't love it.* The beautiful and romantic trappings of a resort can't mask what this retreat is about.

"Lauren? You still there?"

She stops swiveling. "Yeah. Hey, I know you probably need to go. Have a good day at school. Love you."

"Love you too. Oh, and Lauren?"

"Yes?"

"Thanks for giving my dad a chance."

Lauren ends the call and her head drops. *A chance?* Is this retreat really about second chances? Or revenge? Or finally finding *her* voice to tell *her* side of the story?

She glances over to her desk drawer. There's something she promised herself she'd do before the retreat, and now is as good of a time as any. Dread washes over her as she slowly opens the drawer. She lifts out the file containing the worst memories of her life. Her fingers shake touching the papers with Lawson's profile, the private investigator reports, the photographs, the credit card charges and other documents from that frantic weekend. *Look at it.* She rereads all of the reports, looks at all of the photos and totals up the charges for lingerie and alcohol. *Remember that feeling.* She can't get distracted by breezy palm trees, dreamy Mexican sunsets and salty margaritas served with his warm hands and longing eyes. *Remember what you're mad about!*

She drops the papers. *Wait!* How the heck will she get to Mexico without being noticed?

* * *

Beverly Hills boasts mansions with manicured lawns and palm trees so tall they tickle the blue sky. Here live the rich and famous, and plenty of paparazzi eager to photograph them all. Add in tour busses packed with camera-toting tourists and Beverly Hills isn't the best place for a celebrity to go unnoticed.

And that's exactly why Lauren is here.

She and Frank have arrived in California to play airport tag to keep paparazzi from following her to Mexico. Since she mistakenly mentioned on the Daytime talk show that she and Andy were planning a retreat, the paparazzi have been trying to find out where they will be going. Reporters would have tracked her plane anywhere she went, so she might as well go someplace they expected. At least that was the suggestion of their clever accomplice, Josh Spencer.

Right now, people have seen photos of Lauren and Josh and heard Lauren say in an interview that they had a date. Only Frank knows that Josh and Lauren won't be a romantic item. Together they've hatched a sneaky plan.

Josh meets Lauren at a street side café, making them red-hot paparazzi targets. They sit close together at a cozy outdoor table, enjoying lunch, while photographers busy themselves snapping photos from across the street. No one will guess Lauren's next stop is the retreat with Andy after such a public lunch with Josh.

Josh wishes her luck. "Just remember to say everything. Tell him how you feel," he says. "If you wait to tell him later then you're just an old nag."

"I wonder if I can forgive him."

"You may never forgive him, you know," he says, "but that doesn't stop you from moving forward with him, and being happy."

They finish lunch and stand in front of the restaurant.

"This is going to be my favorite part of the plan," Josh says with a mischievous grin.

Lauren smiles. "Kiss me good, baby. They're watching!"

Josh plants a kiss on her lips; friendly to each other but scandalous to the now electrified paparazzi.

"So that's what an actor pretending to kiss someone is like," Lauren whispers, squeezing his shoulders.

"I wasn't pretending," Josh says with a wink. "Off you go now—go get your man back."

It's scramble time.

Josh ambles across the street to his car, which keeps the photographers busy. Lauren heads back inside in the restaurant and slips out the back door, where Frank is waiting in a rental car—a car Josh had picked up earlier in the day. Frank and Lauren drive undetected to a different executive airport. While Lauren's plane remains on the ground in Los Angeles, her rented plane is up in minutes, flying south along the California coast.

"Well done, Frank!" Lauren says of the perfect diversion plan.

"Now remember, I'll be with Craig and Henry at the same resort, but I won't be seeing you all weekend. Andy made all the arrangements, and I feel comfortable with what he's done," Frank says. "But I'm only a text away."

The brief flight gives her time to get her head together. Eyes out the window, she's drawn to the sapphire blue waters of the Pacific below. The simplicity of watching the open ocean helps her relax and clear her mind. But her heart is still mad, mostly at herself for not being able to let Andy go. He ditched her in a hot second but she held on for days and in some ways, she's still holding on now. It's always taken her a while to come to terms with something. It happened when Plebeian was revealed. Years ago it took another pair of feet in Johnny's bed for her to figure out her place as an ex-girlfriend with him. She took way too long to end her marriage with Cory. And it happened again with Andy.

And what if she can't forgive him? She's afraid all she might do is bring up everything he's done wrong. He may have been caught in public, but in private she's not perfect either. She never, *ever* wants a lover of hers to think of her as their mother. She bears part of their problem.

* * *

The sun is low in the sky on a clear evening when they land in Mexico. One of the resort's drivers greets her warmly, opening her door while she settles into the black leather seat. She waves goodbye to Frank, Craig and Henry, getting in the car behind her. Before the driver pulls out, he reaches back and hands Lauren an envelope.

"This is for you, Ms. Logan," he says.

She opens the cream-colored envelope to find a handwritten note from Andy.

Thank you for spending time with me.
I'm looking forward to this.
Andy

Nice touch, and a much nicer note than the last one he left her. She tucks the note in her purse.

The road to the beach resort winds down lower and lower, each turn exposing beautiful views of the Sea of Cortez and the white rock formations of Land's End. She has a full view of the resort now, a classic hacienda-style Mexican resort behind iron gates. There is a main hotel and on the side small groups of bungalows dot the edges of the property. The warm breeze covers her face when she steps out of the car and into the firm handshake of Marco Gonzales.

"Good evening, Ms. Logan," he greets her warmly. "I'm Marco Gonzales, personal attendant to Mr. Hayden and I will be your assistant during your stay."

Marco is a sturdy Mexican man with a huge smile and eyes that look as if nothing will be left undone under his watch. He instructs the driver to deliver her bag to the bungalow, just as the car carrying Frank, Craig and Henry pulls up. Marco holds out his arm to escort Lauren and she latches on, giving a fresh smile back at the guys who are unloading their suitcases behind her.

They stroll inside the resort, through automatic doors that reveal a huge indoor atrium with palm trees and an abundance of natural sunlight. A cantina band plays in the lounge and a few guests are walking around, none of them particularly interested in her.

Marco tells her about the resort, leaning closer for emphasis when he wants her to notice something.

"But the real highlight, Ms. Logan, is the handsome man who waits with your dinner."

"And where is Mr. Hayden?"

"I will take you to him but first," Marco opens his coat and pulls out another cream-colored envelope, "I have this for you."

"Should I open this here?"

"It would be best, Ms. Logan."

She grins while ripping the envelope edges, pulling out another handwritten note.

> *If you are reading this, that's a good sign that you are inside this beautiful resort. I picked this place because it reminds me of you: sunny, bright and happy. I hope this weekend makes you happy again. See you in moments.*
> *Andy*

She smiles, tucking the second note in her purse. Marco offers his arm again and she grabs on as they stroll through the atrium.

Through the massive back windows she can see the sea.

"The water here is magical," he says, leaning in as if telling her a secret. "Each wave brings something new, and the wave that came before it is replaced with the fresh wave in a constant process of rejuvenation."

Glass doors sweep open as they walk outside to a spectacular terrace. A tranquil infinity pool bubbles to the left near a bar nestled under the ledge of a glass-walled restaurant.

Marco guides her farther down the outside terrace towards the sea as he continues his magical story. "And while the water brings in the new, the sunsets here tell us a different story."

He stops to face her.

"What story does the sunset bring, Marco?" she asks, fully cooperating in his story telling journey.

"Ah, the sunsets bring the orange of passion and the reds of love in a different palate of creation every night, much like our personal story of passion and love. Sunsets are different every day, are they not?"

She nods.

"Some days we see the full colors of the sunset, and some days we see no color at all. But true love, Ms. Logan, always sees the full colors, even during the bad days when there is no color," he says with eyes ablaze.

He drops his arm. "And if you are lucky…real lucky…true love will always be a colorful sunset from the heart of the man you love."

Marco gently turns Lauren's shoulders to the right.

Down on the beach, past a path of white candles in the sand, is a tent draped with gauzy white fabric blowing in the breeze, and the love of her life standing beside it.

[TWENTY-SIX]

Lauren's breath leaves her.

Andy's hands are clasped in front of him and his eyes are on her. A brilliant white dress shirt peeks out from beneath his navy blue sport coat. His khaki dress pants look crisp even in the blowing wind. Strands of his straight brown hair move with the nudging of the ocean breeze and his lips are parted in a nervous smile. She may be mad but she's still a hot-blooded woman, and this guy looks good.

"Marco?" She turns to face her escort. "Do you believe one person can be *the* love of your life?"

"Oh yes, Ms. Logan, yes I do," he says with a wide smile. "Now, go to yours."

She takes a big breath in, then turns and walks towards her weekend.

Andy watches every step Lauren takes as soft music blows with the breeze. Her candle lit path leads straight from the terrace and then turns left to reach the tent. Andy walks from the tent, seemingly to meet her at the corner.

Eyes on each other, they slowly walk towards the corner, Lauren timing her steps to the soft beat of the music. She suddenly stops. He stops too, looking concerned.

She takes two quick steps forward and stops. Andy tilts his head in, amused, and takes three steps forward and stops. *Nice touch with the extra step.* She takes three quick steps and stops. He takes four.

Another extra step! She begins to take one giant step backward but his arms quickly sweep the air for her to stop. *Passed.* She continues her regular walk towards him, while he continues his. A few steps later they meet at the corner.

His smile is warm and his eyes are yearning. "I have something for you." He reaches into his jacket and offers her another cream-colored envelope.

"I have two just like it," she says, taking it. She watches him as she tugs at the envelope. She looks down to pull out the card and read the message.

> *If you are reading this, then you are with me now and there is something I want to say.*
>
> *Every day for the rest of my life I will say I'm sorry to you. It may be privately in my mind; it may be vocally with my words; it may be physically with my actions. But every day I will remember the time that I lost my way and chose a path away from you.*
>
> *I start tonight by saying I'm sorry. I didn't value our love enough to see me through the hard times and I have learned deeply by my mistakes.*
>
> *I have one weekend to make it right. Thank you for giving me a chance to try.*
>
> *I love you, Lauren. So much more than I can ever make you know.*
>
> *Andy*

The words blur from the tears in her eyes. She looks into his eyes, also wet with tears.

"I am so sorry for what I have done," he says. "And there is nothing more that I want in this world than to get you back."

She blinks the tears away, nodding. She breaks his stare to look at the ground. He leans in. "Would you like to sit down?" She nods.

He walks by her side, not touching her, and leads her into the tent. Every corner of the tent has billowing white fabric and in the center sits a round table, with two all white china place settings and a glass bowl bursting with bright, colorful flowers. A waiter inside the tent pulls out a white, wooden chair for Lauren, the back of the chair tied with a satin bow. Andy sits across from her as the waiter fills their glasses with water.

She can't focus on what song is playing, but she can hear the sound of the waves crashing on the beach, only a few yards away from this oasis.

"This…this is amazing," she says, looking at his desperate eyes. "So perfect."

"I'm glad you like it," he says. "I imagined the scene you would like the most and tried to make it happen."

"Nailed it."

"Hopefully I'm the right guy in the scene."

"That's what I'm looking for, the right guy."

Food and wine starts appearing from a secret culinary team under Marco's direction.

Andy and Lauren cautiously chat, mostly about their surroundings and the delicious food.

It's dark now and Lauren realizes she forgot to take in the sunset.

"Marco was telling me quite a story about sunsets," she says.

"Marco is an amazing man. I have enjoyed working with him. He has good advice for healing."

"Does Marco know who we are and…um…our situation?"

"He does. He likes your music. And he said he'd do anything he could to help see us back together."

She looks down at her lap. That probably means Marco got them a room with only one bed.

"This beach; this music—it is all so perfect," she says. "What's the weekend plan?"

"I'll take you up to our bungalow next. I thought we could enjoy the rest of the evening just relaxing on our terrace. Tomorrow, I've planned some meals and the spa is ready to do anything you want."

She nods. It's a simple, perfect plan.

Their journey from the tent and up to the bungalow surprises Lauren because no one seems to notice them. There are a large number of international tourists here, so they may actually be someplace where they blend in.

They arrive at their bungalow, one in a group of six small cottages, each facing a courtyard with a splashy, two-tiered water fountain in the center. Andy opens theirs and Lauren walks in to a marble-floored living room, a bedroom to each side and a kitchen to the right of the foyer. Out back, a trellis covers a large terrace with a hammock, a table and chairs, lush potted tropical plants and two lounge chairs. Everything here is about the sweeping view of the sea and white rock formations. Unpack her bags and move her in: she could live here forever.

Andy's things are set up in one room and Lauren's suitcase has been placed in the other. She steps into her room and changes to a comfortable black sleeveless shirt and knit pants while Andy changes to shorts and a t-shirt.

He mixes up a batch of sangria and meets her on the terrace, where she has already found a colorful Mexican serape blanket and settled down on a lounge chair. He positions his lounge chair next to hers, giving him a view of the water but more importantly, a good view of her.

He pours the sangria. "A real friend would have given you a drink by now."

She grins, remembering that line from the party after Plebeian's first concert. She takes the glass. "Looks like an old friend just did. To well-planned retreats." She raises her glass and he accepts the compliment, meeting her glass for the toast.

A calm quiet washes over the terrace as they sit listening to the waves below. If those waves constantly regenerate life, now is as good a time as any to see if she wants to rejuvenate this relationship.

"This is strange, sitting here next to you. At one point, I wasn't sure I'd ever see you again," she says, looking into his eyes. He breathes in deep.

"I didn't believe what you said in the note you left. I convinced myself that you were just out for a drive and after getting a little space you would come back.

"Then the pictures came out. At first I didn't worry because I knew you needed to blow off steam and I was ready to let one night of partying go. I told everyone that you would realize what you did and call to say you were coming home right away."

He breaks her gaze, looking down.

"I had so many people there to help me but I just didn't believe anything was that serious. They all tried to tell me it was: Lynette, Davis, Frank, Tish, Michael, Johnny."

"Johnny was there too?"

Lauren flashes him an incredulous look. "Do you think Johnny would let me go through that alone? We were in full crisis mode, Andy. We saw credit card charges piling up and you weren't calling anyone. When I finally reached you, you were obviously drunk, there was a woman giggling next to you and you didn't seem to know about pictures that you were in. That was so unlike you, and that's when we had to take action."

He rubs his forehead. "I understand why you'd be worried, but why that concerned?"

"Extortion."

His eyes widen.

"Frank pointed out that extortion can take many forms, one being to keep the rich guy drunk and happy while others spend his money. You said you needed space but you weren't calling me back. We didn't know what was going on but the money was going out the door.

"I had to make a decision. We had to find out if you were in trouble. So, I had to…" She stops to choose her words carefully.

"What did you do?"

"I put spies on the ground," she blurts. "We hired private investigators to find out if you were in trouble."

"Wow. Oh my God. I had no idea."

"It didn't take them long to figure out you weren't in trouble," she says, irritation now hijacking her voice. "It was an easy case because you started kissing one of them."

He sits up straight. "I did what?"

"One of the agents was partying at the club and you kissed her."

He sits back, shrugging. "I don't remember any of that."

"It was triage at the house. We had people on computers, Lynette and Lesley working at the dining room table, people sleeping on sofas…it was a full-blown crisis."

Andy slowly lowers his head into his fisted hands.

"You wrote a note and then publicly self-destructed. I wasn't sure if I was still your girlfriend or not. You disappeared but we knew where you were. *I* knew. I saw the charges. I had her damn address, Andy. I had her name. I had pictures. I knew the make and model of her damn car. I knew where she worked. I knew everything about her because she was the girl that got you. She was the one you wanted in your bed. You didn't want me anymore. *You chose her!*"

His bottom lip trembles as his eyes fill with tears.

"Then, finally, you called. Finally you told me. It was the worst moment of my life, ten times worse than finding that note. With one phone call everything I had dreamed of with you—our life, our future—it was all gone."

"What are you talking about? What did I tell you?"

She squints. Does he really not remember or is he just playing dumb?

"You told me you didn't love me. And that you never did."

[TWENTY-SEVEN]

Andy thrusts himself forward. "I said what? No, no, don't say it again. I didn't say that. I couldn't have said that!" He shakes his head, his voice cracking in disbelief.

"Didn't love me. Never did," Lauren repeats with disgust.

"Oh my God, I don't….I don't remember that! I remember telling you to back off just to get you to stop calling, but I don't remember saying that!"

"You broke my heart. That's when I cut off the credit card and moved money from the bank account. I had spent four days worrying about you only to have you tell me you never loved me all along."

He slowly shakes his head.

"You never gave me a chance, Andy. You ran straight into someone else's bed and stayed with her. You never offered to fix us; you never told me we were broken. I was blindsided; embarrassed; hurt. There was nothing left of me. My guy…my love left me. The guy I wanted to be with forever…left me for a blonde, some drugs and drinks, and freedom."

He jumps up. His steps are heavy, agitated, as he walks to the terrace ledge, pushing his hands through his hair. "God, Lauren—how deep of a hole can I keep digging for myself? I did things I don't remember. It's like there are two of me in one body. What the hell did I do?"

His question floats in the air. "You had a bad weekend having a really good time."

Silence blankets the terrace again. He leans on the rail looking at the ocean while she stays in the lounge chair, clutching the blanket.

She didn't think she'd blurt out this much information so quickly. And right now she needs to know something.

"How do I know it would never happen again?"

He snaps his head to face her, taking her words as an invitation to move closer. Slowly he steps back to his chair, sitting on the edge. He reaches for her hands, holding them. It's the first time he's touched her like this since…she can't remember. His touch is warm, pulsing with electricity. And that's a feeling she definitely remembers.

"I fix it. I fix me and it never happens again," he whispers. "Never— please never—doubt my love for you. I am so sorry I ever made you think that I didn't love you, because I do. I do love you.

"Lauren, you are my life. No one has ever given me love like you. No one has ever made me so happy. I was stupid to leave you. I was stupid to throw it all away. There will never be a greater love for me than you."

She nods. She heard him and she doesn't need to say anything else. She doesn't talk about the days that followed his breakup call. There's no mention of the trip to see Dina or meeting Josh. She reels in her urge to punish him with more details, to beat him with more yelling. The sound of the distant waves does the talking now and she leaves it alone as he sits beside her, holding her hand.

Once again, the significant power of simply holding hands. This is how they started.

Andy

Andy turns off the bungalow lights and softly says goodnight. Darkness fills Lauren's room and she doesn't respond. Maybe she's asleep. Maybe she's still awake but has nothing more to say. He lies down in the room across from hers and turns off his light. He's alone with his thoughts, and his thoughts aren't good.

This is a bigger disaster than he realized; what he did is far worse than he remembered. Not only does he have to prove he'll be faithful, now he has to build back her confidence in his love.

He rolls over on his side, facing the moonlit terrace doors. She didn't mention Josh Spencer. He saw the photo of them earlier today in Beverly Hills, kissing. Maybe she's already slept with Josh. Or Josh is just waiting for this retreat to implode so he can be her hero, picking up the pieces of her heart. *You still have to prove you're a better choice than the cutest guy on the planet.*

His ribs feel cracked from all of this crushing emotion. At this point, he'll be lucky as hell if Lauren is still here when he wakes up.

Lauren

Lauren's comforter lies in a wad on the floor. Her sheets are tossed to the side. She can't sleep because she can't stop replaying Andy's words. The facts have sorted themselves out. She knows what Andy did. It was bad. So really, what's next? How many times are they going to talk about it?

She rolls to her right side, facing the moonlit terrace doors. Josh had good advice: say your piece, say it once and move on, otherwise you're a nag. So now she's said it. She's told him how she was hurt. He understands the upheaval he caused. He's apologized. What happens tomorrow? She tells him again that she's mad? *Forgiveness sucks.* At some point something has to spin out of this emotional circle.

She abandons the idea of sleep and gets up for a drink of water. The feel of the chilly Mexican tile makes her tip toe faster as she heads towards the glass doors in the living room. From here she has a good view of the waves surrendering themselves on the moonlit beach.

A few minutes later, she feels his spark. Andy stands behind her. She crosses her arms as he steps closer, finally standing next to her. "Couldn't sleep either?" he whispers.

She nods and stands still, watching the waves. He stands next to her, doing the same.

She will age ten damn years before she stops feeling this pain unless she puts it behind her now. It's time to move forward. Frankly, it is time for her to get what she wants.

"Look…" she says to Andy, still facing the view, "I know there is this line between us, and I respect that. But I want you to know…" and she turns to face him, "that I'm going to cross that line right now."

His head turns fast, his face alive with amazement. These were the same words he said when they first became lovers in a hot tub in Phoenix.

Their eyes lock, icy but hot at the same time in the most powerful and unsettled moment they have ever shared.

Lauren raises her hands, gently touches his chest and takes a deep breath. She wants her bad boyfriend back. Screw common sense, wanting the man who embarrassed her in front of the world. This isn't logical, but logic is as boring as a cargo ship. She wants a reckless cruise with this guy again.

Andy reaches for her.

"My line to cross." She swats his hands. Eyes wide, he stills.

She grabs the bottom of his t-shirt, pulling it up and over his head. Her hands claim his bare chest, a place she never thought she'd touch again. Slowly her hands begins to stroke, leaving a trail of his chill bumps behind her touch. She strokes lower, to his stomach, across his scar from the accident that started this madness.

One time. She has to do this one time and then she'll never do this again.

She imagines Marcia on him, imagines where her lips may have been, where her hair may have been draped. Where Lauren moves her eyes and her hands she imagines Marcia there, and as she passes she imagines her gone.

If Lauren doesn't do this now, the thought of where she was will come later. It will haunt her and make her bitter. It will cross her mind, change her mood and make her mean. Forever it will be an irritating reminder that would chip at their relationship. So she will do this now, once, and be finished.

Her forced self-torture brings her to her knees. The moon's gentle glow lights a path for her as she strokes lower, her thumbs capture the waistband of his sleep shorts and slowly she pulls them down. He's naked for her to review and she's staring right at the part of him she wished Marcia had never used. With both hands she grabs him there, fully arousing him. But she's not ready for him yet.

She gets up off her knees, still holding his rock-solid readiness below. Tense air sucks them closer, their eyes and lips hovering less than an inch apart. One hard squeeze and she could hurt him where he'd never forget. She could give him physical pain so he would understand how hard she suffered. But instead, she lets go of him below. She still has more Marcia to get rid of.

Her fingers gently move up through his hair, her fingertips rubbing his scalp. Then, she caresses his cheeks, one finger slowly tracing his lips. A sickening chill runs through her body as she imagines Marcia's lips on his during those days they spent in bed together.

Do this once; once and then Marcia Lawson is gone forever.

Lauren breathes deeply again, trying to calm the shaking of her body. Andy remains still, obedient to her process, though his nervous, rapid breathing gently moves her hair.

As she reaches for his arms, suddenly he moves. He grabs her head, pulling her to him. Their lips spark with electricity, just like their first kiss in New York City.

She fists her hands in his hair as he thrashes her with his tongue. Their kisses deepen as their hands move down their bodies. They rub, touch, grab, squeeze. They stumble backwards to his room, falling on the bed in a twisting, rolling fit of physical pleasure.

Passion consumes them in moves that are so familiar, yet it has been so long it feels like the first time. Soon their clothes are gone, but their eyes are open, stares are strong. Right now his eyes say disbelief; hers say relief.

Right before he takes her, he stops. "This is it for me," he says through heavy breaths. "I told myself; this is it."

Her breathing steadies. "What?"

"I told myself if I ever got the chance to be with you again, you would be the last woman I'll ever make love to. As long as you are my girlfriend, my lover…my wife."

His…wife? She can't react; his mouth covers hers, kissing her. His body presses tight against hers, and her broken heart welcomes him inside. Two that were apart now share themselves with each other.

Quiet blankets the bedroom as they lie still, resting. The muffled crash of the midnight waves against the shore penetrates through the closed glass doors. Their bare bodies press together. Andy's arms have not let her go. But the final words have not been said.

She rolls to face him. "I've got ten thousand people that will tell me not to say this, but I want you back."

His breath catches. He tenderly moves her hair from her eyes. "And there are going to be a million people that say I'm a lucky guy to get you back."

His fingers slowly stroke the outline of her face; warm, soft, thoughtful strokes. "You gave me a sign that I had a chance. After all that I did to you. I knew you still cared for me when I woke up on the floor at Cal and Christy's. You covered me with your blanket. I knew then I might have a chance to win your heart again."

Lauren smiles. *Busted.*

He pulls up her hands to kiss them.

"I will never break your heart again, Lauren. Never," he promises.

"Please. Don't," she whispers.

He nods.

Sleep finally comes now that she is safe in his arms.

The morning sun arrives in their room, shining brightly through the glass doors. Andy rolls over to Lauren, gently stroking her face.

She opens her eyes to the sight of him. *Him!* "I have missed this so much; my mornings with you."

"Baby, I have missed every minute of you. I can't believe you're still here," he says, kissing her. "Now I want to fuss over you. Ready for breakfast?" An eager smile covers his face as he leaps out of bed.

Within thirty minutes, Marco rolls in a cart containing all of Lauren's favorite breakfast foods. *Yes!* Even a chocolate cream doughnut!

They sit together at the bistro table on the terrace, the bright sun shining right through Lauren's sheer pink slip, a sexy outfit her saboteur Tish must have slipped into her suitcase when she helped her pack. Andy leaves his eggs to lean over her chair. "God, you are amazing," he whispers, kissing her with orange juice flavored lips.

All day his eyes never leave her. He's a step ahead of anything she reaches for; he reads her mind for anything she wants. Massages together on the terrace, naps in the hammock and a no-clothes lunch in bed. It's the perfect day.

Andy has planned dinner in the resort's main restaurant and he wears a very proud smile walking hand-in-hand downstairs with Lauren. Marco greets them with a grin. "Your table, Mr. Hayden," he says, escorting them to their candle lit table with a view of the sea. Unlike last night, eyes follow them to their table.

"How long do you think it will take for this news to hit?" she asks Andy as he pulls out her chair.

"My bet is it already has," he whispers in her ear.

The restaurant is decorated in vibrant shades of red, yellow and blue and a large glass wall overlooks the pool below and the sea afar. The food tastes just as vibrant: corn cake appetizers, original Mexican Caesar salads and fish with roasted shrimp. After dinner and dessert, their waiter arrives with a covered silver tray.

"For you," Andy says.

She smiles, lifting the round silver lid. Inside is a cream-colored envelope. She twirls the card between her fingers, running it slowly across the lip of her wine glass.

He shifts in his seat. "You're driving me crazy."

"Good," she whispers. Finally, she opens the card.

> *Thank you.*
> *I love you,*
> *Andy*

Simple words to wrap up a complicated period of their lives.

When they get up to leave, Lauren proudly grabs Andy's hand, hoping to broadcast her decision to curious diners. They pass the hostess stand where a few couples are waiting for their tables. Marco stands there, holding a large straw bag.

"Mr. Hayden," he says, handing the bag to Andy.

"Thank you, Marco." The waiting guests and Lauren take notice.

"Enjoy the rest of your evening, Ms. Logan," Marco says. She flashes him a flirty smile as they leave.

"What's this?" she asks, tugging at the bag.

"Our after-dinner activity." He smiles, grabs her hand and quickly pulls her out the back glass doors of the resort. They race down the stairs to the sandy beach, near where their tent was last night.

"Here. These are for you," he says, pulling a pair of sequined ballet-style shoes from the bag. "I figured you can't walk barefoot around shells and rocks because of the healing cuts on your feet."

Hand over her heart, she trades her platform pumps for the flats.

They walk for a while down the beach, hand in hand, as the waves take turns trying to get them wet.

"This looks good," Andy says, pointing to a spot near some rocks. He sets the bag down and pulls out a large blanket, two glasses, a bottle of wine and a second smaller blanket.

"Two blankets?" she asks.

"One for cuddling."

Seconds later, he has set up a cozy camp. Nose-to-nose they snuggle, wrapped tightly together with the extra blanket.

They laugh when he struggles to open the wine. She lies back, stretching her feet in the air so the moonlight catches the flashy sequins of her shoes. After enjoying themselves for about an hour, he sits her up and takes her hands.

"Do you remember the first time we sat on the beach like this?" Before she can answer, he continues. "It was the beach at the Sand Club, when we snuck out at midnight."

"Oh, I remember," she says, smiling.

"I made a promise to you that night, that until such time as we were ready, our silver rings would remind us of each other. But I messed it up the first time, so I brought you back to a beach to try it again."

From his pocket he pulls out her silver ring.

"My ring!"

"Our rings meant more to me than I ever believed they would," Andy says, swallowing hard. "The fact that you kept yours even when I didn't made me realize how I have to earn the right to put this back on your hand. I'd like you to have this ring back and I want to make another promise." He picks up her right hand.

"I have to build back your trust. This ring will remind me to keep working. Because it's my goal and my dream for you to trust and love me enough to one day accept my ring of marriage." He pushes the ring on her finger.

Her eyes are as wide as the round ring. *One day accept his—ring of marriage?*

"And," he continues, "I made a big mistake taking my ring off my finger. And I made a bigger mistake throwing it away. But I want to wear a promise ring like yours, so…" He reaches into his pocket and produces a matching silver ring, just like his original, and just like hers. "I had this made. I want to put this on my own hand, because I am not going to break this promise to myself." The ring waits in his open palm.

"Are you sure I can't put it on you?" she asks.

"No…but I want you to see this."

He holds the ring closer. Initials have been engraved inside the silver band: D T L A.

"D, T, L, A?" she asks. "Do time Lauren Andy? Do this Lauren Andy? Dinner time Lauren Andy?"

"Not even close," he laughs. "I had this engraved D T L A to remind me: don't throw love away." And he pushes the ring on his finger.

A soft breeze blows across their beach camp. Their foreheads are pressed together as they both look down at their rings.

"I love my ring. And I love you," Lauren says.

"I love my ring, and absolutely everything about you," Andy says.

It's after midnight and Lauren lies awake, next to Andy. The full moon casts a soft light through their open curtains. And it's just enough light for her to see his perfect, sleeping face.

His rest seems so peaceful. Her forgiveness gave him that peace. They made it; they really made it. Regrets might come later, or maybe they won't. Some people won't agree with her. Many of her fans wanted her to get back with Johnny. But Johnny's love is in the past. She wants Andy.

Still, even with happiness warming her heart, there's a strange feeling in her gut again. She felt it once before, briefly, the night they first came face to face after Plebeian's inaugural concert. It's an odd, unsettling feeling of fear.

But there's nothing to be afraid of. This is the man she's wanted all her life; this is the man she's always loved! Even through her hurt and anger she loved him.

Damn logic and fear. She's going with love.

[TWENTY-EIGHT]

She knows the invitation is hers to extend; she has a hunch he is waiting for it.

Lauren lowers her eyes, grinning. "Do you have plane reservations home?" she asks over their morning breakfast on the terrace; their last breakfast in Cabo. "I know someone who could give you a ride."

Andy's eyes lower too. "I did have reservations but they are so late in the day, and so commercial."

She leans back, holding her cup of coffee. "I've got a place for you to stay too," she says with a teasing smile. "A small fixer-upper but it should meet your needs."

He reaches for the coffee pot. "I know your place. Nice. Comfortable. It could work for me." He slowly pours his coffee. His eyes look devious as he takes a drawn-out sip, "I could make it work for you too."

Before they leave their retreat paradise, they have some important explaining to do. They call Aiden, Lee and Brittney first, and judging from their happy screams they are pleased with the news.

Next is Lynette. "The rumors have already started. I got calls last night."

Then Lauren sends a group text to her closest friends, including the guys in the band. It's a safe bet everyone wants to know how the retreat is going.

"Getting ready to leave Mexico and I'm bringing Andy home with me"

Then she sends a quick request to Tish.

"Can you grab the H pillow? In my bottom dresser drawer. May need stitches on side where I punched the stuffing out. Put on the master bed pls. Tks!"

"I should probably text Josh," Lauren says.

Andy sits still, watching her type.

After a few messages back and forth, Lauren shares her exchange.

"I told him I got my guy back," she says. Andy slowly smiles. "He thinks I should change your contact in my phone to luckiest guy on the planet."

"Now I like this guy," Andy says, just as her phone pings with another message.

"Josh again," she says. "He'd like to have your number. He wants to call you sometime to be sure you know how lucky you are."

Andy nods. "Lauren, I will never forget how lucky I am."

An hour later, Marco arrives to escort them to their waiting car. Several photographers have gathered, finding the resort after Andy and Lauren's public dinner last night and since her plane has been moved. Andy and Lauren walk together, firmly holding hands.

Seeing Frank standing next to the car makes it all the more real. Andy left one Friday in January and two months later he is coming home. She gives Marco a strong hug and a soft kiss. "You are magic, Marco," she says, squeezing his chubby, now lipstick-stained cheek.

Andy shakes his hand. "Perfect execution. I'm very pleased with the result," he says, smiling towards Lauren.

"Me as well, Mr. Hayden," Marco says, smiling. "We do weddings here, I should mention."

Frank holds their door open and they innocently place their right hands on the car door in full view of the photographers. Let these rings send a message to the world: Lauren Logan and Andy Hayden are back together.

* * *

Normalcy returns day by day. The thought of what Andy did often crosses Lauren's mind, but she refuses to let it poison her future. Trying not to obsess over what happened is a hard thing to learn.

Andy continues to work since he had returned to his job when they were apart. He feels work was a big part of his identity that he lost too soon after dating Lauren. Even though his relationship with a celebrity is a distraction, he wants to keep his job. His things are moved back in the house and the lease on his downtown loft is cancelled. Brittney has reclaimed her bedroom and is already grinding on Lee's nerves. The sound of his complaining delights Lauren.

The guys in the band have been hanging around the studio more often lately, working on a song Plebeian will be performing in April. Davis has arranged an appearance on a popular television vocal talent search show and they only have about a month to prepare. The five of them in the band will meet with the show contestants and then play a new song live for the results show.

Life moves along normally for three weeks after their retreat. Until one evening when Ryan's voice comes over the intercom.

"Lynette has come through the hut and will be here shortly."

Lynette arrives just as Lauren and Andy finish dinner with the kids. She heads for Lauren's study and Andy and Lauren follow her.

"The kids can't hear us, right?" Lynette says as Andy closes the doors.

"Right. They're all upstairs now. What is it?" Lauren asks.

"I got a tip that this might come out tomorrow." Lynette opens her email and clicks on a message. It's a draft article for a TV gossip show. The headline reads:

Marcia Speaks: An Exclusive Interview With The Woman Who Stole Andy Hayden's Heart

Lauren pushes back her chair. "Just rip off the scab and squeeze the blood out."

Andy leans toward the screen, his lips mouthing *oh my God* as he skims the article.

Marcia says Andy fell in love with her, and that he never loved Lauren. She has a video where he admits it. He only loved Lauren for her money and fame, but got tired of that and felt trapped. Marcia doesn't want Andy back; she just wants everyone to know the truth.

Andy clicks on the link, looking at Lauren with his eyebrows drawn together as the video loads. "Baby, I don't know what will happen next."

Her chest feels like it's filled with rocks. She nods and he clicks play.

In a dark bedroom, he's sitting naked in bed, with only the corner of a sheet barely covering his lap. His hair is a wild mess, his face is several days unshaven and his eyes are weighted from alcohol. He's speaking right to the camera. And he's talking about Lauren.

"Lauren doesn't fucking get it…" he slurs.

Andy slams the computer mouse to stop the video, jumps out of his chair and stomps out of the room without a word.

Lauren's tears come easy. "What do you call this situation?" she asks Lynette, who nervously fiddles with the smashed computer mouse.

Lynette looks up with sad eyes. "Nuclear."

Lauren's instinct tells her where to find him: outside by the pool, in the safety of their double lounge chair. She eases down next to him and reaches for his hand. It's soft, limp, devastated. He says nothing, his eyes lost in sadness. What a huge embarrassment, naked and drunk in a video. The video is much worse than the photographs that came out before. This…coming out now…might cost him his job. It definitely will be perceived as a setback to their recovery.

But suddenly Lauren doesn't perceive this as a setback. In fact, she sees the opposite.

This is an opportunity to finally crush the woman who slept with her man.

She sits up straight, facing Andy. "I know someone. Let's get inside and get to work." She squeezes his hand and leads him back to the study.

Within ninety minutes Todd Peppers arrives at the front door, not to deliver legal papers but to prepare all legal options to defend Andy. They call in Lesley to be Andy's spokesperson, since Lynette primarily represents Lauren and Plebeian and this is an issue Andy has to defend himself. Frank calls the private investigators that followed Andy and they provide additional details on Lawson's criminal charges, her questionable debt sources and photographs of the drug deal they captured on the beach.

Andy becomes stronger and involved in the process as Todd shows him that he can defend himself, even if his actions seem indefensible. Lauren excuses herself from the room so he can fight his fight.

By ten a.m. the next morning, the story that was to be released has disappeared. Todd had confronted her with so much evidence of her illegal life, she recanted. She told the gossip show producer that the video was a fraud so they wouldn't run it. Lesley was ready to launch a counter-smear campaign to discredit Lawson, but she never had to pull the trigger. It was the worst fourteen-hour crisis they've ever had, that no one ever knew about.

"If Lauren supports you, I do too," Todd says, nodding to Lauren as he shakes Andy's hand goodbye. "I'll keep an eye on everything, Andy. This will be the last time you will hear from Marcia Lawson."

"Good!" Lauren shouts.

After Todd leaves, Andy pulls Lauren close, the warmth of his exhausted body softly pressing against hers. "Oh baby, what would I do without you?" he whispers.

"Me? How about Lynette?" Lauren turns to Lynette and Lesley, who are packing up their things. "How did you ever get that tip?"

"A good favor usually gets returned in this business," Lynette says. "Remember Franz? Your first date night photos we gave him the exclusive on? He made six digits selling those photos and he never forgot it. His brother works for that gossip show and gave him the tip."

Andy pulls back from their embrace.

"Well then, when we surprise everyone and get married, we'll give Franz that exclusive too," he says.

Lesley drops her tablet.

Lynette's face sinks in shock. "If you guys are going to get married, I'm gonna need a whole new set of situation codes."

[TWENTY-NINE]

It seems impossible, but three weeks have passed without major drama, scandal or tragedy. Could this be the beginning of the new normal?

Johnny, Michael, Oliver, Doug and Lauren are back together making beautiful, marketable music. They have worked for two weeks on a song they'll perform for the televised vocal talent show. They chose *You're Never Forgiven,* written from the abundance of drama in Lauren and Andy's lives. On an emotional scale of one being numb and ten being unhinged, Lauren rates singing this song as a twelve. Especially since this will be her first performance since the Andy scandal.

They are heading to Los Angeles for four days. There is one full day of taping where they'll coach the eight young finalists, and then they have a two-day break before their live performance. Andy decides to come after their break, joining Lauren for the live show. This will be the first time Lauren has left Andy alone since they got back together.

When they arrive in Los Angeles, they head straight for the taping. After a long day, the five members of Plebeian have secluded themselves inside Johnny's suite. A buffet of greasy take-out food is spread family-style on the table, except for Lauren's salad which she isn't sharing. None of the guys were interested in a healthy salad anyway.

There's a knock on the door.

"No!" Michael yells. "You still can't come in!"

"I'm hungry too!" Davis pleads though the door.

Johnny smiles. "Only the five of us are allowed in this room. Besides, those blue boat shoes make you look like the harbor master of a yacht club!"

Davis doesn't respond which means they've won, but they know in a few minutes he'll try again.

Lauren returns to the game they were playing. "It's your turn, Doug. And you can't do that eyebrow-raising thing you do with Michael where he magically reads your mind and speaks for you. *You* have to tell us something random."

"Fine," Doug mumbles. "I like someone, okay? And don't bother asking who."

Michael raises *his* eyebrow.

"Whoa! That's bigger than mine of wanting to run a marathon! And way more interesting than Oliver's bourbon collection," Lauren says. "Johnny, you're up."

"Amie's taught me how to bake soufflés and mine are pretty damn good."

"Wowzers, Johnny," Oliver cracks. "We've gone from talking about our next album, to whether we really want to sign a comprehensive deal for a world tour next year, to if we want to add a permanent third guitar player and now…soufflés?"

"Okay, Michael," Lauren says. "Tell us something random and please, make it better than a soufflé."

"Well, by Thanksgiving, I'll have a turkey in the house," Michael says. "And not one for the oven, but a little turkey for a crib. We're having a baby!"

Their silliness shifts to congratulations and the conversation turns to his baby plans. While he tells them Sunny's baby name ideas, Lauren keeps her eyes on Johnny. He's smiling, but he's not talking. Even after all this time, this doesn't appear to be an easy conversation for him.

On the day of the live show, Lauren's stomach is brewing with nerves and even the talent show contestants seem more relaxed than her.

It's tempting to quit rather than sing a song about the worst time of her life and then read scathing reviews about what she wore. If she left this band behind, she could disappear with Andy and enjoy a private life with him and the kids. If she stays in the band, it's eyes, critics and months away on a world tour.

She stands next to Johnny backstage, twisting her silver ring.

"You okay?" Johnny asks.

Johnny. His dreams have all come true. So have the other guys'. How can she let them down? Or the fans? *Plebeian has become bigger than you.*

"I'm a little nervous, but fine," she says, smiling. "You know, you are sweet to always ask but you don't need to for the rest of my life."

He smiles like he knows it. "When you are sad I feel it too and I just always want…"

"…to protect me. I know. My life was a mess but its back on track now."

"Is Andy in the audience? I haven't seen him yet."

"He just got here. He's planning to watch from backstage."

Johnny nods.

After the performance wraps, Johnny huddles them together. "Perfection showing the young people how it's done." Wearing a cheek-to-cheek smile, he leans toward Lauren. "Perfect vocals. Bravo."

Their huddle breaks and Johnny adds more approval by blowing her a kiss before he heads down the hallway.

She'll gladly take that air kiss!

Davis steps closer, giving her a hug. "You did it!"

"Without sunglasses! Or forgetting any lyrics!" she says, pulling back from their hug. "No need to take the plane home. I could skip all the way there!"

She glances down the hall and her celebration ends.

Johnny has Andy backed up against a wall. His face hovers inches from Andy's, his finger pointing in his face. *Holy crap!* She rushes towards them just as Johnny walks away, leaving a pale-faced Andy standing alone.

"What was that?" she says, clutching Andy's arm.

Andy slumps and watches Johnny walk away. "Something I deserved."

* * *

Hours after returning home, Lauren peels back her side of the satin sheets on their bed. Andy lies on his side, blankly staring at the ceiling. Not even the safety here helps him.

She gently rolls onto his bare chest, giving him a strong, warm hug. "You've been very quiet."

"I just have a lot on my mind right now," he says, slowly stroking her hair.

"Will you please tell me what Johnny said?" she asks, again.

He breathes in deep. "It was the obvious: not everyone has forgiven me as quickly as you have. And that I better not ever hurt you again."

"I'm sorry. So many people went through this with me and some still have strong opinions."

"And most of them have already told me. Back when I was working up my confidence to talk to you, I called everyone in the band. I took their punches then but I never did call Johnny. That was a mistake."

She hugs him tighter.

"I feel stuck by my past—still embarrassed," he says. "You moved on; you are so much stronger than me."

They lie in silence.

"I don't think I'm stronger. I still struggle with my fears. But maybe it's time to face yours. Maybe it's time for you to tell your story."

He stops stroking her hair.

"Let Lesley find a magazine or TV news show that would want to interview you."

He lies still, thinking. "But who would be interested in my story?"

"Any of our friends and fans who still doubt you. Plus every guy who did something stupid and couldn't get their girl back," she says, rolling off his chest and snuggling into his side. "And that's probably most men, right?"

Defensive publicity from an offensive position seems to be a perfect game plan for Andy. There is no urgency for him to get his side of the story out; he already got Lauren back. This isn't a tell-all story like Lawson tried to do. Andy is explaining what happened to him after the accident, what he did to fix it and how he still struggles to keep it fixed. Lesley pitches his story and by the end of the week she has several producers and editors interested.

Andy and Lesley choose a feature interview with a weekly men's health and lifestyle magazine. The interview will take place at the end of the week at Andy and Lauren's home.

On the day of the interview, Lauren leaves the house so there's no chance she'll be pulled in for questions or photographs. She's long overdue for a lunch with her old neighborhood friends. But her small lunch with three former neighbors turns into a bigger affair when several other chatty neighbors show up too. Lauren learns that the old lady who constantly watered her dead grass now owns six cats and that the attractive but weird guy in the cul-de-sac now keeps his blinds closed and still lets his kids run wild. By the time Lauren arrives home, she has a headache from listening to their snarky gossip and from smiling for dozens of cheesy selfies.

The closed doors of the living room mean Andy's interview is still going on and chances are they'll be busy in there for awhile. She decides to step out to the pool and her favorite lounge chair to get a little sun, try to get rid of her headache and count her blessings that she still doesn't live back on 'Drama Drive'.

About an hour later, Andy, Lesley and the photographer catch Lauren by surprise, coming out to the pool to take photos. Andy's eyes zoom straight to Lauren's bathing suit, or what he calls his "lucky suit." She is wearing the black bikini he first saw in the Phoenix hot tub and to him, that bikini means "let's play."

She scrambles to get out of their way, quickly tying her black sarong around her hips. But she's no match for Andy's playful grab. His hands quickly wrap around her waist from behind while her straight, damp hair falls across her makeup-free face.

The photographer snaps a flurry of pictures over Lesley's quick objections.

He stops, lowers his camera and looks at the digital images.

"These are amazing; very natural. Are you sure you don't want us to consider these for the layout?" he asks.

Andy and Lesley look at the images on the camera and then to Lauren for approval.

"This is totally Andy's call," Lauren says. "If the photos make me look fat then he's the one stuck in an article with pictures of a fat girlfriend." She shrugs, tightening the knot on her sarong and walking back into the house.

One week later, Lesley comes to the house with a big manila envelope.

"Hot off the press and two days before they hit the newsstands," she cheerfully exclaims, meeting Lauren and Andy in the kitchen.

"And?" Andy asks when Lesley opens the envelope and reaches in for the magazine.

"You are one lucky guy," she says, holding up the issue.

Andy is the cover story! His photo looks so good Lauren kisses the cover.

The headline reads: *Andy Hayden, The Lucky Guy.*

Lauren and Andy start tugging with each other to see who can open the issue first. Lesley laughs. "It's a solid article, I already read it."

The inside spread is four pages total, the first page on the left has an inside headline that reads: *How the High School Crush Got His Girl, Lost Her, Then Got Her Back.*

The entire facing page is the photo of them by the pool.

"Wow, that did come out good," Lauren say, looking fast to confirm that the little fabric on her black bikini covers what it should.

"It really is the perfect photo, because it shows you both very casual, very affectionate," Lesley says.

The other photos of Andy make him look like a professional model and the article is candid where he admits his mistakes without trashing Chase or even mentioning Lawson by name.

"This is huge," Lesley says. "You got your story out, you got to put yourself in a new light and you helped Lauren validate her decision to take you back."

Lauren grins. *Victory!* The press who stalk her life just helped her get it back.

That night they lie in bed holding up the magazine. His eyes gleam; he hasn't stopped grinning. Finally, his story—a brutally honest and difficult story—is out in his words.

She turns the page and points to one of his pictures, slowly tracing her finger over various parts of his body. "You see…after I'd undo that last button, my hand would go right there…"

It doesn't take long for him to want the real thing.

He turns the page back to the photo with them together, pointing to her lucky suit. "Let's play." His hands move from the magazine to the parts of her body the suit barely covered.

She loses her grip on the magazine and it drops to the floor; her hands now busy with an entirely new issue.

* * *

The metal ball rattles too loudly every time he moves the can.

How stupid; he is running out of paint.

He used too much on the art gallery window and might not have enough to finish her apartment door.

He silences the noisy can by holding the bottom with his left hand, as his right index finger pushes the nozzle, freeing the red spray.

All he needs is the last of the four letters and, now, he is done.

This is the first chance he's been able to pay her this visit.

And since she ruined everything, this is what she gets.

This is what she deserves.

He quickly steps down the outside staircase of the apartment, glancing over his pleasing work in the parking lot. The Camry is now flat to the ground, the weight of the car too much for its slashed tires. The side of the car sparkles as the deep creases of the knife marks catch the moon's light.

He quietly slips into his car and lights up a cigarette.

He turns back for a final look.

This will be the last time he will visit 73290 Stockton Street. And he's left her apartment door with blood-red letters perfectly describing her: SLUT.

[THIRTY]

Ever since the magazine article was published, Andy has been wearing a smile from morning to night. Lauren has caught him smiling in his sleep too.

She can hear his humming in the hallway, coming closer towards her study. He bursts into the room, eyes blazing with excitement. "Hey, let's go out to dinner tonight!"

She slumps behind her desk, staring at her phone as she finishes a call.

"Whoa, baby! What's wrong?" He rushes to her side, kneeling. "Who was on the phone?"

Just the grim reaper. "Davis," she says, reaching for his hands. "We're signed; he's booked it. By the beginning of next year, we're going on a world tour."

Andy's happy expression flies right out the door. "Okay, fine. You got this; we got this. It's May now…plenty of time."

She breathes in deep. "I can get ready by then. I mean, Michael and Sunny will have their baby by the time we leave for tour. So if he can leave a baby behind and do this, there's no reason I can't." She swallows the lump wedged in her throat.

He presses his forehead to hers.

Suddenly, he pulls back, his face softens with a grin and his eyebrow arches. "So let's not waste a moment together."

She can't help but smile. "Oh? What do you have in mind?"

"Well, to not waste a moment, let's go to where we've had our best moments together."

Um…bed?

His smile stretches. "Let's go to Clearwater Beach and the Sand Club this weekend."

* * *

The first time they came to the Sand Club they arrived separately to avoid the paparazzi. Now, they arrive together to manager Gregory's warm welcome. Gregory has arranged the same suite they've often enjoyed with the two balconies, two sofas and that great kitchen. The only new things are a fresh coat of white paint and wall-to-wall white plush carpeting, making the room bright and cheerful.

They enjoy a walk on the beach before eating dinner at Saffron's, the hotel's upscale restaurant. On Saturday they eat thick grouper sandwiches for lunch from the room-service menu and then nap on their balcony chairs overlooking the Gulf of Mexico.

For dinner Saturday, Andy has made reservations at a nearby French restaurant.

Lauren plans to wear a short black skirt and black knit top. But right now she only has the skirt on and a frisky idea for how to put on her shirt. "I love choosing an outfit to wear knowing that you are the man who will take it off." She stands bare-chested in front of Andy with a teasing smile, holding out her shirt. "But can you put it on me first?"

"I'd rather stand here and take in this view," he says, his eyes glowing hot. He snatches the shirt and grabs her hips. "Hold still," he wickedly whispers.

Oh my.

Slowly…ever so slowly, he moves his hands up, brushing her bare skin, up higher and higher until he raises her arms. Nose-to-nose with him, her arms are in the air, she's bound by his hold and it's making her hot everywhere. He slides the shirt over her arms and head, lowering his lips for a trail of kisses from her neck, down her bare chest, to her waist as he slowly pulls the shirt down her body and lets her arms go.

Her vision blurs and her heart races. Why hasn't she asked him to dress her every morning?

"Is this good enough for you to remove too?" Andy stands back to model his tight, white button-down shirt and black pants.

She's still trying to catch her breath.

"There's nothing you can put on that I can't take off." She squeezes the bulge she notices in his pants. "I'll take care of removing that later too."

Their delay getting dressed has Frank tapping his feet, waiting with Andy's blue BMW in front of the hotel for the quick drive down the street.

Their table at the restaurant has a splendid sunset view of the Gulf and they eat coq au vin and feed each other spoonfuls of chocolate mousse for dessert.

"This getaway was a great idea," she says, squeezing Andy's hand as they walk down the long hallway leading back to their suite. "I cannot wait to collapse in bed and thank you tonight."

Andy fumbles with the key card, seemingly unnerved, trying several attempts to open the door. *Guess he's excited to see how she plans to thank him.* Finally, he opens the suite door and walks in first. *That's strange.* Usually she goes first. She follows him inside and stops cold with what she sees and smells.

Is this a dream? Everything in their suite, absolutely everything, is now white. The sofas are white linen, the lamps are white with white shades, the cornice boards over the balcony doors and the floor-to-ceiling drapes are now white. Even the dining room table and surrounding chairs are white.

Every surface has a glass vase with white roses. They're everywhere; by the bar, on the coffee table, by the lamps—white roses everywhere!

Andy's "gotcha" grin gives him away. She grabs his hand and pulls him farther inside the living room, looking around.

"This…this!? How did you do this?"

His smile isn't telling.

"You're kidding me! This is so romantic!" She keeps looking around, finding more white things as he leads her farther into the suite. Her hands slap to her face, trying to contain her surprise. She spins around to look at the bedroom. The comforter is white and in the center of the bed is a square white pillow embroidered with a silver H.

"A white H pillow!" she squeals. Two matching rectangle pillows are on each side of the H pillow and they are embroidered too: Mr. and Mrs.

"Even the bed was changed!" she says, turning back to Andy.

Stop. Wait. The bed! What? Her wide eyes turn back to look at the bed.

The Mr. pillow is on his side.

The Mrs. pillow is on her side.

The reason why their hotel suite has been changed to white hits her as if she had been hit with the pillows she's looking at.

Shaking, she slowly turns back to Andy.

He nervously bites his smiling lip, his eyes lit with joy. He reaches for her hands.

"I have something to say." His hazelnut-olive eyes sparkle in the candle lit room and his grip tightens on her quivering hands.

Lauren's heart pounds harder than when she first took the stage as an unknown singer at the Academy Awards.

Andy looks at her shaking hands, then up to her eyes.

"My life is good with you. I've never felt this much love. You've made me strong, stronger than I ever imagined I could be. Something this good is something I want forever. I may be late to the game, but I'm going to seize every moment I can now." He looks down, breathes in deep and then looks back up with flushed cheeks and a beaming smile.

"It would be the honor of my life if you would be my wife." He lowers himself to one knee, squeezing her hands. "Marry me."

Emotion shakes her body. All those years of dreaming of him and now…now this moment of forever. He's on his knee asking her the question she always dreamed he would! Then suddenly she realizes: he didn't ask a question—he told her what he wants and is telling her what to do. Her head turns to the side. "Wait—is that a question or a demand?"

His smile twists as he looks up at her, still on one knee, still holding her hand. "Well, I didn't get you until late and I already screwed up and lost you once, so I thought I'd go with a statement rather than leave it to chance with a question so please just say you'll do it."

"Oh yeah I'll do it!"

He stands and pulls her close for a kiss that leaves her breathless, standing in a room, glowing in all white, smelling like a flower shop.

He reaches down to the coffee table and a white velvet box, opening the lid to reveal a cushion-cut diamond sitting on three diamond filled bands. He slips the sparkling ring on her finger. "Thank you for your trust, your love, your friendship, your strength, your body…"

She stops him. "Thank you for you." He sweeps her into a spinning embrace.

"How…how did you do this?" she asks again, looking around.

"I have people."

"This was an ambush! A good ambush! Who was involved this time?"

"Only Frank knows, actually, and only because I needed to keep you at the restaurant for at least two hours."

They sit on the sofa, her bare legs across his lap. Her short skirt struggles to keep her upper legs covered. She can't keep her eyes off of her left hand and the sparkling ring.

"Lauren Hayden fits me very well."

"You want to take my name? Even with your career?"

"You bet I want your name. I've been doodling *Lauren Hayden* since high school."

She begs him to tell her more about the arrangements and he finally gives in. Gregory was his partner in crime. Andy had the idea to transform a place she loved into a whitescape and had everything redone.

"I couldn't believe you noticed the new white paint and carpet," he says. "Those were the only things they couldn't do in a two-hour turn-around."

Four rooms on this floor were blocked off for this; two of them had all of the white furniture and flowers and the other two is where the old furniture, drapes and bedding went.

"It's a nice feeling to get *this* many roses from a man."

"I was hoping to be the guy who has given you the most."

Lauren softly strokes his cheek. He must have taken the roses Josh sent as a challenge, one he has obviously won.

She tugs one of the roses out of a vase, breathes in the sweet, fragrant scent and then slowly rubs it down the side of his face. "You know, so many flowers, and I've never…" His eyes drowsily blink with her rubbing. "I've never slept in a bed of rose petals before. Maybe we can take some of these and…"

He snatches the rose, suddenly wide awake. "I'm way ahead of you, Mrs. Hayden-to-be." He lifts her off his lap, pulls her up and gently cups her head with his hands. "Come to bed with me."

Her insides quiver. Hand-in-hand, he leads her to the bedroom and every inch of her skin tingles in anticipation with each step. He pulls back the white comforter where thousands of white rose petals are ready to soften their skin. *Oh hell yeah!* She slides into the mass of softness, posing with one hand on her hair and the other on her hip. "How about my new fiancé join me?"

No feeling has ever been this intense: the fragrance, the softness, the white glow of the room with the touch of Andy's bare skin and the fullness of his body.

He is the love of her life and now she going to marry him.

[THIRTY-ONE]

Urban conveniences sit next to archaeological relics, the skyline punctuated by the unmistakable dome of St. Peter's Basilica. Welcome to Rome.

The charter bus carrying the band members of Plebeian has just reached the city. Oliver gets up from his seat and leans over Andy and Lauren.

"The Coliseum—right over there—see?" Oliver points.

"Got it," Lauren says, squeezing Andy's hand.

Who cares about sightseeing or this trip to Rome to announce Plebeian's world tour? She's completely focused on her and Andy's surprise wedding in two days.

It's been two months since they got engaged and Lauren tweeted five words: *"He asked. I said yes."*

Since then, fans have gone crazy predicting when and where the success-failure-success couple will get married. Lauren and Andy's original plan was a fall wedding in Mexico, but even with Marco protecting them, they were worried about their privacy.

Instead, they decided to take advantage of this world tour announcement trip. The entire band, plus an entourage of family and friends, a few select fans, and their record company executives, have been enjoying a Mediterranean cruise. Davis came up with the idea as a way to announce next year's world tour. Andy and Lauren made sure Christy and Cal, Bobby and Cheryl as well as Andy's sister and

Lauren's mom and brother made the trip. Their family and friends have no idea when the cruise stops in Santorini, Greece in forty-eight hours, they will be surprised with a wedding.

Lesley and Lynette greet the bus at the downtown Rome hotel's loading dock, leading the group to the ballroom. A massive metal wire globe of the world with giant pins placed on the locations for the tour is on stage. International media and some local fans and dignitaries are already gathered in the ballroom, ready to meet the members of Plebeian.

Oliver, Johnny, Michael, Doug and Lauren take their places on stage and announce their concert schedule for a twenty-one city tour throughout Europe and Asia.

As they step off stage, Davis whispers to Lauren, "You knew this day would come."

"I can't believe I'm doing this tour next year," she says. "Seriously, if I didn't have the wedding to keep my mind occupied, I'd be going nuts."

"I'm happy for you," he says.

She leans towards him. "Thank you. It means a lot to me. I know you weren't completely on board with my decision to take Andy back."

"I wasn't. And I didn't trust him for a while. But I've seen how much he loves you. He was sorry. And you've helped straighten him out."

She gives him a hug as they continue their walk from the stage. "Thank you, for a lifetime of everything."

Davis is one of the few who knows of their surprise wedding. Aiden, Lee and Brittney know too, as do their wedding planners Frank, Lynette and Lesley, plus one special guest.

That evening the group returns to their cruise ship and instead of having a celebratory dinner at one of the ship's fancy restaurants, Johnny suggests dinner in the casual buffet. Their large group moves tables together and enjoys a casual dinner of pizza, sandwiches and soft-serve ice cream as other passengers smile and take photographs of them.

Their conversation is loud but the laughter is louder. Lauren remains quiet, watching Andy joke with Johnny and some of the guys from their record company. What a relief to see Johnny on friendly terms with Andy again.

While her ears fill with these happy sounds, her eyes stare out the window to the blue Mediterranean water. *How funny!* They are sailing towards Greece, for her wedding to Andy, on a cruise ship. After comparing her brain to a cargo ship and her heart to a cruise, now a cruise ship is taking her to marry Andy.

Andy and Lauren wake early as the ship glides into the calm waters of Santorini. They lie in bed; Lauren gathering warmth from Andy's bare chest in this quiet, peaceful moment before both of their lives change.

He smoothes back her hair, tenderly looking into her eyes. "I finally get the cute girl from high school that always had a boyfriend, don't I?"

She nods. "You bet."

"My greatest fear is losing you again. It makes me sick sometimes when I think of being without you."

She rolls her head to look up at him; her eyes inches from his as her fingertips stroke his face. "I waited too long for you to notice me. I'm not going anywhere now."

"I don't care if it is bad luck to see you before the wedding." Slowly he gives her a kiss that makes her want to fast-forward to the honeymoon.

"You are tempting me," she whispers, nipping his ear. "But I think it's bad luck or something to make love to your groom hours before your wedding."

"Nah…it's not." He kisses her harder.

She stops him. "Oh no…no way you are gonna get this before you marry me." She pokes him with tickles. "And you can't see my dress until I get to the church either!" Her poking pushes him out of bed and the ticking clock gets him out of the suite.

Their surprise plan has begun.

Everyone will meet for breakfast, just like a normal excursion day. Today, breakfast is in a private dining room, where tour guides will meet them to give them the day's sightseeing plan.

Davis will introduce their tour guides. In will walk Aiden and Lee, dressed in gray tuxedos, and Brittney in a pink, floor length formal gown.

The kids will announce everyone has one hour to change because their parents are getting married this morning.

The soft knock on Lauren's suite door means Davis has returned from revealing today's surprise. Frank lets him in.

"Was everyone surprised?" Lauren asks.

Davis grins like he's won the lottery. "We got them good. But you have two visitors that followed me back."

Figures! "Go ahead and let Johnny and Christy in."

Frank barely opens the door before Christy pushes into the room.

"You did this without telling me??" She wraps Lauren in a hug. "I'm so happy; what do you need? What can I get for you? Where's the dress?"

"Lara just hung it in the bedroom—go see."

Christy skips to the bedroom and Johnny moves closer. His shy smile says it all.

"There will be a lot of people staring at you today," Johnny says.

"I know," she says, smiling.

"You're going to be a beautiful bride."

"I know," she says, still smiling.

Lauren looks in Johnny's eyes, sending him a message with just her gaze. Happiness, history, memories: this subject has come up between them before. She launches a zinger to remind him.

"He asked me, Johnny."

Johnny slowly nods. He pulls her into a tight hug. "I know."

After a minute in each other's arms, Lauren pulls back. "Heads up, my bouquet is *so* heading Amie's way." He smiles. Then their special moment is interrupted by Christy's screams.

"Oh my God, how many diamonds are in this belt?"

Lauren drops Johnny's arms. "As many as I damn well wanted, my friend."

Their casually dressed friends who had been planning a day of sight-seeing have now changed to dressier clothes.

A tender delivers passengers to a private dock at Oia, where vans transport them from the pier to the church. A small group of locals has gathered to watch the arrivals for what they think is a typical wedding.

When all of the guests have been transported the tender returns to the ship for the next passenger: the groom. Andy wears a light gray, cutaway tuxedo jacket with a silver ascot, and rides with Aiden and Lee, his best men.

Ten minutes later, the tender returns for the bride and her maid of honor, Brittney. They carefully step into the rocking boat, along with the cruise ship captain who will perform the ceremony, Frank and a special guest; their favorite photographer Franz is getting another exclusive, just as Andy promised.

Brittney and Lauren hold hands as the boat speeds towards the coast. They seem to be heading towards snow-covered cliffs until their travel slowly reveals the iconic whitewashed houses of one of the most beautiful places on earth. Their car is waiting at the pier and within minutes, they pull up outside the church.

Lauren steps out of the car in her sleeveless, white silk, floor-length dress, draped with ivory lace, her waist cinched by a diamond-encrusted belt. The warm breeze picks up the wispy ivory-colored tulle from her headpiece as the five of them walk closer to the small, sixteenth-century church. They pass white homes and village store fronts. All of this white reminds her of Andy's whitescape proposal. Rays from the bright sun warm her skin and brighten her soul. She smiles for the locals and tourists and can tell from their surprised faces: they just recognized this isn't an average wedding after all. And it's no secret anymore.

Michael's impromptu piano playing seeps through the church walls, filling the entry courtyard with happy sounds. Without hesitation, Brittney marches past the weathered wooden church doors to start the processional. Aiden and Lee each extend an arm to their mother.

A few steps inside the church and Lauren can see Andy. His back is turned, facing the arrangement of white roses on the altar and the flickering white candles that light up the late morning air.

As if he can feel her, Andy turns. Now only ten rows of pews keep her from marrying the man of her dreams. With a supporting arm from each of her boys, she begins the happiest walk of her life.

[THIRTY-TWO]

The ferry's horn blows right on cue at seven a.m.

Now on day three of their honeymoon, Lauren and Andy are used to the blaring sound. The marina sits right below the cliff overhang of their villa in Positano, Italy. Andy rolls over to greet Lauren with a morning kiss.

"Your seven a.m. ferry kiss." Clearly the horn woke him up. Again.

The cruise ship still carrying their friends and family makes its final port of call today in Nice, France, before heading back to Barcelona. The newlyweds left the ship the day after their wedding to fly to Positano for their honeymoon: just Lauren, her husband plus a friendly party of four.

Frank and Ryan have joined them for logistics and security, along with their wives. Since Andy and Lauren just want to act like newlyweds, they didn't want Frank and Ryan bored in such a romantic town.

Today, Andy and Lauren decided to exchange wedding gifts. He wanted to wait a few days into the honeymoon, claiming his gift to her will keep her busy for days. Now *that* is a gift that she can't wait to open.

During breakfast on the warm patio overlooking the beach and marina below, he shyly slides what looks like a wrapped hardcover coffee table book across the table towards her.

"Hmmm…looks like a book?" she guesses. *A book is supposed to keep her interest during their honeymoon?* Her interest at the moment is her husband—who looks soft and yummy with his messy morning hair, tight shirt and cozy cotton sleep shorts. If a book is her gift she'd rather skip this whole gift thing and get him back in bed.

He nudges the book closer. She gives him a curious smile and rips off the wrapping paper.

"Best book ever!" she exclaims. "Beach house floor plans!"

"I know your dream is to have a home on the beach."

Right away she flips through the pages of layouts and photos, excited to see what ideas she can find. "You were right, this will keep me busy, even on our honeymoon!" As she quickly turns the pages, an envelope falls out.

"Go ahead. Open it," he says.

It's a copy of a contract. Andy has purchased a lot on the Atlantic coast in South Carolina, on Kiawah Island. "I had some extra money from a bank account and used it as a down payment for this lot."

Oh, baby. She puts her hands on her chest. That account was their original bank account, the one she signed over solely to his name with $200,000. He never spent that money during the time they were apart, saving it instead for something special.

"This will be our dream home; a design project for us both to work on," he says.

"It's perfect. All of my dreams are coming true. Thank you!"

Now she's ready to give Andy his gift. He picks up the heavy package, examining all sides.

"You've got me here; I have no clue!"

"Good!" she says, then becomes more serious. "I want to be sure you know my approach to our marriage and this is symbolic."

He rips open the paper, looking surprised. "You remembered."

Lauren nods. "I want our marriage to be strong, like this, and able to handle anything. I'm not going to worry about what you do and how you do it. It is hard for me sometimes, but I am learning not to obsess about the little things. So, I promise you, I do not care if you ever wash this with dish soap."

He smiles and stands up to kiss her, leaning over the table and the new cast iron skillet.

It is, after all, a second marriage for them both. He had freed himself from the domination of Janie and she had left the indifference of Cory. She's learned from her mistakes.

Sunshine and blue skies fill Lauren and Andy's honeymoon week, along with meals at Italian bistros, evening drinks on seaside chairs under colorful beach umbrellas, and drives up and down the Amalfi coast. Having Frank and Ryan and their wives with them ended up being fun. All of them enjoyed a wonderful Italian pizza dinner one evening in nearby Sorrento.

A little shopping was fun too, Lauren popping in and out of the endless boutiques on the narrow, winding streets of Positano. On the last night of their honeymoon, they return to a small boutique that had a lovely teal, lace sundress she was thinking of buying. Frank decides to wait outside while Andy goes with her to see it.

"Try it on," Andy says. "Now," his smile insists.

She heads to the dressing room and soon finds out why Andy wanted her to try it on. As she steps in the dressing room he slips in behind her, quickly closing the door.

"I wanted to see…you, Mrs. Hayden. And maybe that dress," he whispers, pressing his body against hers, backing her up to the dressing room mirror. His fingers glide down her skirt, his mouth on hers.

She pushes him away. "Stop!"

His hands drop and he frowns.

She grins. "I do believe this is my dressing room, sir. Take your seat." She pushes him down on the dressing room bench.

He sits down hard, and smiles.

Her private dressing room show begins. Every piece of clothing she wears slowly comes off while she teases him with every piece she removes. She presses his shoulders to keep him seated while she straddles his lap.

"Mmmm…you've never given me a lap dance before," he whispers.

Her mouth grazes his ear. "That's not what I was gonna give you."

His eyes bulge.

She unzips his shorts and lowers her head. His groans softly grow.

Minutes later, they step out of the boutique with smiles on their faces and the teal sundress in a shopping bag.

Frank turns to greet them. "Got what you wanted?"

"Just what I wanted," Lauren says.

"Completely satisfied," Andy says with a beaming smile.

* * *

Even a honeymoon has to come to an end and the approaching world tour means Plebeian must start rehearsals. Andy and Lauren head back home and get back into their daily routine. Andy still works every day. They don't need the money, but he likes the challenge and the balance it gives him in his life. Lauren's days are spent practicing with the guys in the home studio, or in a warehouse in Lakeland, thirty minutes from Tampa, where a company has set up the tour stages for their rehearsals.

When Lauren is home, she and Andy immerse themselves in each other and their plans for their beach house. They've chosen a floor plan and construction is about to begin, but Lauren has yet to see the property. They plan a weekend trip with the kids to their South Carolina beach lot.

When they pull up to the lot, her soul feels like it belongs here. Palm trees and sea grasses fill the site and as they walk towards the middle of the lot, the view of the sandy beach appears. Aiden and Lee go exploring down the small hill to reach the beach, leaving a path to show where future wooden stairs could go.

"The metal roof is going to be perfect! All rooms with this view and the pool here. Perfect!" she says, pointing at bushes and survey stakes. Her arms fling around Andy's waist. His hug feels as wonderful as the house she was describing.

"I told you before, Lauren, I'd live in a shack with you."

Brittney sits in a patch of smooth grass, staring out at the water, her beautiful brown hair blowing in the breeze. Aiden and Lee have walked farther down the beach, being nosy by looking in the backs of other people's expensive beach homes. Andy and Lauren stand at the edge of the lot, tight in their embrace. She buries her face in his chest.

Life is so good. She's stronger with Andy's love, strong enough to handle this upcoming world tour. Even if his work schedule keeps him away for half the tour, she can handle it.

But if it was up to her, Andy would quit his job and she wouldn't do the tour at all. She doesn't like the idea of being so far from Andy and the kids, touring for so long.

And someone else she knows doesn't like it either.

* * *

He is all alone, bent over, clutching his stomach, rocking back and forth in the chair.

This is too much, too much.

There are too many details, just too many.

He presses his hands hard to his stomach.

Empty medicine bottles lie in the drawer nearby; the drawer able to hide his stolen and prescription secrets. He's lucky no one can see him like this right now.

The pressure of his hands eases the stomach pain since cigarettes and joints don't help anymore. But it's the rocking that helps him think. He just has to think of something. Think!

She will be gone too long. Too long.

This is just too much.

[THIRTY-THREE]

The late-afternoon clatter of pots and pans in the kitchen has Andy's full attention. He swivels on a barstool, watching Tish. "I'm starving," he says with hungry, puppy-dog eyes.

"But I'm making this chili for tomorrow night," Tish says. "I thought since the boys are out late at band practice and Brittney is at Janie's that you and Lauren were going out?"

Lauren walks into the kitchen. "We were but we didn't have—quote—supervision. Frank is at his daughter's strings concert. Davis is swamped upstairs with tour stuff. I know you have to leave soon and if Ryan went out with us, then no one would be here when the boys came home." She turns to face Andy. "So, your dinner is going to magically appear. I just called Wes from the deli."

"Mmmm…I'd rather have a big steak from City Grille," Andy says with a raised eyebrow.

"Ohhh…that does sound better! But there's no way I can call Wes back. He loves to come over here and I'd crush him if I cancelled our order."

Tish picks up the home phone. "I'll call Wes and break his heart." She walks around the corner to make the call.

"Hey, let's ask Michael and Sunny to come," Andy says.

"They just had a baby!"

"Then they're probably real hungry."

"We should be bringing *them* food!"

"I'm sure they'd come with us."

"Honey, they are overwhelmed. Simone was born three weeks early!" Lauren says.

Tish walks back into the room. "Simone Ivy Casper is such a beautiful name too."

"Deli order cancelled?" Lauren asks.

"Yes, and you were right, Wes was disappointed."

"So, Johnny and Amie just went to North Carolina, right?" Andy asks.

"Yeah, they aren't an option," Lauren says. "But you know, we don't need company and we don't need supervision."

"You sure?"

"You drove me to City Grille on our first date! We'll call ahead to the valet and restaurant manager like Frank usually does. I bet Ryan won't even know we've left the house."

She glances to over to Tish.

"If you don't tell Ryan, then Frank might be as upset as Wes is right now," Tish says, her eyes lowering in a scolding stare as she slices a tomato.

Ridiculous. They'll be fine. If she told Frank now, he might leave his daughter's performance to come drive them! She and Andy can dash in and out of the restaurant. Fans aren't going to bother her. And besides, she's about to leave for a world tour where Andy will only be able to come to half of the shows because of his work schedule. Time is running out for dates like this with her husband.

They quickly change to dressier clothes, Andy in a crisp white dress shirt and khaki dress pants and Lauren in white, low-cut blouse, tight black pants and red wedge heels. Andy tosses the Ferrari key fob in the air, practically skipping to the garage. "We never get a chance to drive this car together."

"Our car looks good and so do we," Lauren says, grinning.

"A simple, fun date with my hot wife." He pulls out of the auto courtyard, one hand on the wheel, the other squeezing the inside of her thigh. Lauren's hands are in the air, waving to the security camera that Ryan is surely watching.

Sixty seconds later, Ryan texts asking where they're going. Lauren responds.

"Andy kidnapped me; requires steak as ransom. We'll be home in a few hours. My phone tracker is on."

The valet manager eagerly shifts from foot to foot as they pull up outside of the restaurant. They are out of the car and inside the restaurant in twenty seconds, not even noticed by shoppers at the adjacent mall. The City Grille manager escorts them to their private table for two.

The warm, butter-seared filet still makes Lauren's mouth water even thirty minutes after she had eaten it. When their dessert and martinis are finished, the restaurant manager confirms their car has been pulled around, and the two head towards the revolving doors.

"Do you remember coming through these on our first date?" Lauren asks.

"The day my life changed? Sure I do," he says. "When we walked through these doors that parking lot exploded with camera flashes."

Once outside, Andy reaches for Lauren's hand and she steps off the curb, glancing down. There, in the gutter, lies a crushed cigarette butt. *How random.* Oh how far they've come from the day when Tish found cigarette butts outside their home. Lauren had thought Andy might be hiding something, or that some stranger had gotten their kicks smoking while they gawked at her house. None of those old suspicions had come true.

Car in sight, Andy leans in, making funny pretend paparazzi camera sounds just like they heard on their first date. She laughs at his hilarious noises as they step towards the car.

She steps closer to the valet manager, standing next to her open car door. But he's not looking at her. He's not even paying attention to her car! For some strange reason he's looking at…

Andy is hurting her hand.

Someone screams.

She's falling.

Her head.

She's hit her head.

Everyone is so loud.

Why is Andy on top of her?

Her chest hurts.

Why is Andy yelling at her?

Fight? Fight??

She doesn't want to fight.

She just…wants…to sleep…

[THIRTY-FOUR]

Andy

Screams pierce the air, drawing diners from restaurants and shoppers from stores.

People start running from and people start running to.

A smiling man is violently tackled by the valet manager; his yells get muffled as his face is pushed to the ground.

Their cries and screams are meek compared to the agonizing screams of one man.

Andy is on the pavement, straddling his wife, screaming NO.

Lauren lies in the parking lot, her blood now staining her white blouse.

"Lauren!" Andy screams, ripping off his shirt, the buttons popping off from the pressure of his horrified pulls. He quickly stuffs the crisp white shirt against Lauren's chest to halt the bleeding.

Two young couples rush to Andy's side. One woman gently slips her shopping bag of clothes under Lauren's head. The other woman picks up Lauren's purse, which lies a few feet away. The men drop to their knees, adding their hands to Andy's to stop Lauren's bleeding.

Valet drivers struggle with the man, his mouth now free from the ground. "Now you can stay home with me!" he yells.

A few feet away, a bystander straddles a gun that had fallen when the valets subdued the man.

The City Grille manager rushes to Andy's side while the valet manager works to push people back. Waiters run from the restaurant with clean towels.

Lauren coughs under the pressure of Andy's hands and her eyes open.

"Fight! *Fight!*" Andy screams. Tears stream down his horrified face. "You have got to fight to stay with me, Lauren!"

Her eyes close.

The police arrive, followed by ambulances a few seconds later.

The valets turn the man over to the police. "You don't have to go now!" he yells as the police load him in the back of a cruiser.

The paramedics forcibly remove Andy and take over Lauren's care. He stands up for the first time, looking down at his blood-soaked wife. His bare chest and hands are stained red. The initial adrenaline rush fades, replaced with an overwhelming feeling of helplessness.

The restaurant manager quickly uses towels to wipe Andy's arms and chest, while one of the men pulls out a polo shirt from his shopping bag. He rips off the price tag and pulls the shirt over Andy's head, guiding Andy's limp hands through the sleeves.

The woman holding Lauren's purse offers it to Andy and asks if she can help him make any calls.

Andy looks up and slowly nods.

"Lynette. Call Lynette," he whispers and then looks back down at the paramedics immobilizing his wife with a backboard.

The woman's hands shake with nerves as she opens the purse, finds Lauren's phone, the contacts and the name Lynette. She presses call.

"Davis. Davis is at the house, Ryan too," Andy says, pulling out his own phone and handing it to one of the men. "The boys are at band practice. Davis or Ryan needs to get the boys."

The man finds Davis in the contacts and presses call.

Andy stands thin, with four strangers by his side. Flashing lights from police cars and ambulances fill the night sky.

The paramedics have Lauren on a stretcher and begin to rush her to an ambulance, gesturing for Andy to run with them.

"Lynette's on her way," the woman says as she hands him Lauren's phone and purse.

"Davis will get the boys," the man says to Andy as he hands him his phone. A police officer standing nearby mumbles something into his walkie-talkie.

Their words sound blurry to him but he slowly nods. The police officer pushes Andy towards the ambulance.

Lynette

"Got it!" Lynette yells to her husband.

Finally, she snapped the ice-cream maker attachment to her stand mixer.

"Let's roll, baby," she says, picking up the vanilla-flavored mix while he starts filling a bowl with ice.

Her ringing phone lies on the counter. *Lauren.*

"Hold on, let me see how she's doing," she says to her husband, answering the call.

"Hey—how are you?"

"I'm not Lauren, my name is Tammy. I have Lauren's phone. Andy told me to call you. Lauren's been…Lauren's been shot! We are outside the restaurant. She was shot outside the restaurant!" the woman says.

Lynette drops the flavoring packet. "What? Who's this? What restaurant?"

"Andy said to call you. They are taking Lauren towards the ambulance now. It's serious; real serious. I have to give the phone back to Andy. He's gotta go. Please hurry."

The call disconnects.

"We have to leave *now*!" she screams to her husband as she runs to her den to get her laptop. He asks no questions and grabs their car key.

They both run out the door, leaving the bowl of ice on the counter.

Davis

"Do you think this is too spicy?" Tish asks Davis, holding out a spoonful of chili.

He just came down from another late night of work in his office above the garage. He stopped in the house when he noticed Tish was still here. He takes a bite and starts fanning his mouth.

"Yeah…it's spicy. Lauren loves it that way but I know Lee won't," he says.

"I thought I should tone it down for him. I've always liked chili when it's served the second day, so I was making a batch for tomorrow," Tish says, turning off the stove and looking for a storage container.

Davis's phone starts ringing. It's Andy.

"Yo, I heard you kidnapped Lauren. Did your steak ransom get paid?" Davis asks.

"No, I mean yes. Davis, Andy asked me to call you. I have something very bad to tell you. Lauren's been shot," a strange man's voice blurts out.

"Who the hell is this?"

"I'm Brian, I have Andy's phone. He told me to call you. This is horrible. The ambulances are here."

Davis stiffens. "Where are you?"

"Outside the City Grille. They were leaving and someone shot her. Andy wants you to get the boys. He told me to tell you to get the boys. They are taking her now to Tampa Memorial Hospital. I have to give Andy his phone back. Please get the boys."

And the call disconnects.

Tish looks puzzled. "Lauren…was…what?"

"Shot? Did you hear what he said? That's what he said, right?" Davis asks. "Go upstairs and tell Ryan to call Frank. I'll get the boys." He grabs the Tahoe keys.

Within seconds he speeds out of the neighborhood and is weaving through traffic in a rush to get to the school. Soon a police car pulls behind him with lights flashing but he doesn't stop. *Throw me in jail later.* Nothing is going to stop him from getting to the school.

The police car works its way through traffic to pull next to Davis. To his surprise, the officer gestures for him to get behind the squad car. The officer pulls ahead and Davis follows, the two of them caravanning quickly down the busy street.

Three more traffic lights until they get to school.

Jesse

"If I have to edit that presentation one more time I will scream," moans Jesse Davidson, Communications Manager at Tampa Memorial Hospital.

"I agree. We are done!" says his coordinator, Rebecca Smith. "Look how late it is!"

They notice the time right as an announcement is made over the hospital's public address system.

Trauma Alert. ER. Star.

Trauma Alert. ER. Star.

Jesse looks at Rebecca; his eyes lighting up with fear. The code has never been used since it was developed over a year ago. *Trauma Alert ER* is a major trauma coming to the emergency room. *Trauma Alert ER Star* is a major person coming in with that emergency.

They created this plan before the city hosted the Super Bowl when they realized they'd need extra communications and security plans for certain patients. Some celebrities, football players and even politicians can attract media and the hospital wants to keep the facility secure. The *Star* code doesn't change the level of medical care, but it does change everything for the security staff and Jesse's team.

"Call everyone on our staff. Get them in here now," Jesse says.

He grabs his phone and rushes to the emergency room, Rebecca at his side with her phone to her ear. They are close to the ER when Jesse's phone rings. His caller ID shows LyBro—his nickname for his friend Lynette.

"Oh…LyBro, I'd love to talk to you," he says to his ringing phone, their pace now close to a run, "but this is not the time."

Then he stops. He and Rebecca look down at his ringing phone.

"You know who she works for…" Rebecca says.

Jesse answers the phone. "Please don't tell me you are on your way to the hospital."

"Oh my God, we are. Something happened. She was shot? What do you know?" Lynette asks.

"Shot?!" Jesse exclaims. "You know more than me. We just had the ER star page so we are on full alert. Her condition must be serious."

"It is, or so I was told by the Good Samaritan that called me. I wasn't with her but I'm on my way. Lock it down, Jesse. You know they'll go crazy to get a photo of her."

Jesse bursts into the emergency room, now filling with a medical team arriving to the trauma bay. Nurses, a trauma surgeon, a respiratory therapist and a dozen others are donning barrier gowns, gloves, face shields and shoe covers, quietly gathering around a vacant bed for the arriving patient.

"Ambulance on campus now, ETA one minute," the nurse behind the desk says.

A police officer enters the ER. "Y'all know who is coming in, right?"

"I do," Jesse says. The doctors and nurses turn to Jesse.

"We have one minute until this emergency room becomes the center of an international story."

Doug

"Band: Ten Hut!" Jason, the band director, calls out.

All 109 teenagers in the marching band snap to attention, except the giggling flute section.

"Eyes on me, mouths on instruments," Jason says.

They stand in the dark, the overhead lights from the high school parking lot the only way they can see.

Doug stands nearby, waiting to release his battery unit of snare, tenor and bass drums for the next movement. Aiden is wearing his snare drum and leans over to Doug. "Isn't it funny how you help us for our band competition next week while you get ready for a world tour with Plebeian?"

Doug smiles. Teaching students has always been a job he enjoys but now it's really just a way to help his brother. Doug looks back up to Jason.

"Let's try it again," Jason says as the sound of an emergency vehicle's siren grows louder and closer.

Suddenly a police car appears, making a sharp right turn into the high school parking lot, pulling next to where the band is assembled. Now 109 pairs of eyes are looking at something other than their band director.

"Is one of you in trouble?" Jason asks.

Lee holds his trumpet at attention as he watches a second police car turn in, this time coming from the other direction, the direction of home. Immediately behind the second police car is a black Tahoe.

Without saying a word, Lee hands his trumpet to his friend on his left, breaking the marching formation to walk towards the arriving vehicles.

That's Lauren's car. Doug starts moving too, tapping Aiden on the shoulder to put his snare drum down and get going.

Davis makes the sharp turn into the parking lot and rolls down the window. "Lee! Aiden!" he yells.

Doug instinctively walks with Lee and Aiden. These boys are his family too.

"*Hurry!*" Davis screams and they start running.

They speed away, under police escort again from an officer who wouldn't normally escort someone to the hospital like this, but this is not normal."

Frank

Grinning fourth graders just finished their string performance.

Frank's wife smiles with pride. "She was so cute," she whispers about their daughter.

"Are you sure we have to stay for the fifth grade band too?" Frank asks, tapping his feet.

His ringing phone is a welcome distraction. It's Ryan. Frank stays in his seat to take the call as nearby parents chat while teachers reset the stage.

"Hey, what's up?" Frank says, his wife beside him now looking on with interest.

His smile disappears and his face hardens.

He stands up.

His wife stands up with him.

He says nothing. The phone remains to his ear and he starts to move, walking into the aisle, heading to the back of the auditorium.

His wife follows.

The adults in the audience have noticed and are now watching; everyone in this close-knit school is aware of what Frank does for a living.

The call ends.

Frank turns and faces his wife, holding her shoulders. He tells her something and she grabs her face in horror as he tries to kiss her goodbye. He runs out the door, leaving her standing in the back of the auditorium, now joined by a few parents.

As the door swings closed he can hear her say, "Lauren Hayden has been shot."

[THIRTY-FIVE]

Andy

The automatic doors swiftly open and a rush of people flood the emergency room.

Paramedics push Lauren's stretcher inside. One of them rides on the stretcher, straddling her, keeping pressure on her chest.

Andy follows behind them, clutching Lauren's purse, escorted by two police officers.

The hospital's patient advocate gently stops Andy from following Lauren. His glassy eyes watch them wheel her into a trauma bay.

Jesse steps up. "Andy, I'm Jesse Davidson," he says, putting his face in Andy's line of view. "I'm friends with Lynette. She's on the way." The use of Lynette's name snaps him out of his trance.

Jesse leads him to a small waiting room. "Andy, please sit here and I will let you know exactly what is happening."

Andy nods.

Jesse takes two steps out of the room in time to see a snarl of brunette hair from a panicked publicist pushing her way through the double sliding doors. Jesse quickly gives permission for Lynette to enter just as security guards pull her back. In seconds she joins Andy in the small room.

"We were leaving dinner," Andy slowly tells her. "I didn't notice anything. The car was right there. I heard shots. I turned to Lauren and she was just…falling. I had her hand—I was holding her hand or she would have fallen harder on her head."

They are joined by police officers eager to get Andy's statement and Jesse sticks his head back in the room. "I think her kids are pulling up now."

Davis, Doug, Aiden and Lee are already running into the room.

A doctor follows them in, bringing everyone to a standstill. They are rushing Lauren to surgery. She is alive but her condition is critical. She has two gunshot wounds to her chest: one under her left breast that penetrated the lung and the second close to her heart, that one more critical than the other. Surgery will take between three to four hours and he will send out updates as often as he can. The doctor disappears before anyone even had a chance to ask his name.

Outside the hospital, the designated media area is quickly filling with television satellite trucks. Lynette gives Jesse her "standby" list, the list she uses for Lauren's closest family and friends.

Jesse moves Andy and his group to the day surgery center waiting room, which is not used in the evening and gives them more space. The day surgery center has two desks, one that Lynette quickly claims to set up her computer. There are several TVs, four of which are used to show a patient's progress during surgery.

During the day, the TVs have multiple lines coded with patient numbers so family and friends can watch the progress of their loved one. The line will be blue to show "in surgery" or green for "in recovery." Right now, the screens are lit with only one blue line.

Andy sinks into a chair and looks up at the TV—a colored line now his only confirmation that Lauren is alive.

A burst of activity at the door draws his attention. Frank rushes in with eyes on fire, running to Andy's side. He looks up to the TV screen, then quietly bends down to Andy.

"I am going to work with the police and get the information you need and work with security here to keep Lauren safe," Frank says. "And if they can't do what I need, I will do it for them."

Andy nods.

He still hasn't thought much about who did this. He can only think about Lauren. His ears still burn from the sound of the gun and his legs hurt from when he pushed his knees into the pavement as he bent over her. But he would have taken the bullet for her in a second. He remains exceptionally quiet, looking up every minute to get comfort from the line on the screen.

Others begin to arrive, including Michael, Oliver, Cory and Lesley. Lesley sets up at the desk across from Lynette, taking Andy's and Lauren's phones to get their incoming voicemails and text messages.

Lynette focuses on external communication, but her shaking fingers are keeping her from typing. She stops, takes a big breath and types the first statement.

> *We are stunned by the tragic events of this evening.*
> *Our main focus at the moment is Lauren's health.*
> *She has suffered two gunshot wounds to the chest and*
> *is currently in surgery. Family and friends are gath-*
> *ering to support her. We will update as we get more*
> *information.*

Her statement ignites a firestorm of followers to Lauren's social media pages, briefly overwhelming one of the accounts.

Lesley looks to Andy. "I have the first batch of messages. Ready?" He nods. She too takes a big breath to calm herself before reading the messages. "Bobby texted and said he is on the way. Christy and Cal are on the way. Tish has turned on every light in the house for good luck and is on her way with food and fresh clothes."

Andy nods again, but says nothing. He looks back up at the blue screen for strength, his mind racing through the horrific events of the evening. Lauren was enjoying dinner and a minute later he was soaked in her blood. He still cannot look over at the TV that has been tuned to a cable news channel—a station that has now gone to a full coverage broadcast of the shooting. Bystanders had taken photos of him trying to save Lauren's life and his bloody and shirtless image continues to be shown on TV.

Suddenly the cable news channel posts a photo of a man they believe is the shooter. Aiden and Lee both jump up.

"Dad! Look!" Lee yells. Cory stands up to see.

"We know him!" Aiden says, pointing to the screen.

Frank hurries in the room with two police detectives.

"Frank! We know him!" Aiden says, still pointing to the screen.

"So…you do remember him?" Frank asks.

"Yes!" Lee says. His hands shake as he explains. "That's one of the dads from our old neighborhood! He always sat around on the driveway when we used to play on the street. My mom said he was always hitting on her or the other moms. She used to call him the good-looking creep."

"I remember him a little," Cory says. "I didn't know him well but I remember Lauren telling stories about him."

"Oh my God!" Lee says. "All my friends think he's weird! One time, he told my friend's mom that he knows what time she goes to bed each night because he sees the light go off!"

The lead detective nods. "His name is Clive Winters and he lives in the cul-de-sac of your old neighborhood. He was arrested at the scene of the shooting."

The man's image now draws Andy's attention. He stands and steps closer to the screen.

Aiden looks to Frank. "He didn't have a job or he got fired or something so he was always around. He always thought he was cool. His kids were younger than us. They were super bratty."

Frank looks to Andy. "He appears to be the shooter and they have already found a treasure trove of evidence at his house."

"What, was he just a crazy fan?" Michael asks.

"It appears there may be more from what we're hearing from detectives at his house," the detective says. "We need to know if he's reached out to you recently or if any of you kept in contact with him after you moved."

Cory, Aiden and Lee sit with him to share their memories.

Andy lowers his head and sinks back into his chair. He has nothing to tell the detective. The light on this damn TV may never turn green because of a good-looking, unemployed creep he's never met.

A nurse suddenly comes into the room with an update and everyone stands to hear. Surgery is going well; one bullet has been removed from her lungs. Now the complicated part to remove the second bullet is underway.

Lynette sends an update to the mass of people who are now following Lauren through the web and social media.

*We have good news: one bullet removed. Surgery continues
to remove the second. We appreciate your support. It's
helping us handle a very difficult night.*

This forthright communication is unprecedented, giving fans real-time updates during a crisis by the people directly involved. Lynette knows Lauren's fans want to know about her life, for better or for worse. Davis has always noted when a scandal hits, record sales soar. It happened in Phoenix when Cory was caught cheating. It happened in Dallas with the car accident. It happened when Andy left Lauren. It is probably happening now.

"I have more messages," Lesley says and Andy nods. "Dr. Tobias is on his way from Dallas. Craig and Henry are flying the plane to North Carolina to pick up Johnny and Amie. And Josh Spencer called." Andy looks up. Lesley's smile brightens the room. "Josh wants you to know Lauren will make it: she is the strongest woman on the planet."

Five hours later, a growing crowd remains camped outside the hospital with candles, stuffed animals and flowers. Power generators from media satellite trucks fill the air with their humming. Reporters and their cameras have staked out all outside corners of the hospital.

Inside the day surgery center, Lauren's friends and family are quiet, texting and talking on their phones or watching the news on TV. Brittney sits next to Andy, their family roles reversed as she holds his hand and comforts her dad.

Oliver rubs his face, his sarcastic tone sobered tonight. He leans in to Michael and Doug. "What do you imagine is the prognosis of a singer who has been shot in her lungs?"

Andy glances over.

Michael leans forward, hands covering his face. "At minimum we don't have a world tour; at maximum we don't have a lead singer. Right now, I don't care about any of that. I just want Lauren to live."

Doug raises his eyebrow, but this time, he doesn't wait for Michael to speak for him.

"To me, it's clear," Doug says. "There is no Plebeian without Lauren."

The three exchange troubled glances.

"I agree. Plebeian ends tonight if she doesn't make it," Michael says. "She could never be replaced."

"And Plebeian ends if she lives but can't sing," Oliver adds.

"If Johnny was here, he'd agree," Michael says.

Doug nods. "If Johnny was here, he would have suggested it."

The television screens that have bathed the waiting room in a soft blue light suddenly change, covering the waiting room in a warm green shade. All eyes look up to the screens—the blue line for surgery has changed to the green line of recovery!

Andy stands, putting his weary hands to his face in joyous disbelief. "Green!" he whispers. "She made it! My baby made it!"

Everyone rises to look at screens, hugging and smiling, quietly celebrating the green line's arrival.

Several minutes pass before they're joined in the waiting room by two doctors who performed the surgery. They bring news of the surgery and the plan for recovery.

Both bullets have been removed. Lauren is fortunate; the second bullet was deflected by her sternum. While this is good news, they advise caution in celebrating. She is critical and on life support, and will remain on life support until she stabilizes.

Then the doctors offer more good news: Andy can go see her now.

[THIRTY-SIX]

The doctors lead Andy down a maze of hallways to the surgery recovery area. Before they head through the double doors, one of them pulls Andy back.

"Remember: the machines you are about to see may be frightening but they are keeping her alive. Talk to her as if she is awake. You can't stay long; only two minutes," he says, pushing the double doors open.

Curtains partition the large recovery area, circling a nurse's station. Most of the lights are off tonight since only one patient is here. A chill runs through Andy's body when he feels the temperature of the room. Everything is still and quiet, except for some beeping and suction sounds. Those sounds mean Lauren is near as he is led closer to the only pulled curtain in the room.

The doctor escorting him gestures that it's okay and a nurse standing by the curtain nods encouragement.

Andy takes a few steps and now has a clear view of a hospital bed, sheets, blankets and machines. Somewhere under there is his wife. He takes a few more tentative steps closer to see the side of Lauren's face, her head wrapped with a bandage and her mouth covered with tape and the plastic tube of her ventilator.

Dizziness blurs his vision. He gulps down air and steps closer, gliding his hand under the sheet to hold hers. One of the nurses comes by Lauren's other side. "She may be able to hear you; let her know you're here."

Andy stands taller and bends over her. Her hair smells medical and her cheek is difficult to find under the tubing, but he sees her ear. He lowers his mouth, kissing her ear gently and slowly.

"Hey, it's me. It's Andy," he says sweetly, hoping his voice can find a way inside her. "I hope you can hear me because I need you to do something important; really important. I need you to wake up."

He squeezes her hand and tries to put his other hand on her hair but pulls back, afraid that he might hurt her head. He breathes in deeply and continues talking with his mouth over her right ear.

"You see, there is this line between us right now, another damn line, but I can't cross it for you. I really, really need you to cross that line and come back to me. There are people who love you; people who need you. And I'm one of them. Baby, I can't do this without you. I love you, Lauren. Fight and come back to me."

The nurse indicates that it's time to go. He steps back and watches her adjust something on the beeping machine.

"Thank you for keeping her alive," he says to the nurse. He turns to speak to the other nurses. "Thank you all."

One nurse kindly smiles. "Well from what we understand the only reason she made it here to us is because you saved her."

Andy reluctantly nods. He slowly walks through the doors to leave and as the doors swing closed, he looks back through the rectangular window. He stares inside at the curtain shielding Lauren in a room where her body and spirit lie, but where machines are keeping her alive.

He's alone in the hall, the first time he has been alone since the shooting.

Slowly he begins his walk back but suddenly his legs weaken. He stops as a burst of feelings that sum up his life begin to physically take him over. He staggers against the wall, crying the cry that is years overdue. With his hands on his face, he slides down the wall to the floor, sitting and sobbing.

What now? How will he have the strength to help her recover?

He's not the strong one—Lauren is. This is when Lauren would dig deep and produce some strength he never knew she had. He remembers watching her on TV at the Academy Awards, and then in person at her first concert, where she found some pocket of inner strength to calm her fears as millions of people in this curious world watched her. She took their stares—those critical, hateful stares—and she sang on.

Her strength has helped him, and has taught him. He thinks about the embarrassing video of him that almost came out and how Lauren literally led him to fight it. Then the death of baby Anna; Lauren fused her sadness into lyrics of a hit song. It was Lauren who suggested he tell his side of the story for the article that helped him heal. And he remembers a chase through the woods, when Lauren's strong will pushed her faster than he could run. How could he ever be as strong as her?

His position on the hallway floor has gone unnoticed by the energy-saving lights. They turn off, leaving the faint glow from the recovery room the only light in the dark corridor.

The weak moment in sudden darkness brings it all back: the screaming voices in his head. *You are nothing. You are worthless.* He thought the hurtful voices he knew as a boy had been silenced in the freak car accident that had killed his parents. Yet he continued to hear their doubting voices echoed in the mistakes he made throughout his life. As an adult, beauty turned out to be another bad choice, adding a new voice of torment. *You are worthless,* she said. *You are nothing,* she told him. He worked hard to silence these voices, to forget his abusive parents and to leave Janie behind. It was Lauren's love that quieted the voices of doubt. Lauren believed in him, even when he didn't believe in himself.

But history tried to repeat itself in a car accident eerily similar to the one that killed his parents. Chronic pain and depression opened the door for the voices of doubt to return as he struggled with his recovery. He never told Lauren how the accidents were so similar; he was too afraid. Lauren herself had become a voice in his head; hers not of doubt but one of obsession and excessive worry. He ran away and released his pain with alcohol and a stranger and he almost lost it all. He shut up the voices and proved himself to win Lauren's trust again. He cannot let these voices come back; there's too much at stake now.

Andy looks down to the door at the end of the hall. The light from the small rectangle window struggles to brighten the dark hallway. The love of his life is down there, in the fight of her life. She will need him. He still needs her.

"Until such time," he says to himself in the dark hall. "It's still *our* time."

He stands up, wiping his face with the palm of his hand. Motion sensors detect life in the hallway, filling it with bright, energizing light. He looks back at the double doors of the recovery suite.

"I'll be damned if someone else thought our time was over. Now we fight," he says and he turns his back to the recovery suite and quickly walks back to the waiting room.

Everyone jumps in surprise when Andy bursts through the doors of the day surgery waiting room. He stands tall and with purpose, his breakdown over, his thoughts refocused, his entire life redefined.

"Davis!" he calls out, surprising everyone. Davis steps closer.

"I need your help to build the best legal team ever assembled. Start with Todd Peppers and then add more just like him and better. Money is no object."

"Frank," he calls out a little less forcefully. Frank steps forward. "Anything you need to investigate this with police; more people, more money, use of the plane, anything you need, you get it."

He says to them, "I want to be clear: I want the guy that did this to my wife to stay in jail forever."

"With pleasure," Frank says.

Then Andy looks at the group of family and friends.

"So someone decided to set Lauren back, but she didn't listen. She made it. She's alive. There are machines helping her, but she's alive. She's going to have the fight of her life ahead of her, and that's why we're here. We fight with her. And we fight for her.

"I'm not sure I have always been the smartest or strongest guy, but I've learned from Lauren. She taught me how to be strong. She was strong for me when I wasn't. Now, I plan to return the favor."

"Me too!" Oliver says, raising his hand in the air to volunteer for the fight. It relieves the tension as the waiting room full of weary family and friends comes alive again.

Then Lynette sends out the message fans around the world are waiting for:

> *Surgery done; bullets out; Lauren made it! Critical condition and difficult road ahead. Andy has seen her and we are energized for the fight ahead.*

Shortly after nine the next morning, Andy steps out of the ICU, where Lauren was moved an hour earlier.

Bobby is waiting for him, standing outside a hospital room now assigned as a private waiting room for Lauren's family. He holds two cups of coffee and hands one of them to Andy.

"I'm so glad you came last night," Andy says, leaning his aching body against a wall and taking a drawn out sip.

"How is she?" Bobby asks.

"Same. No changes. I think that will be the news all day today. She has to be completely still so they are keeping her sedated. At least the ventilator is gone."

"How did the boys do when they saw her?"

"They were quiet, but fine. I left so they could have some private time with her now. The nurses are going to let them stay back there for a few more minutes."

"Then this is a good time to clean up your act," Bobby says. "You have been wearing this polo shirt since the guy in the parking lot gave it to you. Tish brought you stuff and I'm going to stand right here outside this room while you take your shower."

Bobby has a way of being able to manage Andy, in a good way. They both step into the hospital room, which has been converted into a makeshift private waiting room with extra chairs plus one bed for someone to sleep on. Bobby asks everyone to clear out so Andy can clean up.

His timing was perfect because an hour later, Dr. Tobias arrives.

Dr. Tobias has flown in to offer emotional support for Andy. Now Andy has his trusted doctor plus his best friend here, a combination that helps him feel stronger.

He will need that strength for the meeting that is to come.

[THIRTY-SEVEN]

"Have a seat. Here, pull up a bed," Frank offers to Todd Peppers, who just arrived to the converted hospital room. Frank, Todd, a police detective, a state prosecutor, Andy, Davis and Lynette are meeting to hear the latest on what has been discovered about the shooter.

"It's not fancy but it's close to the ICU and keeps us happy," Frank says of the accommodations. Since Todd is the last one to arrive, the few chairs in the room are already taken. Todd shrugs and sits on the bed's edge.

"We have a very strong motive emerging from the evidence collected so far," the prosecutor says. "The hearing on his bail has been pushed back to Friday, so we still have plenty of time to sort through the many leads we're getting."

"So was he just a nutty fan?" Davis asks.

"More than that," Frank says. "Andy, this may be difficult for you to hear."

Andy sits up straight.

Frank continues, "This guy became obsessed with Lauren the minute she was revealed as the lead singer of Plebeian. He evidently always liked her when she lived in the neighborhood and was upset when she suddenly moved to the new house when she became famous. He was driven to try to get closer to her."

"That's so similar to what happened with me," Andy says. "I had always liked her, even before she was famous, and after we reconnected, I wanted to get her into my life."

"It is similar because it is what happened."

"What do you mean?"

"He thought he got into her life because he thought he was you."

"Me?"

"He had convinced himself that he was Andy Hayden."

The police detective leans in. "He attended the first concert with some other neighbors, even sat in the same section you did. He followed her on several trips, including New York City and Phoenix. But he couldn't get noticed by her. Then the two of you went public as a couple. It appears sometime after the Dallas accident he began fashioning himself in your image. He went to almost every concert on that first tour; those were concerts that you didn't attend. It looks like he "replaced" you during that time by pretending to "be" you. His fantasy continued even after you healed. He traveled to Los Angeles for many of the awards shows Plebeian attended and even went to Boston for the Daytime interview. We found evidence that he followed the two of you locally and also tracked your plane."

Frank nods. "Usually someone like this would be jealous of you, but he bought clothes like yours, he styled his hair like yours, he somehow bought a car exactly like yours. You were never in any danger, Andy, because he thought he was you. He watched you and felt it was him."

"I never would have expected something like that," Andy says. "So why hurt Lauren?"

"It evidently came down to the world tour," Frank says. "This guy could follow you almost anywhere in the country and keep the intent behind his travel hidden from his family, calling the trips job searches and interviews. But he couldn't travel the world because he couldn't afford it. It drove him completely crazy that he was not going to be able to be with her on the world tour."

"So he decided to hurt her so she'd have to stay home," Andy says.

"That appears to be the strongest motive," the prosecutor says.

Todd asks. "So did the tip from Lawson pay off?"

"Wait, what? Lawson? Marcia Lawson?" Andy asks. He thought he put that woman and his epic bad weekend behind him.

"Yes," Todd says. "She called me last night."

"And yes, thanks to her tip we may be able to charge him with vandalism too," the detective says.

"Okay, now I'm lost," Davis says.

Frank once again connects the dots. "Not too long ago Lawson's apartment, car and workplace were vandalized. She isn't exactly loved by everyone, so she didn't report it to police. She had Todd's number from the legal matters against her and she called him last night to tell him what she thought. She thought if this guy was nuts enough to shoot Lauren, maybe he vandalized her stuff. When actually, he was acting on what he perceived to be Andy's behalf."

"And we found a speeding ticket he got on Interstate 95, just outside Ft. Lauderdale, late on the night when the vandalism occurred," the detective confirms.

"So if he thought he was Andy, he vandalized her as revenge for messing up his life with Lauren?" Davis asks.

"Exactly," Frank says.

"This is creepy," Andy says.

"There's more," Frank says. "In his mind, evidently an enemy of yours also meant a threat to you, Andy."

"What do you mean a threat to me?"

"A romantic threat," Frank says. "Anyone who may steal Lauren away from you."

"Okay, so he was acting on my behalf to vandalize someone who screwed up our lives and then he was messing with other guys he thought I was jealous of?" Andy asks.

Frank and the detective exchange glances.

"He kept a binder with photos and notes of men in Lauren's life. Men he thought were a threat to him, um, you," Frank says.

"Oh great. Was I in it?" Davis asks.

"Yeah but way in the back, lucky for you," Frank quips.

"So this book was in order of guys he didn't like?" Andy asks.

"Correct. We have evidence that he was planning to hurt some of the men in the book," the detective says, "and he was very close to attempting to kill the first one."

"Who was first?" Andy asks.

"Josh Spencer," Frank says.

Andy buries his head in his hands. "We've got to tell Josh."

"We will this morning. We need to talk to Josh about any threats he may have received; threats he might not have considered important until now," the detective says.

"And I have turned over some additional evidence that may be helpful," Frank says. "There were some cigarette butts we found in front of the house some time ago and Clive Winters was a smoker. If his DNA matches, then it will confirm he was trespassing at the house too. The good news is with this much evidence, it shouldn't be difficult to keep this guy locked up until trial."

"The bad news is, somebody, at some point, is going to have to explain all of this to Lauren," says Lynette.

[THIRTY-EIGHT]

Lauren

That smell. She knows that smell.

Rubbing alcohol and floor cleaner. Antiseptic wipes and a scent like heated canned chili.

It's hospital smell.

Lauren's crusty eyelids are hard to open but she finally pushes them free.

She's in a room. A hospital room. Good God, someone is loud. Andy is standing at the door, talking to him. The loud guy looks like a nurse. *Could they be quieter?* She's…so…sleepy…

Lauren blinks her eyes open again.

The loud guy is *still* talking.

Yep, he's a nurse and he sure has a lot to say. Why the heck is she here? A fall. She vaguely remembers falling. She blinks a few times.

The loud guy adjusts something over her head and just keeps talking.

"And the only thing worse than sending a tell-off text to the wrong person is having someone deliberately overhear your conversations, like right now," he says, looking down at Lauren. "Well hello, sunshine, we've been waiting for you! Turn your head that way to see someone more interesting."

She does as he says, slowly moving her head to the right and her vision fills with Andy's happy, smiling face.

"Oh my God! You're awake! Oh my God, Lauren!" And then her face fills with Andy's head, falling hair, and kisses.

Lauren tries to talk but she can't. Her throat feels horrible. It hurts worse than her head. Actually, she doesn't feel good anywhere.

"I'll go tell the doctors she woke up," the loud nurse exclaims with his hands in the air, rushing out of the white room.

"What...happ?" She scratches out the sounds just as two doctors hurry in.

"Lauren!" a doctor says. "How wonderful to see you awake!"

Everyone seems pretty damn excited to see her. Then a big problem walks in the door.

Dr. Tobias steps in her view. "Hi, Lauren! Welcome back."

Tobias? *That's not good.* Did she hurt her head like before? *Oh shit!* A seizure? Is she in Dallas?

She clears her throat to stop their celebration.

"Where am I? And who's the new guy?" she says, looking over to the doctor she doesn't know.

Andy leans over her, whispering, "Honey, that new guy just saved your life."

"Saved my..." Lauren starts to ask but she's interrupted by three more people coming into the small room: two policemen and Frank.

"No, not now. She just woke up," the new doctor tells the cops. "I will tell you when." The policemen leave. Frank comes up to the side of her bed.

"Those open eyes are the best thing I've ever seen. You got her back, Andy!" Frank says, looking up to an ear-to-ear grinning Andy. Now Frank has the happy bug too?

Her head hurts and she can barely feel her throat and everyone is so damn happy about it.

All she wants to...do...is...sleep...

She wakes up again to the sound of Mr.-Happy-Talks-A-Lot-Nurse.

"Whoop! She's awake again!"

Andy is immediately in her view. "Hey, baby, how are you feeling?"

"My throat hurts," Lauren struggles to say. "Why am I here? What…happened?"

Once again, her room fills instantly with doctors and Frank.

Didn't this just happen a minute ago?

"Okay, this is how this is going to work…" she tries to demand in her coarse, whispering voice.

Tobias finishes her thought. "We are going to tell you the truth, exactly what you want to know and not sugar coat anything," he says, repeating her demand from Dallas when she wanted to know Andy's condition.

"Now is good," she whispers.

Happy nurse comes back with ice water. Lauren drinks through the straw like she's never had a beverage before. Oh the delight of cool water when you have a sore throat.

"So I messed up my head? I remember falling," she says, her voice still growling.

"You do? Okay, yes, you did fall. Do you remember where we were?" Andy asks.

She thinks for a minute. "Leaving dinner?"

"Amazing recall," the new doctor says to Tobias.

Andy holds her hand with both of his and fidgets in his chair, getting as close to her as possible. Frank leans in behind him, practically putting his head on Andy's shoulder. She's sleepy and hurting but close to laughing seeing them look so dramatic.

"Why did I fall?"

"You fell," Andy says, "because you…you were shot."

The room falls totally silent as her brain processes a surprising four letter word. "Shot? With…a gun?"

"Yes, with a gun. Someone shot you as we were leaving dinner.

They got him. He can't hurt you now and everyone is safe. Even the kids are safe."

She sits quiet for a few seconds as everyone in the room looks around at each other.

"Where…was I shot?"

The new doctor steps in and points to her chest. "Your left lung and your sternum, and both bullets have been removed. This one here was a very serious wound," he says, pointing to the center of her chest.

"So why does my throat hurt?"

Tobias says, "You were on life support; a ventilator to help your body start to heal. Your throat will start to feel better soon."

Now she sees why everyone is so happy. Life support? *Oh God, Andy! The kids? This had to be a nightmare for them!*

"Oh no—Andy! You must have been going crazy while I was out of it…" she says, trying to lift her head up.

"No—stop," Andy snaps, squeezing her hand. "We are not going to do that. You are not going to worry about me. We are not going to go down a road like we did after Dallas. Baby, I am fine and even better now that you're awake. I get to worry about you—you don't worry about me."

She lays her head down. He's right. Something big has happened to her and she launches an emotional rescue team for Andy. *Worry about yourself.* She lets go of his hand, reaching up to touch his stubbly, unshaven face; smiling. His hands gently cup her cheeks. Andy is so strong right now, strong for her.

"I guess this might have made the news?" she asks. Andy, the doctors and Frank share a laugh.

Happy nurse comes back to place the straw in her mouth. "Sweetheart, you have been the big story for days now."

Days now?

"I remember…we went to dinner on Monday. So today isn't Tuesday?"

"No, baby," Andy says. "Today is Thursday. And we have a big day ahead of us tomorrow."

[THIRTY-NINE]

"I'll be there as soon as we are finished in court," Andy says. "I love you, Lauren."

"I love you too, Andy," she says, disconnecting the call. Christy takes her phone away. "Big day in court," Lauren says, taking a deep, calming breath.

At least she's alert and feeling better; much better since she woke up yesterday. She's surrounded by Christy, her mom, Amie, Brittney and Sunny while the guys go to court to fight to keep her shooter in jail until the trial. Anticipation that he could go free today has her worried.

Christy notices Lauren's expression. "Hey, creepy Clive proved he's a threat to you and others. He'll stay locked up."

"That guy was always so smug, so cocky. I can't believe he thought he was Andy. They are worlds apart."

"And Andy will show him that when he comes face to face with him today," Christy says.

"All Andy would tell me is that he's handling this in a way that would make me proud."

And she's got big news that will make him happy. Mr. Happy Nurse just moved her to a private room. Her new room is larger than normal, at the end of a hall and on a floor a patient in her condition wouldn't normally go but this floor is not full, so her large party of visiting family and friends won't disturb others.

Lauren is still very weak and unable to move much. But that doesn't stop Christy, who has arranged a few treats for her best friend.

Christy puts on Lauren's makeup, brushes her hair and massages her favorite perfume lotion on her arms and legs. She had Tish bring some fashionable loungewear Lauren can wear instead of the flimsy hospital gown. Tish also brought Lauren's comfy Mrs. pillow. After several days in the Intensive Care Unit, these are million dollar treats.

But the priceless treat is the tasty one that just entered her room.

"Wes!" Lauren says.

Her favorite deli manager wears a sneaky grin, clutching two white paper bags. "The nurses didn't catch me!" he says. He unpacks a round of turkey melts for everyone and baked potato soup for Lauren. He looks around the room. "Isn't Lynette here? I brought her jalapeño cheese puffs and extra sour cream."

"She's at the courthouse," Christy says. "But sure as shootin' she'll be back here soon."

"I hope you feel better, Mrs. Hayden. Anything else you need, just call!" Wes says, turning and leaving the room.

Soup in her tummy, Lauren settles in to watch the one p.m. hearing. Thanks to cable news cameras camped out on the downtown courthouse steps, she can watch the arrivals and departures live from her hospital bed. Cameras can't go inside, so Davis will call them from inside the courthouse once the ruling is made.

Andy's arrival is being broadcast live. Suddenly, all of the cars parked on the street in front of the courthouse pull out of their spaces, instantly opening all of the front parking spaces for an arriving fleet of black Cadillac Escalade SUVs.

"That's pretty slick," Brittney says.

"That reminds me of the Sand Club," Lauren says, remembering the time the manager Gregory dispatched his valet drivers to make an instant traffic jam to slow the paparazzi who were chasing her. "I wonder if those are Gregory's drivers."

"They probably parked in the spaces early this morning," Amie says.

Doors on the four SUVs start opening and out steps the most impressive display of men in suits Lauren has ever seen.

"They look like they mean business!" Christy says.

"All of the important men in my life," Lauren says.

Cameras focus on the first SUV. Andy steps out, looking fit, groomed and ready to kick ass in his charcoal gray suit, white shirt and blue tie. With him are Bobby, Dr. Tobias, Frank and Bill.

Another SUV has Aiden, Lee and Cory, plus her brother and pilots Craig and Henry.

The third SUV looks like the Plebeian mobile with Johnny, Michael, Oliver and Doug getting out.

And the fourth SUV draws a lot of attention now that the door is open. Out steps Davis, Cal, Ryan and Josh Spencer.

"Josh…is here?" Lauren slaps her hands to her face in joy.

"Davis…Oliver…have suits?" Brittney says, laughing.

This can't be happening: Andy is pulling off the Todd Peppers maneuver! This may not impact the judge, but he's going to send a strong message to the shooter by sitting these impressive men front and center in that courtroom. Way to go!

They watch the group make their way inside the courthouse and now Lauren must wait. A battle wages on her behalf and she can only pray that justice prevails. She can only hope a dangerous person is kept off the streets so he can't hurt anyone else. Nothing is in her control, including the potato soup gurgling in her nervous stomach.

Christy is holding Lauren's phone when it rings only thirty minutes later.

"Held until trial! No bail!" Davis yells. "We got him where we want him. Holy crap, Lauren, the State Attorney is good but Todd Peppers is a legal beast."

"You have no idea how happy I am!" Lauren says. "Can you tell Andy I've got a special reward for him? I'm in room 612, out of the ICU, with a bed big enough for two."

"You're out of the ICU? Thank goodness! Okay, when he stops

talking with the lawyers, I will," Davis says, ending the call.

Oh how excited Andy must be! He's literally gone from the pavement trying to save her life to victory in the courtroom in the short course of a week.

Outside, cameras are broadcasting live as Andy comes out of the courthouse. He and his entourage walk down a flight of marble steps, straight to a group of microphones that Lynette and Lesley have set up for remarks. Andy's never spoken to the media like this! He stands behind the microphones while all the guys in their suits cluster behind him. Lauren tries to pull up her knees to hug them to her chest but her sutures tug at her skin.

Andy begins:

"Thank you all for your support today and all week.

It's been a remarkable week for us. There have been some horrific lows and then today, two terrific highs. The first of those being that the person accused of shooting my wife will not be a threat to her or the public as he awaits trial. I will be leading that fight to see that justice is served.

I'm joined here with the men in Lauren's life. We are the men who love her. I asked them to come and stand with me. We will stick together and stand up for Lauren until justice is served.

I have two people who also want to speak to you, the first being Josh Spencer."

Lauren breathes for the first time since Andy started talking. Her eyes light up like a high school girl with a crush on a guy she wants to marry.

Josh steps to the microphones:

"It's a bad day when you get a call that your friend has been seriously hurt. It's a worse day when you get a call telling you that you could have been next.

I'm not okay with the thought of someone free in this world with plans to hurt other people. I'm joining Andy in this fight and plan to stand by his side for the duration of this trial.

I think there is someone else here who has something to say..."

Josh has a big smile as he turns to help Lee to the microphones. Everyone in the room gulps in surprise.

"I'm Lee Logan, Lauren's son. My brother Aiden and I, and our sister Brittney, want to thank everyone for all of the support. It really has been helpful to us and I know my mom appreciates the emails, calls and vigils. I hope that no other kid has to go through what we did this week and our fingers are crossed that the trial will bring justice."

Brittney stands next to Lauren's bed, pointing at the TV. "He just called me his sister! Did you hear that? He's never done that! He finally called me sister!"

Their eyes turn back to the TV as Lee steps away and Andy steps forward again.

"I know there are a lot of questions and I hope to be able to answer them sometime, but the other good news we had today is that Lauren has been moved out of Intensive Care and into a regular room. So if you don't mind, I think right now there is someplace else all of us would rather be. Thank you!"

Andy waves to the media, leading the entourage of men back to the waiting SUVs.

Happy shock has stunned Lauren's body. That just happened! Andy was so strong; he rallied those men and spoke so confidently. Lynette and Lesley have to be standing on the courthouse steps, high-fiving each other. She rests her head on her Mrs. pillow. How can she ever thank Andy? How can she thank all of them?

She sits up straight; a crazy idea forms in her mind.
Ah…perfect.

As soon as Christy returns to confirm that the arrangements for Lauren's thank you plan have been made, they hear the crisp click of men's dress shoes coming down the hall. These guys must have forgotten they are in a hospital; they are talking so loud. If others on this hall didn't know Lauren was a patient on this floor, they do now.

Christy clears everyone out of the room just as Andy stops outside. "Everyone wait here. I want to see Lauren first," Lauren hears him say.

She sits up in her hospital bed, alone, watching the door. Andy steps inside and her mouth dries when she sees his combed-back hair and impeccable charcoal gray suit. She may be medicated but she could still help him take off that suit right now. His face brightens when he sees her fresh and cleaned up; the days of blood and despair are behind them.

They say nothing; their eyes fixed on each other. He slowly walks past the end of the bed to her right side. Their flirtatious smiles and inviting eyes are doing all the talking. Finally he reaches her side, adjusts a rogue, dangling strand of his hair with one of his trademark hair swings and leans down to press his lips to hers. His kiss is so insanely slow, surely the machines monitoring her just sounded an alarm at the nurses' desk.

Lauren softly rubs his cheeks.

"Andy, you are my hero," she whispers. "You saved my life and now you are my hero protecting it. I'm so glad I already married you." Tears of gratefulness fall from her eyes. He strokes her hair and smiles.

"Lauren, *you* saved *my* life. You are the only person who ever believed in me. Your forgiveness gave me new life," he whispers, continuing to stoke her hair. "I told you before: I love you more than I can ever make you know. Losing you is not an option. No one is ever going to get between us again."

Then, one by one, her room fills with smiling people. They stagger themselves around Lauren's bed, squeezing in for Lynette to take a photo. Then Lynette posts the first photo of Lauren since the accident to social media with the caption:

On the way to healing.

All this smiling has left Lauren too weak to talk, so she has Christy gather the guys together to thank them.

"The best way for Lauren to show her appreciation is to have you get out of the hospital and go have a fancy steak dinner, her treat," Christy says. "It's all arranged, so get back in your rented SUVs and take Andy out for a nice dinner, please!"

Reservations have been made for all eighteen of them. But only seventeen will go.

[FORTY]

Andy

It just got very loud at Healey's Steakhouse.

Lauren's boisterous group of men, with Andy at the helm, just arrived at the heavily wood-paneled restaurant. They each claim one of the burgundy velvet chairs at a mahogany table reserved for them. A distinguished waiter promptly arrives, carrying a tray of drinks.

"Good evening, gentlemen," the waiter announces. "These have been selected for you courtesy of Mrs. Lauren Hayden."

"Where is Mr. Cory Logan?" he asks, and Cory raises his hand. "A Blue Eyes for you, sir." Cory smiles, his blue eyes picking up the table's candle light reflection.

"Mr. Aiden and Mr. Lee: a Roy Rogers for each of you," the waiter says.

Lee raises his hand. "But these don't have alcohol!"

The waiter nods. "As your mother wishes."

"Mr. Josh Spencer: a Little Green Man from Mars." Josh smiles at the inside joke. As long as no hot men from Mars appear, he keeps the cutest guy on the planet title.

"Mr. Frank Allen: an Incredible Hulk," the waiter says.

Frank puffs out his chest. "I think I like the way that sounds."

"Mr. Oliver Brink: a Little Dinghy," the waiter says.

Frank laughs. "I think I like the way that sounds too."

Oliver's face wrinkles with displeasure. "She thinks my dinghy's little?" Josh spits out a mouthful of his drink in laughter.

The waiter completes his personalized presentations around the table, leaving one orange highball glass garnished with colorful fruit on his tray.

"And this is for you, Mr. Andy Hayden," the waiter says.

"That's no martini."

"No sir. This is what Mrs. Hayden wants. It's a Sex on the Beach."

Andy raises the glass high to toast that idea.

It should have been a party of eighteen for dinner but they are missing one. And right now, he's in bed with Lauren.

Lauren

Johnny has found a spot at the end of Lauren's hospital bed, and he sits in his jeans and bare feet, softly strumming his Hummingbird guitar. He's singing some lyrics and melodies. The lights in the room are dim; the sound of his voice so soothing.

A guard stands outside her door but she thinks Johnny wanted to stay here to protect her. She feels safe with him here; she's always safe with Johnny.

He hasn't asked her if she's okay. And he usually does. Maybe it's because there was nothing he could have done to prevent this. He was out of town; helpless. And according to Amie, after it happened he was inconsolable.

He hasn't even mentioned the postponement of Plebeian's world tour. But he has asked a lot of questions about the trial. Out of everyone, he seems to be the most vindictive towards her shooter.

The words he softly sings are not words he'd normally use: odd, bastard, creep. His dark lyrics are about the shooter and clearly he is struggling. He has plenty of time to play around with the words; it will be a few hours until Amie and the girls come back. Christy has taken them out to dinner too, just like the guys.

His singing makes her sleepy and she can't help but yawn. Before she pulls her feet under her covers she notices her toes and feet at the end of the bed, next to Johnny's bare feet as he sits with her.

Four feet.

It was over a decade ago when she peeked in Johnny's bedroom window and saw that extra pair of feet in his bed. The set of four feet meant another woman was with him, that he'd already moved on from her. Those feet instantly made her the has-been ex-girlfriend.

But that is not what she became.

What an amazing journey she and Johnny have taken together. He picked her in the very beginning to help him form this band. Together they wrote their Academy Award winning song. From there, Plebeian took off. They got rich, really rich, together.

She never expected to have fame with the money. Maybe that's why Johnny is so quiet. If they had never revealed themselves to accept the Oscar, she never would have been famous. If she had never been famous, she would have never been shot. Of course, if they had never revealed themselves she wouldn't have caught Andy's eye, forever being just a girl from high school he never asked out.

She's lost a lot being famous, but she gained everything in her new life with Andy. Her future is with Andy, from a journey started by this man in her bed.

Lauren pulls her feet under the covers and Johnny stops playing.

"You okay? Anything I can do for you?" he asks.

Finally.

"Actually, there is."

[FORTY-ONE]

Two months later

The sky is a stunning shade of blue and the breeze smells like salt water from the upstairs balcony of Lauren's Kiawah Island beach home. What a perfect day for a wedding. She stands on the upstairs balcony, listening to the music from the pool terrace below and the chatter of their close friends and guests.

Lauren is ready, wearing a sleeveless taffeta black dress with a simple white ribbon around the waist. The high-neck dress hides her scars which, thanks to plastic surgery, are healing nicely. She picks up her bouquet of white roses tied with sheer green ribbon and walks to the guest room, quietly knocking on the door.

Johnny is ready now too, in a simple black suit with a skinny black tie. He's rubbing his hands up and down his thighs, but stops and smiles when Lauren steps into the room.

"Let's do this," she sweetly says to him, straightening his tie.

"I'm ready," he says and they lock arms.

Downstairs, Michael's fingers are making their musical magic on the living room piano. Their friends quickly organize themselves in chairs when Johnny and Lauren appear. The two walk side by side, arm in arm, making their way to the edge of the outdoor patio, where a local judge waits to officiate the ceremony. Lauren takes her place next to Johnny and breathes in this moment.

She's so happy right now, savoring the beautiful evening. The pains in her body are healing. The one who hurt her has confessed and has now been convicted. By this time next year, Plebeian will be on their rescheduled world tour. During the tour she will be carrying extra baggage: scar tissue in her lung that makes it harder to sing and now a deepened fear of people staring at her. She'll worry about the world tour later. Right now, she's enjoying the simplicities of love. Lauren winks at Johnny, then turns to face the crowd.

Amie appears from the back of the terrace and Michael's music cues everyone to stand. "Beautiful" could only begin to describe the bride, her curves hugged by a simple white lace gown with a black ribbon at her waist, her red rose bouquet bunched in the shape of a heart.

Lauren looks at Johnny, who nervously twitches his worn guitar-playing hands. She knows why he chose her to stand beside him. She'll slap him if he tries to run now.

Step by step, Amie comes closer. *Thank goodness Johnny finally listened.* Lauren knew he loved Amie and wanted to be married, but he's always been afraid of taking the next emotional step. This is exactly what happened to Johnny and Lauren back when they dated. Had he been brave enough and asked Lauren to marry him, she would have done it. But he never did, and they never were. That was the real reason why they broke up. He hesitated to make a commitment when Amie got pregnant too. He denied he wanted to be a father until Anna died, and then he realized what a good father he would have been. When it comes to matters of the heart, Johnny holds his close. It took a trusted friend to help him force it open.

Amie and Johnny clasp hands and the judge begins the proceedings. Lauren faces forward, towards the open ocean as the judge talks of love, commitment and honor.

A wave on the beach below crashes on the shore just as Johnny starts to say his vows. Lauren remembers Marco's wise words, about each wave bringing something new, and the wave that came before it is replaced with a fresh wave in a constant process of rejuvenation. This perfectly sums up her life since Plebeian was revealed.

It's Amie's turn for promise-making and Lauren turns to watch her. Amie smiles from her soul; she has waited so long for this stubborn man. She endured so much with the death of baby Anna and she had to filter out the negative people in her family, choosing today to surround herself with the few that are supportive of Johnny. And she's had to put up with Lauren, the always present ex-girlfriend. Lauren smiles at Amie with her complete approval.

Johnny and Amie kiss and the friends cheer. They make their way through the crowd while Michael starts jamming a lively song. The air fills with the smell of smoke from Oliver's already lit cigar. The beach front home comes alive with celebration.

Lauren remains in her ceremony position, looking around to take it all in. This house! These people! So much happiness.

Then she notices a good-looking man, tall and well dressed, standing by the edge of the terrace. He, too, is standing alone, surveying the happy crowd. He notices her and smiles a warm, inviting smile. Lauren smiles an appreciative smile in return. *He's here!* She can't believe he accepted the invitation to come. Maybe today *is* about new beginnings for them all. Their glance is broken by Aiden and Lee, who have rushed up to him, eager to show off the pile of roast beef slices stacked on their plates. They tug at his arm to lead him to the buffet, in a playful, all-too-familiar pull. After all, Cory is their daddy.

Lauren turns to the open doors of the living room where two people are laughing and smiling in a flirtatious dance. She's never seen Doug act like this and apparently neither has Amie's younger sister Ashley, the two of them looking like the next match made in heaven.

Simone approves of the wedding, her loud baby squeals delighting everyone. Michael stops his piano playing to pick her up while Sunny looks on, smiling beside them.

Lauren stands at the edge of the terrace, enjoying the ocean breeze on her skin, clutching her flower bouquet while Plebeian music now plays on the stereo. All of what she feels, hears and sees was made possible by taking a crazy risk to start a secret band with Johnny.

She completes her visual sweep of the party by looking to the right now, towards the outside bar set up by the pool. Leaning on the corner of the bar is the best looking man here, and he's got one drink in each hand.

He smiles and begins to walk towards her, the ocean breeze slowly blowing his straight brown hair. He offers her one of the martinis.

"A real friend would have given you a drink by now."

"Looks like an old friend just did," she says, accepting his gift. Their glasses gently clink in a toast. "Until such time," she whispers, sipping and never taking her eyes off his.

He steps closer.

"I know there's this line between us, and I respect that," he says, his eyes devious and confident. "But I want you to know, I'm going to cross it right now."

And Lauren's husband leans forward to give her a deep kiss: slow, sexy and in plain view of whoever is looking. He doesn't care who sees and frankly, this is his house so he's going to do whatever he wants.

Andy. Her hero. The love of her life.

Other Books by Debbie K. Lum

PLEBEIAN IN DANGER (BOOK TWO)

Lauren thought her stage fear would be her largest challenge during Plebeian's world tour. But a series of bad luck has given her bigger problems. The world tour is unraveling and it's all according to plan. By the time Lauren discovers the enemy within, she's already fallen into a trap. Now she must face a killer to stop this, and resist his love.

PLEBEIAN REBORN (BOOK THREE)

Lauren Hayden has survived remarkable challenges as the lead singer of Plebeian. Now she faces her biggest challenge yet—her mistakes from the past. When tragedy strikes and secrets are revealed, she unravels in a downward spiral. Only one man can save her, and Plebeian, now.

THE DOCTOR, THE CHEF OR THE FIREMAN

A small-town girl running from a big-time secret finds herself in the middle of danger, and in the arms of an unexpected love.

I CAN HANDLE HIM

Quinn Corbin's got nothing to lose – except her life.

She's finally got the attention of the man she's always loved, Nick Allen. But Nick has a reputation for trouble. And after a car explosion killed his last girlfriend, many people in San Antonio, Texas think Nick got away with murder.

But Quinn, a twenty-four-year-old elementary school teacher and bubbly optimist, believes Nick is innocent. So does her best friend Tory, a law student and sarcastic realist. Soon Quinn and Nick find their relationship growing when suddenly their world upends. Now Nick is in major trouble again and Quinn may have made the biggest mistake of her life.

With incriminating evidence mounting against Nick, Tory works to prove his innocence. But Nick finds himself in a bigger battle when he must fight to protect, and win, his true love.

About the Author

Debbie Krueger Lum has enjoyed a 28-year professional career in marketing, where she loved turning big, complicated problems into smooth, organized programs. She's traveled from the beaches of Turkey to the volcanoes in Italy to the bricks of Red Square, Moscow. And no one can drink more unsweetened iced tea than her.

After seeing a self-esteem campaign encouraging little girls to dream big, she wondered why not grown women too? She challenged herself to do something she knew little about: reading and writing novels.

PLEBEIAN REVEALED is her debut novel, first in the PLEBEIAN series. It's a journey about common people launched into something new. Just like her.

www.debbielum.com